FORT PRIVILEGE

By Kit Reed

Novels

FORT PRIVILEGE
MAGIC TIME
THE BALLAD OF T. RANTULA
CAPTAIN GROWNUP
TIGER RAG
CRY OF THE DAUGHTER
ARMED CAMPS
THE BETTER PART
AT WAR AS CHILDREN
MOTHER ISN'T DEAD SHE'S ONLY SLEEPING

Short Story Collections

OTHER STORIES AND: THE ATTACK OF THE GIANT BABY
MR. DA V. AND OTHER STORIES

Nonfiction

STORY FIRST: THE WRITER AS INSIDER

FORT PRIVILEGE

KIT REED

DOUBLEDAY & COMPANY, INC.
GARDEN CITY, NEW YORK
1985

For: Richard Purdy Wilbur

surprise

All of the characters in this book
are fictitious, and any resemblance
to actual persons, living or dead,
is purely coincidental.

Library of Congress Cataloging in Publication Data
Reed, Kit.
Fort privilege.
I. Title.
PS3568.E367F67 1985 813'.54
ISBN: 0-385-19405-6
Library of Congress Catalog Card Number 84-21182

Printed in the United States of America
First Edition

In April of that year, the exodus from Manhattan became a rout. There had been so many riots and fires over the years, so many murders and disasters and subsequent departures that reporters wrote no more than an inch about this new spasm; TV newscasters did not bother. Over the years, with a sinister speed, the refugees had been replaced by scavengers and opportunists, the lawless, the violent and the pathological, so that one night in early May the balance tipped, changing the city almost overnight, and forever.

The middle-class escapees of the 1960s and 1970s had been followed by the working poor and even the destitute in increasing numbers, which left behind only the very rich, who could still afford every comfort, and the helpless. What had begun as a trickle became a fatal hemorrhage. Overpowered and outnumbered, threatened and afraid, the last of the honest citizens began to flee in cars and on foot, through tunnels and over bridges, by helicopter and by boat, taking what they could and leaving the rest for the spoilers. For the city was by no means empty.

If the people of the Parkhurst, a splendid fortress on Central Park West, were too preoccupied to notice, what did it matter? They were New Yorkers all, protected by power and privilege and the granite walls of the landmark whose anniversary they were preparing to celebrate. The hundredth birthday gala was going to be the most magnificent party in the history of the city.

1

The invitation was engraved on a Parkhurst correspondence card almost a quarter of an inch thick, with the family crest embossed in gold so heavy that Bart was tempted to scrape it off and find some girl to pin it on. Instead he was in the haberdasher's, letting it slip out of his book with a murmured "Ooops."

"The Parkhurst." The clerk's expression went from scornful to deferential in one twitch. Even he could still be impressed.

On the principle that you could make anybody keep talking if you were quiet for long enough, Bart glanced at the ersatz beams in the ceiling, considered the mahogany fittings, began counting the little brass knobs on the glass-fronted cases filled with expensive shirts.

"Black tie," the clerk said finally, because Bart wouldn't say anything. "You shouldn't have waited so long to come in, sir. Not much time for proper alterations if it's going to be ready tonight."

No need for him to know the invitation had come only this morning—a mystery, because nobody from his old life knew where Bart was. It was on the front table in his rooming house when he came down. He smiled.

"So I suppose you'll want everything. Shirt, tie, studs"—the clerk went on uncomfortably—"cummerbund."

Bart nodded. Everything. He had bailed out of the Institute for Living without even a toothbrush; his Cambridge wardrobe, assembled in the last three months, was a mixture of Army surplus and early Goodwill, which was one reason he was here. The other was almost accomplished. Pretending to pick up the card and the book, he let the invitation fall backside up, exposing a purple blur.

"My goodness." By this time the clerk was so unnerved that he babbled, "What nice handwriting. Isn't it nice handwriting, sir? You must be a very special guest."

"I'm surprised you made out the handwriting. Most people find it hard to read."

"Hard to read? Why no sir."

"I bet you can't really make it out."

"Of course I can. It's plain as day. It says, 'Please come. You are needed here.' "

"Mmm," Bart said. "You're better than I thought." Grinning, he scooped up the card and slipped it in the book. So he had solved his other problem so smoothly that the clerk didn't even know. It was one of the reasons he'd ended up in the Institute for Living, he supposed, along with the fact that after whatever happened to Mardella happened, he'd done—whatever it was. The immediate problem, that he'd cleverly circumvented, was the fact that he'd been reduced from banner student and budding architect to functional illiterate in the sweep of a bat's wing, which meant whatever was engraved on the Parkhurst invitation, whatever was printed anywhere, was only a blur to him—a kind of black hole. The larger problem was that there were often black holes where he least expected them: in the place where his lover Mardella had been, for instance, and in the patch of time right before he woke up at the Institute. He went over the back wall because they'd messed with his head for what began to seem like years, and he still couldn't read a word.

On the principle that if you looked OK you would be OK, he'd dropped back into Cambridge and picked up a job as a bagger at a local super, not bad work for a guy who couldn't read. He told them he was a law student working his way through. So the book was part of his disguise. Also, in odd moments, waiting for the trolley or eating in some diner, he would open it and try to sneak up on the words. He would pretend to be thinking about something else and suddenly snap it open and pounce. Sometimes he could surprise an entire word that way: *the* or *an,* before it dissolved and sank back into the hole. He was in Cambridge on the premise that since most of his past was here, he might run into an old self coming around a corner any minute, he could grab it and shake the truth out of it. As it turned out, everybody who'd known him and Mardella had graduated; everybody he cared about was gone. Which was why this invitation had come at such a good time.

It would be like going home without any of the aggravation. He had played with Sarah Parkhurst since nursery school days, she was with him and Mardella at Harvard before . . . Right before it happened he'd spent a month in the Parkhurst library, researching a paper on the building, which he had drawn in detail for the last class project he ever turned in. If he loved the Parkhurst and found reasons to go back to it this probably had something to do with who he really was, what he had been going to be before the black hole swallowed Mardella and certain parts of his life quite simply began to disappear, threatening to pull the rest in after her.

In addition to which, he now understood (thanks to the clerk), somebody down there needed him enough to send for him. An idea he liked a lot. Standing in front of the long mirror in his first choice, with the clerk fussing with the break in the trousers, Bart was pleased by the difference between his outsides, as reflected, and his insides. He was big to begin with, black-haired and maybe a little bit sinister, and he thought he looked a little like a dressed-up gorilla in the tux; in short he looked tougher than he was, which was definitely good. *Nobody would guess I'm nuts.*

"It looks fine," he said to the clerk. "I think I'll wear it."

"But sir, the alterations."

"No time for that now."

"If you'll just give me time to take this tuck . . ."

And check out his credit rating? Not a chance. "Sorry, no time. They're expecting me. You saw the note."

"Very well. Will you pay by card or check?"

"You can bill my father." That would throw a scare into the folks. What if they traced him this far? He would be long gone, holed up in the Parkhurst, boogying.

"I'm sorry sir, I'll need further identification."

Bart had no choice. He drew himself up like King Kong, balling one hand into a fist like a sledge hammer and with the other flashing the Parkhurst invitation once more, relying on the combination of physical threat and appeal to base snobbery to spring him. "You have my address. You have my word as a gentleman. If you're still anxious about this you can bill me care of Abel Parkhurst. I'll be staying in his suite."

This seemed to do the trick. The clerk handed back his sweater and the fatigues, which Bart put on over the tux. "Yes sir. Goodbye, sir." He twitched uncontrollably. "Be careful in New York."

Was it really that dangerous? Bart didn't think so. People exaggerated because they had to defend their choices, starting with his folks. They packed up and pulled out almost overnight when he was twelve. He came home from Sarah's house one day and the moving men were carrying things out. He and Sarah used the Parkhurst as an enormous plaything: jungle gym and park and dollhouse and play fort, in which everything was possible and everything was perfectly safe, but there was his mother wrapping china in newspaper and wiping her nose with newsprint-blackened fingers because the city wasn't safe any more. What was he supposed to do? They were carrying him off to Cincinnati when the city was his whole life, and the Parkhurst was the biggest part of it.

It was also, he realized, a gigantic educational toy. He drew most of the architectural details with Sarah's colored pencils, and white-haired Abel Parkhurst gave them both a short course in art history, taking them around the family collection on rainy afternoons: "This is the picture Sargent painted of my grandmother in her ball gown, and this is the Whistler of the east façade, you know Bernard Berenson did a short catalog of the collection, and Henry Russell Hitchcock wrote about us in 1939. . . ." He showed them the illuminated manuscripts in the library off the grand ballroom and when he left them Bart and Sarah rode their skateboards across the parquet floor. He and Sarah were best friends; they ranged the Parkhurst from the lofty garret to the wine cellar and the underground garage; he thought he loved the place more than Sarah, who was careless of her things, and when his parents bundled him out of the apartment, he begged to be allowed to go and live in the Parkhurst, but they would not be swayed. Something about being mugged on the way home from the opera, they said. Some foolishness about the air. They stuck him in Cincinnati in a house with trees, which he suffered for two years until he was old enough to go to boarding school; they had to beg him to come home for Christmas, could never get him to stay. You paid your money and you took your choice, he thought with a leap of the heart. Being safe and bored, or really living, at some risk.

Which was why he was so excited. What if things were as bad as everybody said? The Parkhurst was impregnable. The worse things were outside, the harder you danced. There was a kind of bizarre recklessness about this that pulled him along. They danced before the Battle of Waterloo, he thought; the night before the Sepoy uprising at, he thought it was one of the stations north of Delhi, there was one hell of an officers' ball. Better have fun tonight; no telling what you would be called upon to do the next day. Those stout British soldiers in dress uniforms heavy with gold braid escorted beautiful doomed ladies in their pastel evening gowns, knowing they were being watched, celebrating as if their lives depended on it. They sat down to the banqueting table in the middle of the night because it was the only cool time in that part of India, sweating in their finery and stoking on roasts and puddings because this was, after all, a feast, and sweltering or not, this was what one ate. They had to have this party, would move out in the grand march because civilization as they knew it was teetering, the natives were simmering with discontent and it was important to remind the world that no matter what forces moved in the shadows outside, no matter what befell them tomorrow, they were in control. What were they doing at Lucknow right before it all came down on them, he wondered, and wondered why he was so excited now.

The last ride he hitched took him almost to the Triboro Bridge, where the driver said, "OK, friend. This is as far as I go."

"I thought you were . . ."

"I unhitch my trailer. They come and pick it up. Nobody goes in that doesn't have to. It isn't safe."

"But I grew up there."

"Things change. What's the matter, don't you watch the news?"

Bart shrugged. "You shouldn't believe everything you hear."

He scrambled onto the back of a pickup truck heading in. They made it to the 96th Street exit before traffic stopped for good. The city seemed to be approaching terminal gridlock, with everything on wheels out on the road and jammed to overflowing with people and goods. Ski racks and luggage racks were piled with suitcases, cartons, garbage bags, and the cars and trucks were packed so tightly into every intersection that the only way out of the clog was over fenders and hoods.

Still the FDR Drive looked not much worse than it did at rush hour on any other day. When he came down to do his paper—when was it—two years ago? When he got to this point on the FDR Drive, he asked his ride to let him out and went the rest of the way on foot because it was always quicker. If there was a difference today it was in the mood of the drivers, who kept their windows rolled up and shook fists at Bart as he scrambled over their hoods. They crouched with embattled looks, while passengers with blunt instruments kept watch on all sides. So what if they were in gridlock? Night would fall sooner or later and the police would sort it out. It was only later that he realized what was wrong with the scene: every car he saw on the East Side was heading out of town.

Being turned loose in Manhattan was like being unpeeled. He knew better than to try to read street signs or hastily lettered placards, but even where there was nothing written, holes threatened to open, which he did not understand. Mardella. Had they come to the city together? Did it happen here? Even though there was nobody on the sidewalk he began to trot, with the uncomfortable feeling that he was being watched from the shadows. He became aware of things moving behind the boarded-up windows and doorways—somebody in there, looking out. He heard footsteps behind him, somebody closing in with a sinister scuttling sound and without turning he picked up a broken brick and wheeled and lofted it, breaking into a run without waiting to see whether he had hit his mark. By now he understood that he had better keep moving and moving fast, or some crazy kid with a Saturday night special and pinwheels for eyes was going to move on him and make all his questions immaterial; unless he got out of this neighborhood in a hurry he might not make it to the ball.

What had happened to 96th Street, he decided, was an extension of the blight that began in the Bronx. The contagion had leaped the river and was creeping toward Fifth Avenue. A few buildings were reduced to rubble; others were burned out. The rest were boarded-up, showing blank faces to the street. Bart heard things stirring in heaps of cartons and debris, could not know whether there were rats or people rustling inside. It was better not to know. The problem of the buildings was more complex. From outside there was no way to tell whether they had been disguised by the original occupants, to foil blockbusters, or whether they were already occupied. The new chic was to look poor so you wouldn't be bothered; on the same principle it made sense for buildings to look deserted. Inside life might be going on as usual, middle-class people in complete comfort in their decorator living rooms. If he tried to knock he could get his head blown off. If the buildings were already occupied by blockbusters, gutted and more or less used up, he could get his head blown off anyway. On Park Avenue, stalled drivers had gotten out of cars and in some places were mixing it up with sticks and fists, fighting to defend—what? Their cars and belongings or their lives? With nightmare speed three men darted out of the shadows and dragged a driver out of his Lincoln like an oyster out of a shell. Bart started toward them and was stopped cold, frozen in his tracks by something he did not immediately understand.

It was worse than trying to read a book.

He couldn't see where they were.

And where were the police? There were no police anywhere. In the old days people screamed blue murder every time a fire station was closed or a police detachment cut to keep the city out of bankruptcy. That was in the old days; now it happened all the time. What would happen when they were all gone?

"Never around when you want them anyway," he said bitterly, and something in his head buzzed so loud that he thought his vision must be just about to clear. When he looked back at the tangle of people outside the marooned Lincoln, he saw a flash of arms and legs and then nothing, or something less. It was shimmering slightly, and then it became a version of what he saw every time he looked at a page: a vacant blur, another hole in his universe.

It gave him the creeps.

Maybe Sarah could help. He was going to pick her brains and not quit until she helped him figure out what had happened to Mardella, what he had done; until he did his landscape was going to go on being blighted by these holes.

He plunged into the park with a sense of relief. To his surprise the unbroken stream of cars continued; in the underpasses he had to vault hoods and scramble over roofs. From above came sounds of people milling, bushes crackling as if from savage battles being waged just out of sight; he heard reports that might have been shots. There were pervasive cooking smells and here and there rose columns of smoke. He came out on Central Park West bunched for combat, but to his surprise traffic was still moving and things looked more or less normal. He made his way across the avenue, concluding that the business on the East Side was true only in that neighborhood—one of those isolated instances of decay. *Maybe it was my imagination. People making things sound worse than they really are.*

Before long he was able to make out the Parkhurst, looking like a miniature Dover Castle; he could see the gold pennants flying from the corner turrets, even from here. He was already anticipating the blooming shrubs in the courtyard, music coming out of the mullioned bay windows, which would be open to the spring air. If the place turned stern granite walls to the side streets and the avenue, with medieval-looking slitted windows shuttered in lead, the interior was all graciousness, dozens of casements opening on the beautifully landscaped courtyard inside. He would go around to the two-story bronze gates and announce himself to Dawson in the wicket; in just a few minutes he would be greeting Sarah's father, who would be much too polite to mention the Institute for Living, if he even knew about it. Bart grinned. He could play returning prodigal if he wanted to, because the old man had always treated him like a son. He . . . felt a light touch on his arm and jerked away.

"Mister."

"Go away." He might have been shrugging off a grasshopper.

"I just want to come with you, OK?" It was just a little kid, fat and funny-looking, with a trail of snot across his upper lip.

"Who are you?"

"Just get me up the next block and around the corner. I'll give you my watch."

Bart looked over the kid's head for the concealed weapon, the adult partner in crime. "Come on, what do you really want?"

"I want to get home in one piece, all right?" He was jiggling Bart's elbow and tugging and trying to hide behind him all at once. "I'm just going up there and around the corner. The gates open on the side street."

"You can't go in there." Bart tried to shake him off. Who did he think he was?

"Like hell I can't."

"That's the Parkhurst. They don't let anybody in."

"Dummy, that's my house." By this time the kid was pulling Bart along, more or less hugging the wall of the building they were passing. "I was looking for my dog and these guys . . . what they did . . ." He was not altogether coherent. "It was only my wallet."

"We'll get a cop."

"Don't put me on."

Before Bart could ask why this was so funny, he was aware of a dark shape above them and he lunged, pushing the kid against the wall. The falling shape separated into two shapes and hit in a spatter of broken glass, which surrounded a terrible wet thud, because the TV set landed seconds before the person did. Bart pulled the child's face into his side and edged away from the mess, backing to the corner, where he was stopped in his tracks by the shimmering outlines he had learned to dread. There was another of those damn holes opening right where the body had been—if there was a body, he thought, and wondered why he couldn't move. When he did get moving again it was because the kid had pulled out of his grasp and was pushing him along. They crossed the street and hurried the length of the east wall. By the time they rounded the corner and reached the bronze gates he could not be sure if he had seen a body at all.

The kid said, "Thanks for the ride."

"Wait a minute. I'm coming in too." They were standing in front of the bulletproof wicket where Dawson stood. He had been coming here since he was little, Dawson would be thrilled to see him, he thought, but he was troubled. Had he almost been hit by a falling body? He didn't really know.

"Master Archer! What are you doing out there? How did you get out?"

"Never mind. I brought a friend. Hurry and let us in."

"But I didn't see you go out." Dawson opened the wicket for Archer, slammed it on Bart. "Not so fast."

"Dawson, it's me. Don't you remember me?"

"He's my friend, let him in."

"Master Archer, your tutor is looking for you. You're in trouble."

"Dawson, it's Bart Cavanaugh. Come on and let me in."

"Let go of that, Master Archer, and scat. That's it. Now, as for you . . ."

"Don't you remember? I was Sarah's little friend."

The guard's voice rattled the speaker. "You could be anybody."

"I had a purple down parka," Bart said in rising exasperation. "I looked just like this except I was short. I came back a couple of years ago, to do my architecture paper?"

"I'm sorry, you're not on the list."

"Somebody just got killed out here, at least I think they did. Come on, I have an invitation to the ball."

Dawson glanced at Bart's card and then looked down the list. "There's a penciled note here at the bottom, but I still don't know . . . You'll have to wait while I ring upstairs."

"What if I get murdered in the meantime?"

"I'm sorry, you're going to have to wait."

It made him frantic. He had not come this far to be snuffed while Dawson hung on the phone. He shoved his hands in his pocket and tried to look like a bum with nothing to lose. Finally he heard a click and a hiss as Dawson covered him and he slipped inside.

Everything was as he remembered. Flowering trees dripped petals; there were fresh pebbles in the walks and the staff had added bright pennants and strings of Japanese lanterns. Workmen were putting up a bandstand in front of the ornamental fountain on the north wall. Somewhere in the west wing, the orchestra was rehearsing an air Bart recognized. Sarah's great-grandfather Anson had commissioned it for the fiftieth. Her piano teacher had taught them both the tune, and when she had children they would learn it, along with the new piece Abel Parkhurst would introduce at the hundredth anniversary bash. Here in the Parkhurst, tradition marched as surely as the sun rose. Bart was overcome by a sense of peace and order that made him wonder whether the disorder in the streets was an illusion, one more product of his own psychic hype. Whatever they gave him at the Institute had left him with flashes—bizarre visions, so he could not be sure whether the trip across town had been technically augmented by the machinery inside his head. Maybe a guy didn't fall on him. Maybe everything was fine. Maybe he could go up to the library and pick up a book and begin to read aloud.

"Mr. Cavanaugh."

"Hey, Randolph!" The aging majordomo looked like Boris Karloff on a good day, looming with his craggy, seamed face softened by a welcoming smile. Lights glinted in his cropped silver hair.

"Mr. Bart, you've grown up." Randolph looked abashed. "I mean . . ."

"Boy, am I glad to see you."

"Mr. Parkhurst will be so happy you've come."

"Me too." Bart studied Randolph as they crossed the marble lobby. Somebody had sent for him. Could it possibly be Randolph? Or was it the old man? Wedged in the family elevator with Randolph, who seemed to be bulkier than he used to be, Bart didn't have a clue. As the elevator jerked to a stop they bumped for a moment, in which Bart understood that Randolph was wearing bulletproof underthings. That was probably a shoulder holster making a bulge in the Parkhurst livery. "You don't happen to know if Sarah sent me a . . ."

"Miss Sarah? She just came in."

"What I'm trying to say is, somebody sent me a note."

"Oh look, here we are at the door." Randolph busied himself with the bell. A slit in the door opened and he and the Parkhurst houseboy exchanged sign and countersign. Two cameras lodged in the bellies of Abel's *putti* monitored the little hall.

"We didn't used to have to go through all this."

"Times change, sir."

The houseboy regarded Bart with horror. It must have been the fatigues, he thought, and grinned disarmingly. Even so the houseboy made him stand in the front hall. He defended the doorway to the rest of the apartment with his wiry body, ready to fight to the death. Bart tried to think of something winning he could say but was spared because there was a flurry behind the little man and then Sarah was in the hallway, her bare shoulders rising out of a green gown that took his breath away.

"Bart Cavanaugh. Imagine! I never expected to see you here."

He just opened his arms and they hugged.

The houseboy was lingering in a fit of anxiety and she gave him a shove. "Oh Setsu, go away. Barty! What are you doing here?"

"I heard there was going to be a party."

"I thought you were locked up in the . . . you know."

"Well, I'm not." He decided not to mention the note. She was still beautiful, even with her hair in a bogus Afro and her skirt caught up on the edges of her woolly socks and cleated rubber-and-canvas shoes. Her neck was dirty, he saw, and understood this was one more body blow in her battle with her patrician father. He had missed a couple of rounds and wondered what stage they had reached. "Besides, you're here."

"Not for long. I had to talk to Daddy, but he wouldn't listen. He just shoveled me into this dress. The next thing I knew he was maundering about the head table and sending for Grandmother's emeralds. What I hate is, he can still do this to me. It isn't fair."

"I thought you might be home for good." He was trying to get around to Mardella, but she cut him off.

"You must be out of your mind. Oh hell, Barty, I thought I might get him out while there was still time."

"I thought you hated him."

"That too." She had a long history of rebellion, got herself arrested while she was still at Brearly, filled the Parkhurst with strange, shaggy friends, confounded her father by leaving Harvard with a handsome, sour guy who trafficked in—something, Bart was sure, stayed with him even though more than once Bart had caught her nursing bruises that she'd gotten, she said, by accident. Too many things happened to her by accident—it was her way of getting back at Abel, who wanted nothing more than for her to be happy and surrounded by beautiful things.

"But you're here. What happened to Lawrence?"

"Oh that." She shrugged. "We broke up."

"Good old Lawrence, he was a bastard from word one."

"Well he doesn't like you either. Listen Barty, I want to do you a favor. Why don't you get back in the elevator and get out while you still can?"

"Do what? I just got here."

"Hurry. Before it comes down." She went rigid. "Shh. Here he comes."

"Bart Cavanaugh. How wonderful to see you." The old man opened his arms in a feint at an embrace. He was tall, not so much angular as delicately made, as if a sharp blow would shatter his bones. His white hair fell away from the part in a youthful shock and his face was ageless, lighted from within; all the excess flesh had burned away, leaving Abel clearly visible. "I would have put you on the list, but I thought you were . . ."

"I was, but now I'm not."

"Barty was just leaving."

"Nonsense. I won't hear of it."

"Have it your way." She spun, turning to go. It was interesting. Here was Sarah, the beloved daughter of Abel's old age, heiress to everything generations of Parkhursts had collected and preserved; he loved her more than anything and she could hardly bear to be in the same room with him.

"Sarah, wait."

She was tossing excuses over her shoulder like used-up Kleenex. "I have to get out of this damn dress. I have to do my hair."

"But you'll be back, so we can go to the cocktail parties, and you'll let me seat you at the head table, just this once," Abel said to the empty doorway. "What's the matter with her? I planned this party in hopes she would come back for it, I wanted her to dance and be happy just this once . . ."

Bart looked at the empty doorway. "I don't think that's what she wants."

"I've made a house party around it—Mellons and Whitneys, all our friends and friends of friends—I even told her to bring that person, Lawrence, and made a special place for him. The caterer has been here since Monday and the orchestra since yesterday, and now . . . I don't even know whether I can get her to stay."

"I don't know if you can either, Mr. Parkhurst. It's hard to make somebody want something they don't want." This was complicated by the fact that more than once Abel had described himself as an unwilling prisoner—yanked back from the world to take care of matters here.

"Come in the library, I want you to see sketches of the restorations. We replaced the damask in the ballroom with some new stuff—it's a perfect match. And those gargoyles in the courtyard have been restored . . . And I'd like you to have a look at the lists . . ." He was like a child numbering playthings to attract another child.

The library was Bart's favorite room. When they were little, he and Sarah rode up in the secret elevator that opened behind what looked like a shelf of incunables, playing at being spies. Over the fireplace was the Sargent portrait of Abel Parkhurst's grandmother: Sarah's gleaming profile, the same slant of the neck and bosom rising out of the satin gown. If Sarah wore burlap and work boots now it was to spite her father, to get even with him for bringing home a young bride to this silken prison; *No wonder she ran away,* Sarah said. *I would too.* Everything about the Parkhurst legacy had to do with prison or escape.

From the day of the grand opening the Parkhurst had been not so much a gift as a prison for the family. Anson Parkhurst created it as a setting for his bride, laying out a Manhattan fortress that occupied two thirds of the block. Behind the west wall a tiny park spread like an apron between the building and Columbus Avenue. He may have imagined her giving parties for the neighborhood children out there under the trees, hiding eggs for them in the grass. Emulating the builders of the Dakota, he had created apartments where the cream of the Four Hundred could live, and as he designed the grand ballroom and the mahogany-paneled library he may have envisioned a time when the Parkhursts would proliferate and fill all the apartments: his special people in their own world.

As it was, Anson had only one son, who had a single son, who had a single son, a string of only children that ended with Sarah, the child of Abel's old age. Outside the world changed; the nature of the residents began to change. In the early days only the best families lived here, and if the Parkhursts could not be completely surrounded by family, then they were surrounded by the next best thing. Some proper descendants of the Four Hundred still lived here, but so many had died that Abel was forced to sell to strange new elements from industry and even show business, and, lately, to his intense discomfort, to the Arab sheikh who was the only bidder for the late Mrs. Van Weil's place. From the beginning the Parkhurst had been a beacon, rising over the park; now it was more like a citadel, an island in the middle of a deteriorating world. It was a monument to both style and survival, the last bastion of the old, good life on the island of Manhattan; this was both the Parkhurst legacy and its curse.

If Sarah fought this it was understandable. Abel's own hopes, the promising career as an actor, or even a filmmaker, had been nipped in the bud by the death of his father. What could he do but come home and take up the reins?

"If you didn't want to, why didn't you just say no?"

Abel and Bart had talked about this more than once. "Because we are the custodians. When this goes . . . everything goes."

Bart remembered saying—once—"Would that be so bad?"

Abel remained calm but his voice quivered with anger. "If you don't learn anything else you must learn this. Insofar as you are gifted, so are you responsible." So there it was: the iron rule, or was it the trap? *Noblesse oblige.*

He was reminding Bart gently now. "I've taken on an extra hundred for the party. The checks ought to ease things for some of them, and the money I've paid to the artisans alone . . ."

Bart said in a low voice, "Sarah says it isn't safe here."

"I've promised the city a party," Abel said. "And a party we shall have."

He had unrolled a sketch and was waiting for Bart to comment on it. What could he say? There was another of those damn blurs. He smiled, waited for the old man to lead.

"The reconstruction of the east parapet," Abel said finally. "Don't you approve?"

"Looks exactly right to me."

"And this?" Abel was tapping another blur which Bart thought might be a list of some kind.

"I've been having trouble with my eyes. But really, it looks fine."

Abel did not even notice. He said, relieved, "I thought you would approve. Oh Bart I'm so glad you've come. Maybe between the two of us we can keep her here."

"You mean for the party," Bart said. Long enough for him to find out what she knew.

"Even beyond." The old man's voice dropped significantly and his next words rocked Bart in his socks. "I've always hoped that you two . . ."

"Mr. Parkhurst, I don't think I'm exactly what you want. I have problems you don't even know about. Listen, I did come for the party, but"—he decided not to mention the note—"it was only partly that. There are some things I am trying to find out. For instance, Mardella Pearson. I brought her to one of your parties once."

"Mardella Pearson. Poor thing. It was very sad."

"What was very sad?"

After a long pause, the old man said, "That's the trouble, nobody ever really knew. You may just have to try to forget it, and carry on."

He was staggered by a flash: a bloody arm rising out of . . . then the black hole, just another blur. "If I can't remember, how in hell can I forget?"

"Don't use that tone with me." The old man's fingers were like steel under velvet, clamping his arm. "And whatever you do, don't flail. The most important thing in life is knowing how to carry on. Settle down." He reached for one of his lists. "Look here."

Bart shook his head impatiently; it was only a blur. "That isn't all. Outside . . ."

Abel overrode him. "About these cocktail parties. The bishop is counting on us, but so is Ransom Hickox, the singer person, but so are some of the old guard."

"In addition to which, outside . . ."

"And the sheikh, of course . . . We won't really be welcome, but if we don't make an appearance, we'll never hear the end of it. . . ."

"This guy almost fell on me, at least I think he did, and if I can't even tell whether or not somebody fell on me, how am I supposed to read this page?"

Abel waited only two beats and then simply went on. "On second thought, maybe we should separate, three of us could go to three parties each . . ."

"There are bad things happening outside, and you . . ."

Abel said, sharply, "There are always bad things happening outside. That's what's so important about what we are doing here. Look, here's Sarah, back in her awful wardrobe. Please, for me, see what you can do with her."

Which was how he ended up in the back bedroom of the suite Abel kept for her. There were heavy silk swags over the windows and the bed was covered with a matching spread. The carpeting had been woven in Belgium to match the pattern in the fabric and the Louis XIV furniture sat uneasily with the angry abstractions Sarah had painted at Brearly, which Abel had framed at great expense and hung on the glazed wooden paneling. The Roman shades glowed with afternoon light that softened Sarah's drawn face and blurred the faces in the photo album she had on her lap. Bart sat next to her, haunch to haunch, and discovered that while printed words and drawings escaped him, he could make out the faces here. Underneath the layers of smelly clothing Sarah was as soft as ever, and as they picked out faces in a birthday party picture he leaned until their shoulders touched. Could he get her to tell him the truth about Mardella? Did she know?

"Look, Mr. Haywood's dancing class. Can you still waltz?"

"You look," she said. "Pinky Hughes. He used to huff in your ear."

"Not in my ear." He grinned. "That was Pinky, not me."

"You."

"Hot hands, maybe." He used the old nickname. "Sarah. Say."

"I don't even know why you're really here."

"That's what I came about."

"It doesn't matter. Listen, you can still get out in one piece."

"Come on, Say. We grew up together."

"And we grew apart." Her voice was suddenly cold.

"That's not exactly true. It was that guy." Lawrence. He could make women do anything. Even things they didn't want to do. "It was that guy. The thing about him was, he was bad business."

"That's because you didn't understand. Besides, you may remember, you went off your rocker. You're hardly in a position to judge."

"OK. If you want to know the truth, that's why I came. I'm trying to find out what happened to Mardella, that I was in love with."

"Oh, her," Sarah said indifferently. "What happened to her?"

She was exasperating him. "That's what I'm trying to find out."

Sarah said, vaguely, "I heard something happened to her. I'm afraid that's all I know. I really would like to help you, but if you want to know the truth I was so wrapped up with Lawrence that I didn't have time for details."

"Details!"

"Shh. Don't look at me like that. If that's what you came for, why don't you just pack up now and get out while you still can? I can't tell you anything, I honestly can't. If you leave now you can still . . ."

"Still what?"

She wouldn't answer. "I've been trying to tell you ever since you got here. The city isn't safe."

"You're here."

"That's different."

"I don't see how."

"Let's just say I know something you don't know."

"Out there in the street then"—Bart said in a flash of clarity—"a guy really did fall on me."

"Believe me, a lot worse things are going to come down." At the sound of the door opening, Sarah's voice lifted and she touched Bart's arm, pointing to another snapshot. She could have been a little girl again, Daddy's darling, back home where she belonged. "Oh look, Barty, here we are in Harry's boat. That's back when I was in love with you."

"You were?"

"Sort of, but you were too stupid to know."

Behind the Roman shades the light made a subtle change, so that Abel, coming in, would see a late-afternoon glow striking highlights on their two bent heads. They were of an age, more similar than they would have admitted, both beautiful. They had grown up together, Bart had played here almost every day of his life up to a point and the old man would regard the two of them with flooding eyes because now that they were here together he could hope to get them to stay. He wished they could stay like this forever.

Several floors below, in a fussy guest suite with padded walls and draperies in matching fabric, Regan Millane paced uneasily. She had been lifted out of her environment, the routine of home and hospital that kept her going, and plopped down in this pretty, plushy room decorated in pinks and roses that clashed violently with the color of her thoughts. At home she had been more or less shored up by routine, moved from one appointment to another so fast that she didn't have much time to think. She could be Dr. Millane, who had a function. Here in Billie Beckett's pretty little French provincial guest room, she was only Regan, who was getting over a bad divorce. She was high and dry in Billie's fussy little bower, with her mouth sandy and her eyes wide and she couldn't figure out what to do with her hands.

Was she out of her mind?

She went to the dressing table, put both palms flat on the glass surface and finally looked up, into her reflected face. To her surprise, all the bad times with Jake had passed without leaving a trace. The eyes she looked into were bright; her color was good and the two or three white hairs springing away from her temples could be pulled out in seconds, leaving curls that were more red than brown. If she looked closer, she knew she could anticipate her face in a few years: how she would look if she kept on the way she was, but right now the face looked all right and so did her body in spite of all the things it had been through, everything she'd lost. Which meant that she smiled at her reflection, feeling somewhat restored, and returned to the artificial charms of the room Billie Beckett had designed for guests, wondering why the peach satin eiderdown, the flowered canopy over the bed filled her with such dread. As an intern, she had treated a dying old woman in a designer gown. She was wearing full makeup and all her jewels but in spite of the cologne Regan could smell the corruption of disease. Looking around the room, Regan thought the surface was as pretty as usual, saccharine; downstairs in the courtyard everything was in perfect order, the flowerbeds weeded and freshly planted, and the cobblestones hosed, but outside—what? Outside . . .

Why had Billie made Arthur pick her up in Greenwich in the Parkhurst limousine, and why did lead shutters whump down over the windows as they rode into town? Arthur said it was a routine precaution, but the sickening zigzags and swerves they made getting here indicated there was something more, and the occasional thump of a hard object on hood or fenders made her know Billie had not been straight with her. For Regan, knowing was always better than not knowing and she went to the heavily curtained window, thinking to pull up the shades and find out what was going on outside.

It was not as simple as she thought. The draperies were secured by a series of complicated hooks and when she had them opened she was thwarted by a heavy shade, which was latched to the sill. When she tried to peek around it she was stopped by what appeared to be a metal shield. She suspected it covered the entire window, but unless she could get the shade up, she wasn't going to find out. Going through her things, she located her surgical scissors and began working on the latches. Why had Billie gone to such pains here? Was it to keep people from getting in or guests from getting out? She managed the last hook and the shade rolled up, exposing a pair of lead shutters. *What's the matter here?* It was like being in a trap.

"Well, Regan, are you unpacked?" Billie's voice was not exactly warm. Had she heard Regan fumbling with the shutter, or was it marginally possible that house security had a hidden camera? Billie crossed the room quickly and pushed her aside. "Here, let me cover up that ugly thing."

Regan stood back as the shade came down, followed by the layers of draperies, and the room was restored to its relentless appearance of peace. Accepting Billie's invitation for whatever reasons, she had put herself in Billie's hands, and now she was going to have to wait and see what Billie had in mind. Her friend was flushed and pretty, a little rounder than Regan remembered her and, she thought, agitated under that fussy housewife manner.

"There, that's better. You've been alone for so long that you've gotten weird. How about a drink?"

Regan's mouth began to water and her knees quaked. "No thanks."

"Are you sure?"

"I don't think so," Regan said with her remaining strength.

"I don't know about you, sweetie, I don't think you look well. You know what your trouble is? You've been alone too long. I know exactly what you need, you need a new man."

"It's kind of peaceful without one," Regan said, because her insides were still scored by the wounds Jake had inflicted. "It's . . . It's *quiet.*"

"So's being dead. Is this your *dress?*"

Regan blushed. She had spent days shopping for it, trying this color against her skin and then that one, in hopes. She'd spent three times as much as she'd intended because she was staking more on this weekend than she was willing to admit. "I liked the color."

"Well, it's fabulous. Ted will love it, and so will Al."

"Al?"

"A business friend of Ted's. Frankly, you'd be doing us both a favor, if you just . . ."

"I didn't come here for that," Regan said. It was true. She . . .

Then Billie snapped, "Then what are you doing here?"

I wanted to see if I could get through this weekend without taking a drink. It was true. She had left her flask behind, made certain resolutions because she had been going through the motions for a long time now, hated Jake for making her this way. She was Dr. Millane who needed a little *cassis* in her before she could get going in the morning, a little Scotch from a flask at noon, more than a few drinks at night, but she was also Dr. Millane who was going to begin slipping if she didn't take herself in hand, Dr. Millane who was going to slip and hurt somebody if she didn't cut it out. ("I've found somebody who makes me feel alive," Jake had said, filing for divorce. This was only partly true. He had found a girl who would cry virginal tears for him. *Even in pain,* she thought, remembering his knuckles and fingernails, *you get jaded after a while.* "It was fun playing doctor with you, but that's not enough to make a life on. Here, have a little drink.")

Well she would show him.

Billie was saying, "I thought you wanted to put a little *zing* in your life. Meet some gorgeous man."

"That's enough, Billie. We haven't talked about the window shade, or why you're so upset with me. What's the matter here?"

"Matter? Nothing's the matter." She twirled her hand. "Ted and I are happy as ever, close as two clams."

Regan was on the offensive now, anything to keep Billie from pushing her into telling her too much. "You know that's not what I mean."

"I don't know what you're talking about. Now show me your shoes."

Regan ignored her. "Yes you do. You've been strung tight ever since I got here. I know there's something wrong."

Billie faltered. "Between me and Ted? That's ridiculous. We're happy as . . ."

"With the city. With this place. What's going on?"

Billie rucked up her pale silk shirt, tucked it back in, rucked it up. She looked distracted and pretty in the lilac cardigan, the matching silk slacks. "How could there be anything wrong."

"When Arthur drove me in it was like coming through a combat zone. If everything's OK why wouldn't he let me see?"

"Aesthetics. Abel wants to give us pleasant memories."

"Lead shutters, Billie. All the guards are armed."

"Oh well. You know."

"No I don't."

Billie was wavering. She had kept her figure, but since Regan saw her last something had happened; all the lines in her face had relaxed slightly, so that she looked not pretty so much as silly and frivolcus, beginning to get old. Regan touched her own face. "Billie?"

"They just make us feel a little more secure."

"Against what?"

"Whatever." Billie laughed girlishly. "That's half the fun."

"Lord!"

"Don't listen to everything you hear on the news."

"Why wouldn't Arthur let me see out of the car? I think there were people *throwing* things at us."

"Oh stop it, you sound like a tourist," Billie said with a New Yorker's practiced calm. "Living in New York has its little inconveniences, but there are no blockbusters in our neighborhood, and if there were—this place is like Gibraltar."

"Or Corregidor."

Then Billie wheeled on her, saying angrily, "If you're so worried about every little thing you read in the papers, why did you bother to come?"

"I'm trying to do something!" Lord her mouth was dry.

"Well, for heaven's sake stop brooding over things that don't matter and make yourself pretty. I've found you a perfectly gorgeous man."

Regan put both hands to her face. "I don't know if I can." She could not tell Billie about the dry mouth or the shakes, could not figure out how to get away from here and go home until Billie was ready to order up the car and let her go. She did not really want to, when it came right down to it, because she had a three hundred-dollar dress in the closet, she had gotten this far without a drink today; it had been too long since the last time she was not Dr. Millane, with all her troubles, but a pretty girl getting ready for a party. She thought all she wanted to do right now was have fun and be happy—for now, at least. She dropped her hands and tried to smile. "All right."

"That's better," Billie said. "Now a little lipstick. We've kept him waiting long enough."

Did they dance the night before the French Revolution? Billie's carelessness had a kind of mad charm. Regan put on lipstick and said goodbye to the face in the mirror. Then, perhaps because of her troubled passage through the city this morning, or the discovery of the lead shutters, or curiosity about what Billie was trying to hide, Regan was compelled to say, "I don't know why you still live here. Why don't you just move out?"

Billie turned those wide blue eyes on her. "And leave all our pretty things?"

"You could take them."

"It wouldn't be the same—even if we could get them out." Regan jerked her head around but before she could say anything Billie locked steely fingers around her arm, moving her along as she continued. "There's no point in living, if you can't have the very best. You ought to take a few risks yourself, honey, you're getting all wrinkled from being so safe." She raised her voice as they came into the long drawing room. "Regan, this is Colonel Al Brody."

"I'm not really a colonel," the colonel said.

"Al, this is Regan Millane."

The colonel sprang to his feet with his back straight as a guidon and his chin tucked into his neck. He was too neat in the gray suit with the white shirt, one of those officers who would probably die at ninety without ever looking right in anything but the uniform. His blond hair was too short to be parted and he looked stifled and out of place amid the soft contours and subtle whites of the Beckett drawing room. Billie pushed Regan forward and then headed off with a knowing look and a wiggle of her behind that made Regan wonder which of them the message was for.

"Colonel?"

"Not any more. Ted just likes to needle me."

Regan thought she was going to like him. "Ted Beckett was in the Marines?"

"For about ten minutes. Not exactly his idea—there was still a draft, we hid out in the ROTC."

"And you both ended up in the Marines."

"Yeah. Ted liked all the wrong things about it, I think. Ran his men ragged just to prove something. Somebody got hurt and he got out."

"But you stayed in."

"Twenty years. I'm out now, but in a way I'll never really be out. I was going to be a painter," he said with a complicated grin. "I thought I could make money this way, and paint in my spare time, which was my first mistake. After which I thought I would get out after twenty, you know, forty-something and on retirement pay, and then I could paint. I turned out to be too good at what I was doing."

"You mean painting?"

"Tactical officer. They kept promoting me. Don't look at me like that, I know you're right. I should have quit anyway. If you want to know the truth I liked it. Probably I liked it more than I wanted to paint because it was all—they laid it all out for me, by the numbers. What I was supposed to do. Then, in my last year . . ." He broke off, looking troubled. "Would you like a drink?"

"Just Perrier."

"I never did manage to start painting, even after I got out. Instead I run a design firm in Detroit."

"I might as well warn you, Billie thinks we ought to get together. I just didn't want you to feel obligated on my account."

"My pleasure." The colonel handed her a Waterford tumbler. "It's one of the problems here. She thinks everybody ought to get together, which is one of the reasons why Ted . . ." He shook his head and began again. "You know you shouldn't be here."

She got up abruptly.

He touched her arm, drawing her back to the pale velvet sofa. "No. I'm sorry. That's not what I mean. I mean in the city, right now. It's not exactly the best place."

"That's what I've been afraid of ever since I came in. All the *precautions* here. What do they expect?"

He grinned. "Not half of what they're going to get."

"What do you . . ."

"Don't worry. Since you're stuck here, I'll take care of you."

"Stuck? I'm not stuck. I'd really better leave," she said without getting up; she was thinking, *The party. My dress.* "Do you suppose you could convince Ted to order me a car?"

"That wouldn't be a good idea. By the time I came in this afternoon it was already too late to try anything like that."

"Too late?"

"You know."

"Then why did you come?"

"A couple of debts to square, I guess. I thought I might be of some help here." He went on with a crazy grin. "If you want to know the truth, I get off on this kind of thing."

"You . . ." Her heart was fibrillating; she touched her throat.

"Shh. Quiet. Here they come."

It must have been his jungle training; he had heard Billie and Ted approaching long before she did. Turning to the archway where they would appear, she wondered what had happened to him that made him so quick and so troubled, and in which war. "Shh," he said to her unspoken questions. "Not now." Then he drew her back into the lush sofa and the comforts of companionship in this beautiful room. Billie came in first, pink from her bath and the attentions of her masseur, in a silk thing that yielded her outline when she paused in the doorway with the light at her back. Ted was next, ruddy and a trifle cross but so much the master of his house that Regan knew it would do her no good to ask him to order a car or even have the front gate unlocked so she could leave on foot. She realized as they sat together and the maid brought in a series of hot hors d'oeuvres that she did not want to leave after all, and was almost relieved that the decision had been taken away from her. The room itself seduced her with its pale, soft overstuffed furniture, the indirect lighting and soft draperies, the Chippendale pieces and the abstract paintings Ted liked to collect. Everything was so perfect that she could imagine the evening was going to be perfect too. For tonight at least, she could forget her losses, the pressure of her ambitions, suppress the thirst that had made a hell of the past few months. She could be pretty Regan, with nothing more pressing to do than bathe and comb her hair and slip into her golden party dress, careless Regan, who was going to the ball. So for a time at least she and the colonel would give themselves to the life in the Parkhurst, the elegant fabrications of their friends, forgetting everything but the beauty of the room, the pleasures of the evening to come. Their talk made a gentle rise and fall that was undisturbed by the occasional muffled sound outside; they were perfectly safe here, and right now, at least, this seemed to be enough.

It was only when Regan went back to her room to change that she was reminded that it might be otherwise. There was a flash of beige at the closet door as she came in. When she went over to it she found a maid inside in full uniform, crouching among her things.

"Why Rose! What are you doing here?"

"Nothing." The girl tried to dodge under her arm, but Regan held fast. "I only wanted your coat."

"Why would you want my coat?"

She grimaced. "I needed it."

"Yours is probably twice as good. I've had this old thing for years."

"I need a disguise."

"Disguise!"

"To get past the guards. I'm running away, all right?"

"Right now?"

Rose said, "It's way past time. Now will you let me go?"

Regan's hopes for the evening were slipping away. "All right. Rose, wait.

I'm going to make the Becketts get me a car first thing in the morning. You can come out with me."

"No ma'am."

"I'll make her give you references, and severance pay."

"I'm sorry, ma'am, I don't want to wait."

"Not even until morning?"

Rose was jittering like a helicopter about to rise. "Morning's going to be too late. If you're not going now, then you'd better let me go."

"Where are you going? What are you going to do?"

"Out. It doesn't matter where."

"If it's that important to you, take the coat. Here's some money you can have, and I'll call Boston and get you a place to stay."

"You can't, the phones are out."

"But I just heard one ringing." She grabbed for Rose and tried to hold her down. "Just wait for one minute and let me try to make this call." She gave the girl a little jerk and picked up the phone. The operator came on the line at once. "Hold still! Operator, this is Dr. Millane, in the Beckett residence. Are you taking any outgoing calls?"

"Of course we are."

"I want to make a call to Boston, the number is . . ."

"I'll put your name on the list and call back as soon as there's a circuit available."

"I'm kind of in a hurry. Can I wait?"

"I'll call you as soon as I have a line, Dr. Millane." Regan started to protest but the operator cut her off. She turned to the maid with an apologetic shrug.

"Doesn't matter," Rose said sourly. "Probably won't make it anyway."

"Regan?" The voice came from the hall: Billie. Regan sprang for the latch as Billie rattled the door. "Regan, let me in."

Rose looked frantic. Regan shushed her. "Billie, is that you? By all means, come on in."

"I can't, it's locked."

"Nonsense." Regan stalled, whispering, *"Rose, what are you going to do?"*

"Find some way."

"Take this." Regan stripped her watch. "Billie, I'm coming! *Take care,"* she said to Rose, who slipped into the bathroom; she would get out by the other door.

In the hall, Billie was rattling the knob. Regan undid the latch with an apologetic murmur. "My foolishness. I must have turned it the wrong way."

"Party flutters?" Billie was dressed for the ball in white organza that drifted from her shoulders and exposed most of her back. She looked like an outsized camellia, going to seed.

"Something like that." By now Rose would be on her way down the service stairs, and to her surprise Regan found herself anxious to forget about her and put on her own party dress. She had come a long way for this, and now, in spite of all warnings, sensed or stated, she wanted to have a good time. Her friend was studying her with a calculating look that made her pick up a brush and begin working on her hair, humming, warming to the dance. She was as ready as Billie was for the party. What was the matter with her? All she could think about were the colonel's eyes on her in the gold evening gown, herself close to a man for once, safe from . . . from the bar, for one thing. Maybe it was this she had been drinking to supply for all these months, the warmth of a man's eyes on her, and if the city outside was not safe, she had the colonel's promise that he would take care of her. "I won't be long, Billie, I have to dress."

"By the way," Billie said, leaving the room with a disturbing look over her bare shoulder, "we'll get your things back from Rose. You know how servants are—you can't believe a word they say."

"Billie, how . . ."

"If we are perfectly safe here," her old friend said coldly, "it's because we pay people to attend to everything." Then, to Regan's astonishment, she said, "By the way. If Ted—does anything, please take it in the right spirit."

"What?"

"I'm counting on you to keep him happy. It's one of the reasons you're here."

Before she could find out what Billie meant, whether it should make her sympathetic or furious, the door closed and Billie was gone.

The first thing Bart discovered after Sarah's father scooped her up and took her to look at the cake in the grand ballroom was that, except for the Centrex, the phones were out. Who was he going to call anyway? Dr. Foster, at the Institute? *Hi, Doc, I'm fine, but I still can't read.* His folks? *You may not remember me, but . . .* Mardella? What could he say? He didn't even know where she was; he backed away from the blur. Or whether she was. It gave him the creeps, but so did staying here alone. He got up quickly and went out, took the family elevator in the hallway outside the apartment, going to the second floor.

The grand ballroom occupied most of the east wing; in the old days Bart and Sarah could stand at its long windows and look down into the park. The north and south wings faced the side streets, and on this floor were given over to billiard rooms and a gymnasium on the uptown side, where he got out of the elevator, and on the downtown side, the sumptuous library which rivaled the Morgan in its holdings and outstripped it in size. There was no access to the west wing from any of these public rooms; on this floor, as on most of the others, the west wing was occupied by the help, from household servants to maintenance staff to groundskeepers who tended to the gardens in the courtyard and still went out under guard to prune and plant anew in the park facing Columbus Avenue. All the public rooms on this floor flowed from one into another. Bart knew from his childhood forays that it was possible to start at the far west end of the gym and walk three quarters of the way around the block indoors, fetching up in front of the baronial fireplace at the far west end of the library. The gym led into a series of game rooms that met the bank of elevators here on the northeast corner.

A liveried servant challenged him. "This floor is not open until eight o'clock."

"I have a message for Mr. Parkhurst." Bart knew he could go to his right into the Victorian hush of the first billiard room, or cross the hall and enter the grand ballroom. He stood listening for a minute, until a distant clatter told him that the caterers had set up in the gym. He wasn't sure why, but he didn't want to see anybody right now, and he went into the ballroom, lying— "I think he's in here."

It was like a museum setting, a habitat waiting for civilized man to be stuffed and mounted and set down in it. The gold damask on the walls gleamed and the crystal chandeliers were like exploding stars. Anson Parkhurst had designed them and had the crystal cut in Bavaria, to be assembled in New York by the artisans who came with it. His son Ansel had them electrified and they were lighted now, making the room glow and studding the ceiling with points of light. The orchestra's little gold chairs and music stands were set up on a platform at this end of the room and in front of the platform was a table protected by a gold shroud. The cake, Bart supposed, and resisted the temptation to lift one corner and snitch at the frosting. The parquet dance floor was so glossy that he was reluctant to walk on it. Instead he threaded his way among the little round tables that were scattered along the interior wall, each with its damask cloth and fresh flowers and an outsized vigil candle set in a cut-glass container. After dinner and the unveiling of the cake, the guests would sit here to watch the dancing. At the far end of the ballroom stood the bar. The handsome fruitwood folding doors that usually separated the ballroom and the library were open tonight, so the two rooms formed a single magnificent L. In the library, all the leather lounge chairs and small furniture had been moved aside to make room for the banqueting tables. Bart noticed with mixed emotions that every one was place carded. More blurs.

It crossed his mind that he was going to have tough work finding his own place, and so without remorse he selected a spot near the head table, also conveniently near the doorway, in case he wanted to make a quick exit— why? He took the place card out of its holder and reversed it skillfully, writing his own name, which disappeared as quickly as he put it down. No matter. He knew where to sit now, could point to his name on this card, that he had doctored, and if this left Mrs. Turnesley Woot, the grandest matron, or even the resident Anglican bishop out of place, Abel Parkhurst would know how to handle it. He was, after all, the past master of the grand manner. *If you handle it right, you can overcome anything.*

"Oh really?" Bart would say, grinning brashly at any challenge. "I'm sure there's been a mistake. If the bishop is here, then where am I supposed to be?"

After which somebody would have to consult the seating chart and move him to his place. He became aware that he was not alone in here. There was somebody sitting at the far end of the farthest table, snuffling. Moving quietly over the palace-sized Persian carpet, Bart saw that it was a girl in a maid's uniform, collapsed in tears.

"Hey."

"Oh. Oh lord!" She leaped to her feet in stages, toppling her chair and flailing in failed gestures of apology.

"Nothing can be that bad."

"Oh yes it can." Wailing, she backed into a bookshelf and began edging along it to the door.

"What's the matter?"

"Nothing. I'm so sorry. It's nothing sir."

He contorted his face, in a stab at looking kind and trustworthy at the same time. "You can tell me the truth."

"If you want to know the truth, it's all just too much is the truth, if you want to know the truth." He had her backed into the fireplace so she had no choice but to continue. "All I want is to get out of here."

"Oh hell, is that all. Why don't you go home? Hey?" She had her face in her hands; she was sobbing again and would not talk to him. He was going to have to try a different tone: master-to-servant. "Pull yourself together," he said.

"Yes sir."

Grinning, he said, "You're a disgrace to the uniform."

To his absolute surprise she took this seriously and answered it in all seriousness, with little sobs snagging at every word. "Oh, sir! I never wanted to wear it. It isn't even mine. I'm only here because my sister Maud was sick and couldn't come." She was slipping; in another second she would disassemble altogether. "They made me come so the family would get her pay. Mama said all I had to do was help with the food and then run away before the party started, but now . . ."

"Easy."

"Uh-hup. Uh. The main gate is guarded. They won't let anybody go until after Sunday brunch."

Bart managed not to say: *You know how hard it is to keep good help,* because he could see this girl was beyond kidding; she was terrified. "That doesn't sound so bad."

"That's the least of it. The thing is . . ." Even in the dimness the rings around her irises glittered white. "It's tonight."

"What is?"

"You know." Her eyes were rolling. "It's tonight."

What had Sarah . . . "How do you know?"

She was wild, shivering. "Because everybody says it is. Oh lord. Mr. Parkhurst!" She was looking over Bart's shoulder. "Mr.— Oh!"

"Bart, I'm afraid you're not welcome here until everything is ready. It's a little thing, but I like all the work to be done—behind the scenes?" The old man's voice was cold.

"I was looking for you and Sarah, when I . . . Look, this girl just told me something I think you should know."

"I did not," the girl said. "Please can I go?"

"Of course, my dear." Abel had maneuvered himself between Bart and the girl, so that Bart was caught in a head-on collision between manners and curiosity. "Perhaps you'd like to come to the kitchens with me, Mrs. Maddox is asking for you."

"Don't you want to know what she said to me?"

"It doesn't matter," the old man said smoothly, "we're getting ready for a party here. Right now, I don't have time for anything else." By this time Abel had Bart's arm and they were going back the length of the library to the fruitwood folding doors that opened on the ballroom. "She's really outdone herself this time," the old man said fast, to keep him moving. "She was hoping Sarah would come and spend a few minutes with her but Sarah . . . she seemed to be so busy with one thing and another and . . . Mrs. Maddox would be so pleased to see you."

Bart said evenly, "I thought if something really was going on, we ought to be informed."

Abel turned, ashen and determined. "And what difference would it make?"

Bart shot a quick look at him. "What do you mean?"

"It doesn't matter. I'm committed here." With a visible effort the old man drew himself up and lifted his voice at the same time. He said, in a moment of disclosure that almost toppled Bart, "You don't know how much I'm counting on you."

Bart angled his head slightly, as if that would help him hear. "You didn't, ah, happen to write something on my invitation?"

Abel was already heading back through the ballroom toward the north wing. "I didn't even send you an invitation. I just thank the lord you're here."

2

Enormous in her traditional black dress with the pink cabbage roses, Mrs. Imelda Maddox rushed Bart, almost crushing him in her delight. "Oh Mr. Parkhurst, I'm so happy to see him. Barty, look at you!"

When he could speak he said, "Well look at you! You're thinner, right?"

"I wish that was true. I just don't understand why I keep on gaining when I don't eat enough to stuff a squab."

"It's being around food all the time." At her expression he added tactfully, "I mean, food's in the air; it probably gets in through your skin."

She beamed with discovery. "Good heavens, you're right. I never thought of it. Imagine, Mr. Parkhurst, all this time, and I never thought of it. You're a wonderful boy, let me show you the menu, the trucks never got here with Mr. Parkhurst's ices, Barty, so this is what we're going to have instead . . ."

Looking at her lists, Bart smiled and nodded, nodded and smiled. This nice big lady had catered hundreds of parties in his childhood, many of them at the Parkhurst, and if she did most of her work in Connecticut and New Jersey now, it was another sign of the times. He followed her from station to station in the enormous temporary kitchen, saw where the plates of salmon pâté would be set up, for the first course, admired her ingenuity in calling for the crystal banquet set to replace the ice sculptures, which were supposed to come by truck from Hyde Park, and had not arrived. In one alcove three people were hastily cleaning the last of the crystal bushes and two others were polishing silver trees and attaching strings of crystal leaves.

"Had to bring these all the way down from the garret when the ice sculptures didn't come. It was going to be the building in all its stages, just lovely, but lord knows what happened to the trucks. You can't count on anybody these days." She clucked and shook her head. "I had to bring in loads of backup food, it's all stored below in the freezers, just in case, although heaven knows I'd rather die than serve defrosted food . . . Still, venison and *boeuf* Wellington, just in case . . ." She was moving through the ranks of heating tables, ticking things off. "My bakers are pressed to the limit now because the bakery trucks didn't make it through, between hijackings and all those damn holes in the streets, it's a wonder I have anything to serve . . ."

Bart began. "I was just talking to this maid."

Three busboys passed with crystal trees. "One per table of eight," she said. "Two for the twelves. You should have seen that arrangement in the old days, one enormous glass garden on the big table, but everything's informal now. For my money, it's all downhill, you know? I hardly come to the city any more, it's worth your life, but for Mr. Parkhurst, anything."

"This maid said something was about to happen . . ."

"We're going to have this party," Mrs. Maddox said.

". . . but she wouldn't say what."

"By the way, what happened to that pretty girlfriend of yours? The blonde dancer, you know. I could close my two hands around her waist."

"Mardella? You knew Mardella?"

"If that was her name. You brought her back to meet me, after Mr. Parkhurst's birthday dinner, I never heard anybody be so nice about the food, she even took two of my recipes."

"She did?"

"If you want to know the truth, I thought you two would be married by now, you both had that look, plus which she had a very sweet nature, unlike some girls that I won't mention, but their name begins with S."

"Mardella was here?"

"Along with that boyfriend of Sarah's, but if you think she brought him back to meet me you're mistaken, after that scene he made at dinner, I would have pushed my chocolate mousse right in his face, and you and that nice girl . . . What's the matter? Don't you remember?"

"No." Bart lurched; it was like going from sixty miles an hour to a full stop; he thought it was probably one of those things that sometimes happened in his head, but when he looked everybody else in the kitchen was lurching too; they were like passengers on a pitching ship. "What was that?"

"Oh lord!" Mrs. Maddox was rushing away from him, bearing down on two terrified assistants with the strength of ten. "If you put the pâté on the toast points now, we're going to be serving mush."

Abel was at Bart's elbow. "We'd better go dress."

Bart jerked around. "I'm wearing it. What was that?"

"What?"

"Earthquake, maybe. Explosion. I don't know."

"We've never had an earthquake, and I'm sure we won't." Abel was maddeningly calm. "You're wearing what?"

"Tux already. Underneath."

"Good lord." The old man wrinkled his nose. "Perhaps we'd better get you a fresh shirt. Setsu will press everything while you shower and shave."

"Yes, sir."

As it turned out, they went to the cocktail parties without Sarah. She pleaded a headache, said she wasn't ready, said she had to do makeup, said she was waiting for a call, said she got dizzy at parties where too many people stood around and drank. She promised to be at the library door at eight-thirty, when the guests were expected to sit down, to which her father agreed, finally, instructing Randolph to call for her. He and Bart began their rounds.

There were dozens of cocktail parties going on, at least one on every floor, and where there were smaller apartments, two. The resident Anglican bishop, the Most Reverend Bertram Rumsey, came to the door himself to usher them in, producing roasted hummingbirds on melba rounds along with a crabmeat fondue. They seemed to sink into his richly paneled drawing room, where wine-colored velvet draperies met priceless Persian carpets; lush tapestries absorbed the clink of glasses and the chatter of the guests. His circle was mostly male; younger clerics mingled with certain figures from the literary establishment, and if everybody ate and drank heavily without a thought for the future feats of eating and drinking that would be demanded of them tonight, it could be put down to the festive atmosphere. The bishop was a man who enjoyed the earthly pleasures that remained to him; if he had forsaken women, he had found ways to compensate. His assistants, the sepulchral Dexter and Brewster, were wearing velvet bibs with their clericals tonight, and as a special concession to the occasion, had put on patent leather dancing shoes. They hovered, the only somber notes in an otherwise festive scene, and Bart found something not exactly off-key but somehow unpleasant about the way they scrambled to hold doors for the bishop or lunged to light his cigars.

The Ransom Hickox party was something else. His place was done in gray everything, floor, platforms, cushioned corners, all sparkling with lights that appeared from nowhere and flashed off the mirrored columns and the mirrored walls, multiplied and set dancing by the mirrored ceiling. Instead of the bishop's rich food and sweet wines, the rock star was offering a heady mixture of coke and uppers and cracked lobster and champagne, and if Abel did not linger it was only partly because of this. He seemed uncomfortable in the presence of the Hickox groupies, horny little teenagers of both sexes who lounged among the pillows and jittered and danced to the hyped Hickox sound, under the flashing strobes. Bart thought he saw what the guy was doing: he was eighteen and he had made it big, he wanted to impress his guests, who, depending who they were, were already high as kites or rigid with *politesse;* to him the kids were just decorations, no more than living furniture. Bart touched one little girl on the cheek and thanked her as his determined host waited for him to finish so they could go.

"We'll finesse the Becketts," Abel said. "Some of the people Ted knows . . . When Ted decided to make a new business, he lay down with the wolves." Because Bart was bewildered he added, "New money. You understand. They'll be so busy with their models and race drivers that we'll never be missed. But we will stop in at the Livingstons', and then on to Mrs. Turnesley Woot. You remember Mrs. Turnesley Woot."

She was a horror. "I'm afraid I do."

The Livingston apartment was on a vertical plan, two stories with balcony overlooking the tall living room. Bart disliked Mrs. Livingston on sight; she was gaunt and chic in bottle-green satin that accentuated her bony haunches and she fell upon him with sexual greed. Her husband was a portly man in a velvet smoking jacket who reminded Bart strongly of the little boy who had brought him in. Mrs. Livingston was introducing Granger, the live-in tutor, a plaster dummy with a bogus English honk, when a woman near them brushed her cleavage with a piping shriek. Bart looked up and caught Archer in the act, dropping finger sandwiches from the balcony with deadly aim. He excused himself and headed upstairs, moving fast because the little boy was scurrying for his room.

"Wait up."

"I can't." Archer was about to close the door to his room, but Bart managed to intercept him. Behind him the TV news was on: somebody with a red snowball mike interviewing a crowd.

"But it's me."

"If Granger catches me he'll murder me."

"Because you went outside?" Bart was distracted by a scene change on TV: boats. A documentary, maybe, the evacuation of Saigon, but the skyline looked . . .

"They don't like me much." Archer saw something he didn't, bulged his eyes significantly. "Bye." He looked frantic.

"You mean we can't talk?" There was somebody approaching but Bart kept trying to snag Archer and get a clear look at the TV.

"I didn't do it, Granger," Archer trumpeted, and dodged into his room. The tutor plunged after him. He slammed the door and snicked the lock before he began the spanking.

As a result, Bart did not see the TV screen go from one last shot of an explosion in a tunnel to blank snow, and Archer, who was fighting Granger with his usual concentration, would not see it either. Nor would the others in the Parkhurst, who were busily celebrating or preparing, according to their station. Except for the oldest resident, who was too feeble for the party, nobody had time for TV at all. The ancient and honorable Dame Nora

Featherstone, who was propped on a satin bolster with a house phone nearby in case she needed help, had been left well fixed by her maid, with a tray of sweets and a four-hour tape on the VCR, already running. When she finished watching *Pumping Iron* for the thousandth time, she would go on with less enthusiasm to *Conan the Barbarian.*

Back downstairs with the Livingstons' guests, waiting for Abel to give him the sign that it was time to go, Bart wondered how firmly entrenched this Granger was, whether the family knew how mean he was to Archer. He thought he might bring this up with Mr. Livingston after the party; he could think of worse things than taking Granger's job and keeping Abel company on this island of civilization in the middle of a world that had not treated him badly, exactly, but that was a little like a Swiss cheese, with significant hunks missing. He was ready to put the arm on Archer's father when Abel Parkhurst pulled him away because they were expected downstairs: Mrs. Turnesley Woot.

Bart went reluctantly. He had been to Mrs. Turnesley Woot's as a child sacrifice, squirming at the tea parties she'd held for him and Sarah. He could still taste the cambric tea and the zwieback: she made them finish every crust while she lectured on the evils of waste.

"Abel, dearest," she murmured; she had come to the door herself, and when the entire building lurched she caught her balance with the ease of an old salt who is used to rough seas. "And who is this?"

"I just felt something."

"Erma, you remember Bart Cavanaugh. He used to play with Sarah."

"Didn't you feel . . . Oh how do you do, Mrs. Turnesley Woot. It's wonderful to see you."

He was strangely lulled by the indifference with which these people let the moment pass. New Yorkers all, they had lived here all their lives, unscathed, and would pass off disaster as a temporary inconvenience. What was a slight concussion in the larger scheme of breeding and position and possession? If there were disruptions outside, what difference would it make to them? The old guard was assembled here in evening clothes they wore as carelessly as bathrobes, dowdy in rumpled tuxedos and rumpsprung dinner dresses that were a tad too large because the owners had shrunk. The dowagers' jewels and the men's diamond studs were cloudy with neglect but still magnificent, and although he had more style than they did, Abel Parkhurst relaxed here, among his own. The cambric tea of Bart's childhood was replaced by Scotch and the zwieback by crackers and cheese, but the rest was constant. Sitting among them, Bart could imagine that everything here might always be constant. Tomorrow he would approach the Livingstons, he thought. He could think of worse ways to spin out his days.

He might have managed it, too, if it hadn't been for the occurrence in the archway. With exquisite timing, Randolph waited for them to come away from Mrs. Turnesley Woot's. He was standing in the hall with an agonized expression, and he looked at Bart with concern as he bent and began to whisper to his master. After a brief flurry they turned and headed down the stairs to the bank of elevators on the main floor. Without hesitation, Bart followed. The door to the utility stairs was around the corner from the elevators and Bart was surprised when Randolph stopped in front of it, blocking it with his body.

He studied Randolph. "I won't, if you'd rather I didn't."

Randolph's face was a puzzle. Did he want Bart along or didn't he? The majordomo was so well schooled in concealing his feelings that there was no reading it. He said, deferentially, "Mr. Parkhurst?"

Abel was distressed; in this light he looked almost fragile. "What do you think, Randolph?"

"We may need an extra hand," Randolph said, with magnificent indifference. "But if you'd rather I called Arthur . . ."

"There isn't time. All right, Bart. You must never tell anyone that this exists. We need"—his voice broke—"We need to keep our few secrets."

As it turned out there was a door leading off the service stairs. As a child Bart had passed it by dozens of times because it seemed to open on a closet. Now Randolph swept aside the barricade of cleaning paraphernalia and opened a second door. They stepped into a high stone archway. It cut through the building from avenue to courtyard, but somebody had sealed it at both ends with heavy metal plates so long ago that nobody remembered. Bart had been around the building without ever guessing—a tribute to the skill with which workmen had veneered the outside with matching granite. He was surprised to see a smaller door in the plate that shut them off from the street. Lying on the stone floor just inside was a runner; from the way he writhed on the stones, Bart guessed he was injured, and some protective instinct kept him from looking closer. If he could get through this without *looking* at the guy, the runner might not turn into a blur. He fixed his eyes on the opposite wall of the arch and discovered another door. *Well I'll be damned,* he thought, because he and Sarah had spent most of their childhood looking for it. *It's the entrance to the northeast tower.*

Randolph drew them closer to the injured runner. "There was a commotion down here, sir, and I took the liberty of investigating."

Abel was bemused. "But nobody knows about this entrance."

"He had a key, sir."

"My God. Do we know him?"

"He's from somewhere in the neighborhood. I'm afraid he's badly hurt."

"And he has a key. Where did he get it?" At an anguished sound from the victim, Abel said, "We must get him a doctor."

"He's trying to talk."

On the stones, the runner writhed and bubbled and because he wanted to help, Bart made a mistake and looked at him. His throat had been punctured by a stick, he saw as his belly began to revolve and the victim's outlines blurred in the beginnings of a process that was as familiar as it was dizzying. He heard a woman screaming.

Who was she? Where was she? He had to help her but he could not move beyond the great hole that had opened in the spot where he knew the runner must be lying.

"Please don't talk," Abel said to the runner. "Save yourself until we can get you to a doctor. He's trying to tell us something."

Bart could not see the victim; he just heard the woman, screaming and screaming somewhere in the void.

"We'll get this fixed and then you can talk to us. Randolph?"

Through the screaming, Bart heard the runner gurgling. The bubbling sound of blood and unrealized words mingling canceled the woman's screams, finally. He looked from Abel to Randolph to the emptiness in the sickening realization that he alone had heard her screaming. "What's he trying to say?"

"Please don't," Abel said gently to the runner. "Whatever it is, it can wait until we get you to a doctor."

Randolph said, "I don't think he should be moved, sir."

"But he needs a doctor."

"I think it's too late for that."

"Please don't turn your head like that, you're losing too much blood as it is. Oh please stop moving. Randolph, send for Dr. Millinger."

The runner made a last bubble of desperation.

"I'm sorry, sir."

"And Dr. Millane, she's staying with the Becketts."

"I'm afraid it's too late, sir."

Without seeing, Bart knew. "He's dead, Mr. Parkhurst."

"But he can't be!" Abel staggered and Bart reached automatically to support him.

Randolph was saying, "I'm sorry I troubled you with this right now, Mr. Parkhurst. I thought we could still do something for him."

"You're sure we can't?"

"It's clear he's beyond it."

"But he was trying to tell us something."

Through the buzz in his ears, Bart heard Randolph. "We'll have to go ahead in any case."

"You don't think it was a warning."

"Even if it was."

Abel said, "You're right, of course. Even if it was."

Bart could not stop the buzzing in his head. He had seen the runner in the flash before . . . today he had flashed on a bloody arm rising out of . . . just now he had heard her screaming. He had been yanked back from the lull, or respite, and plunged into the present. His throat tore. "What are we going to do?"

The old man's strength surprised him. "Why, for the moment, we are going to carry on. If you will help Randolph move this poor man as far as the utility room, we can call Dawson and Dr. Millinger to see to him. As for the party . . ." He turned to Randolph.

Randolph and his master were of an age, hovering somewhere around eighty; they had both grown up here; Randolph's father had worked for Abel's father. In spite of his age, Randolph still stood almost six-foot-six in his stocking feet and he was as much a monument as the Parkhurst. Bart realized with a shock that there were tears running down the seams in his craggy face. "You won't want to disappoint your guests, sir."

Bart was aware of Abel's weight on his arm, and felt it lift as the old man collected himself. "Certainly not. Whatever happens, the Parkhurst is perfectly safe." If he did not believe this, he gave no indication. "They're expecting us upstairs. Oh, Randolph, this poor man . . ."

"There's nothing more we can do for him. I suggest we leave him where he is for now."

"Then cover him."

By the time Bart and Randolph had put a blanket over the runner and let themselves back into the utility stairs, Abel was composed and organized. Dawson and Arthur appeared almost magically with fresh evening clothes for both of them and in a matter of minutes they were both restored and ready to go back to the party. They came out of the stairwell and crossed the marble floor of the lobby, heading for the grand staircase to the ballroom. From above came music and the ripple of conversation and laughter. Bart took his host's elbow and they went up the stairs together. At the top, looking like one of the family portraits, Sarah stood waiting in silver slippers and the emerald gown.

Abel said, "My dear." He seemed close to tears.

Bart was reminded of the lacquered dolls sailors brought home from the Orient; she was gorgeous and impassive. Her black hair had been arranged so carefully that there were no tags or unexpected curls; it was as smooth as her face. On her neck and bosom, the Parkhurst emeralds caught fire. "Sarah"—his voice caught—"Say."

Abel spread his arms to his daughter. "Sarah."

She said, in a velvety voice, "Where were you? We've been waiting."

"By all means." Abel was not answering her. Instead he bent gallantly, and crooked his elbow, tucking her hand into it.

Dazzling in the aggregate, flushed and joyful, chattering in anticipation, the dinner guests filled the hallway, falling back to make an avenue for their host and his daughter. Over their heads, Bart could see the candlelight glowing in the door to the library. *Lucknow,* he thought, remembering the explosions, the fresh blood of the runner. Were they doing the right thing here? They were doing the only thing under the circumstances. Whatever was going on outside, they were protected by the Parkhurst militia, by Abel's system of locks and double gates, by the integrity of the building, and if they were not protected, they were going to have to go in to dinner and move on into the dance as if they were. Even in his dizzy state, flashing on black holes and isolated fragmented sounds that were beginning to reveal themselves, Bart understood that there was more at stake here than the success or failure of this particular evening, or even their safety. If he stayed here long enough, it was going to come back—everything that was hiding itself from him, and like it or not he was going to see clearly.

It's not what you're doing, he thought, giddy and shaking. *It's what you look like you're doing.* Outside something exploded.

To his astonishment, Abel Parkhurst had fixed him with his eye, motioned him to come closer. He spoke in a low, compelling voice. "To remain unassailable, you must look it." He turned to his daughter, whose face was changing as he spoke. "Now shall we lead the others in to table?"

For Regan, the most disturbing thing about the Becketts' gathering was not the bar. She had armed herself against questions with a glass of Perrier, and made her way so far with an occasional pang—nothing she could not control. What troubled her, then, was the accidental discovery of Billie wedged in an alcove with the Southern gentleman in the brocade vest, which was closely followed by an encounter of her own. She had managed to back out of the little sculpture room before the couple came unglued and saw who she was, but she was shaken and needed time alone. She was heading for her room when Ted Beckett caught her in the hall.

"Well Regan, are we boring you?"

"Oh, no. I just . . ."

"I'd hate to think you weren't having fun." He slipped a hostly hand around her waist. "Come with me, let's get you warmed up. What is that, soda water?"

"Gin-and."

"I have a bar in my study. Come and let me freshen you up." His hand dropped a few inches and she jumped.

"Oh look, there's the colonel," she said quickly and slipped away, but not before his fingers dug into her rump with a lustful twist of the flesh. She made a mental note too complicated to decipher and plunged into the safety of the living room. The disturbing thing, then, was not her discovery or Ted's approach; it was the way Billie looked at her when she came back too soon—the pattern it made. She saw the colonel by the window and went to join him with a sense of relief.

He said, under his breath, "Problem?"

"Nothing I can't handle. I'm just sorry I came."

"I'm not." He said, so quickly he must be prescient, "Did Ted?"

"Some kind of transaction. I'm the poor relation, and Billie expects . . ." Regan broke off, troubled by what this made of her—Billie's assessment of her life. Was it as bad as Billie thought?

"They don't play nice. They never did. Will you relax if I promise to keep an eye on you?" The colonel took her elbow. "That's better. Count on me. Now cheer up, we're going to the ball."

She could not help smiling as she moved out on his arm. The Becketts' guests were spilling into the hall to join guests from other apartments in a procession to the grand staircase, which led down to the hallway outside the ballroom. Chattering brightly in the carnival atmosphere, other guests from other floors had chosen the staircase over the elevators, so that Regan and the colonel joined a glittering parade already in progress. There were handsome women in elaborate gowns and diamonds flashing fire, going along with men in every variety of evening clothes: some had on large medals and sashes and they were all flushed with excitement, laughing and talking as they descended, conscious of the handsome splash they made. Regan joined them with pleasure, and if her heart lifted now it was partly because of the colonel's kindness and partly because of the music and the sound of laughter coming from the floor below. She felt giddy and festive in spite of herself, high on the excitement of the event and surprised to find that right now this seemed to be enough. Coming down the last few stairs, she skipped a few steps with a lighthearted feeling she almost failed to recognize because she had not been really happy for so long. There were worse things, she thought, than having fun for once. On either side, people were noting just who had come from whose cocktail party, and speculating on where they would be seated—how far from the head table, and with whom. Would she sit with the colonel or with some terrific new man, she wondered with a lifting heart. Right now it was the most important question in the world; she suppressed a giggle because this was all she had to worry about. *I really am at a party,* she thought, and took her place in the spot the colonel found for her, as grateful and unquestioning as a girl. The place card amused her: it would have taken some thought on the part of the person who lettered it to come up with the formula. It sat in its little silver holder, bordered in gold, with the Parkhurst crest in gold centered above the exquisite calligraphy, which identified her not as Dr. or Mrs. or ex-Mrs., but simply as: MISS MILLANE.

Al Brody was indeed on her left, but there seemed to be some confusion over who was sitting on her right: a huffy cleric with a big belly and a glossy beard arrived seconds after a handsome kid who looked like a dressed-up gorilla in his tux. He slipped in next to her and when the cleric protested simply kept on saying, "It's right there on the card."

It was on the card, she saw, lettered in ballpoint that was definitely not the work of the house calligrapher; it might have been done by a clever child. The cleric, who turned out to be a bishop, muttered about the seating chart posted in the doorway, but the kid just smiled blandly and when that didn't work bunched his shoulders and scowled from under heavy black brows, by which time a footman who must have been instructed by their host gently guided the bishop to a place between two of the women from the sheikh's entourage, who batted their eyes at him over golden masks.

"What was that about?"

The kid shrugged and grinned. "Is that your right name?"

"On the card? Sort of. It's not Miss, it's . . . Regan."

He tapped the hand-lettered place card. "That's mine." He was waiting for her to read it aloud.

"Bart Cavanaugh."

He seemed to relax. "See? It was never his place. It's mine."

"You have a lot of nerve."

"I'm glad you think so," he said, and turned at the insistence of the bony dowager who was rattling her jeweled arm at him from the other side. She would foil any attempt Regan made to rescue him.

The party was brilliant, Regan thought, giving herself to the progress of the feast with a sense of duty to the riches being lavished on the Parkhurst guests. After the seemingly endless succession of meat and fish and fowl and sherbet and cheese and fruit and sweets and the presentation of the *bombe*, waiters hastily filled champagne glasses and the toasts began. Abel Parkhurst spoke briefly, welcoming them all on behalf of the Parkhurst family, and he was followed by the bishop, who turned out to be the Most Reverend Bertram Rumsey, a gracious speaker who welcomed the guests on behalf of the residents of the building, who had gathered them here. Then Al Brody rose to respond for the guests. Regan angled her chair to look at him, amused by his serious aspect, the way he filled his chest and braced himself before he spoke. He glanced down at her and then swiveled, looking rather like the figure on one of those memorials to extraordinary feats in battle performed by Marines. He let his breath out and filled his chest again and then, sounding strangely moved, he growled, "Here's to it," a toast so abrupt and heartfelt that everybody laughed. After that the laughter was general and everybody toasted everybody else in happy confusion until their host tapped his gold goblet with a fruit knife and called everyone to follow him into the ballroom for the unveiling of the cake.

Because the colonel was used to being first in war and first in peace he managed to make a place for Regan in the front row. When Abel Parkhurst lifted his hand, the orchestra struck a chord and the golden canopy dropped to reveal the cake. Then he introduced a pudgy ten-year-old who, as the youngest resident, would cut the first piece. Archer Livingston had been stashed in a far corner of the banqueting room. Regan had seen him yawning enormously and writhing with impatience during the toasts. Now he was looking perky and purposeful in his blazer and neat slacks and she was close enough to see his mouth working hungrily as he made the first cut. As he did so a cheer went up and their host used the diversion to fade back into a doorway where Randolph stood with an implacable glare. She could not imagine what he was telling their host, but it caused the old man to give hasty instructions and then stand for a moment with his back turned. When he faced the party once more it was with a smile so carefully constructed that only Regan would wonder whether it was real. He thanked Archer profusely and at his signal several maids came forward to finish cutting and distributing the cake, which appeared to be a replica of the building whose birthday they had been called here to celebrate. The maids were slipping bits of cake into tiny silver boxes—anniversary keepsakes. When she turned hers in the light, Regan saw the outline of the building etched in the cover. She let Al Brody slip it in his pocket so they could dance. It was rather like dancing with that Marine monument, and after a minute she pulled back. "Hey. Don't do me any favors."

"Ma'am?"

"I don't know where your mind is, but it isn't on me."

"Look, I'm really sorry." He seemed embarrassed. "I've—I got myself into a hell of a thing in South Carolina, and I can't quite shake it. Be patient?"

"Do you want to talk?"

He shrugged ambiguously and pulled her back into the dance, circling with his chin on her hair and his mind in South Carolina. Still, it was nice having somebody to dance with and she let herself drift until he said abruptly, "Oh hell, I did something really stupid. I fell in love with somebody I had no business wanting. Southern girl. She's a general's daughter. Made a damn fool out of myself, kept dropping around, offered to do her portrait."

"She didn't love you?"

"You know how Southern women are. Nice to everybody. I didn't have a pig's idea. I just had to be with her."

"If she didn't, she should," Regan said generously.

"I kept going to her house for these sittings, had her dress in fatigues, thought it might turn me off, thought listening to that Southern talk might do it, but . . ."

"I'm sorry."

"When the portrait was done she said thanks and goodbye, I just went crazy, declared myself, all that crap, I would have given her anything, her father threw me out." He tightened his arm and she gasped. "Oh I'm sorry, did I hurt you?"

"It's OK, I think."

"So do you know what I did? It was so damn stupid."

"It couldn't be that bad."

"It was. I tried to steal her."

"Good lord!" She didn't know why this was funny; it must be the contrast —the military bearing with all this passion. "I'm sorry."

His voice dropped. "The hell of it is, she's only fifteen. The hell of it is, I think she loves me."

"Oh, Al."

"Which is why I can't go back. Son of a bitch pressed charges. If I were still in, he'd have me court-martialed. So I have nothing to lose, and nothing to go back to."

"If she loves you, maybe you can work it out." Regan was distracted by a large figure hovering in step with them, turning as they turned: the black-haired kid from dinner, who broke into a tap dance as soon as he saw she was watching. The colonel was about to go on when he moved between them like a running back, made a swing with one arm and whirled off with her. She found herself spinning away, a little angered by the assurance with which he had done this, and made angrier still by the way her body responded.

"Do you ever knock first?"

"I'm sorry." He hugged her tighter. "I just need . . . You're just . . ." He was sputtering with false starts. "Oh excuse me. You're just so nice and warm."

"You mean like a teddy," she said drily.

"You know that's not what I mean." His grin went out of control. "Don't mind me, OK? Mr. Parkhurst just . . . he just wants to be damn sure nothing ruins his party."

"Should it?" She was fishing; they both knew it.

"I . . . don't think so. I hope it's all right, me cutting in like that." He dipped masterfully. "He didn't look too fun."

"He has a problem." Brody was heading out of the ballroom—for a phone, she guessed, to try to make up with his loved one. She hoped he could. She was struck by how very young her partner was, and how old this made her feel. Why had he chosen her anyway? Maybe she did look good from a distance, the severely cut golden dress outlined her body, which was still good, but what did he see now that they were this close? There were beginning lines around her eyes, certain marks left by the trouble with Jake, the price tags attached to living, and she thought, *Oh baby, you are just a baby.*

"He's not the only one. Look I'm not as young as you think."

"What?"

"Not hard to figure out what you're thinking. I've been through as much as anybody . . ." He faltered. "I can't tell you the half of it."

"You can tell me anything you want," she said kindly. For some reason she did not add, as she usually did in confessional encounters, *After all, I am a doctor.* It would betray her age.

"Not until I know what I have to tell." He seemed to be debating, blurted, "Would you believe I can't read?"

"Tell me another."

"Really."

"You mean you don't like to read." He shook his head. "Really?"

"That was why you had to tell me what was on the place cards."

"Dyslexia?"

"Beats the hell out of me." She recognized his manner: the friend at the party who wants to be told it isn't cancer. Or in this case . . . "It just—came *on* all of a sudden."

"You ought to see somebody."

"I got seen, up to here," he said impatiently. "It doesn't matter anyway. Not now."

She was afraid to find out what he meant. "You mean we are in danger." He would say no, and they could go on dancing.

"Your guess is as good as mine. Wrong, my guess is better. Something that happened, before dinner? I promised not to say anything, I . . . oh hell."

The lights had gone out. It was like a blow on the head. They froze. She heard herself yipping because her partner had almost cracked her ribs in a reflexive attempt to protect her. "Let go!"

"It's all right," he growled. "I'll take care of you."

"What is it?"

"Happens all the time," he said, and would not release her. "Power failure somewhere, they'll fix it in a minute. Plenty of candlelight anyway."

He was right. The candles in the little crystal holders on each table glimmered, and the music resumed. As it did the young man turned his arm slightly, spreading his fingers at her waist as they resumed the dance. Warmed, she let herself lean.

The servants brought candelabra and the dancers cleared a space as liveried footmen lowered the chandeliers, one by one, touching flames to candles that had been renewed every season since the place was electrified. The orchestra did not miss a beat and the ballroom glowed with whirling skirts that spun like opening flowers. Faces lost years in the candlelight, so that everybody glowed now, and every woman could be beautiful. It seemed appropriate for the orchestra to segué into the waltz, so that all over the glistening parquet floor couples swooped and dipped in four-four time, with skirts flaring wider and wider and women's faces opened in beginning laughter. The candlelight made boiled shirtfronts gleam and struck sparks from diamond studs, and for a few minutes Regan and her partner whirled and laughed with as much abandon as anybody, careless and giddy with the spirit of the moment. When this dance was over they could leave the floor together, arms entwined, and in the intoxication of the moment they could both be of an age, and anything could . . .

There was a sound as if the world had cracked. Without warning and against all the laws of probability, a black projectile tore through the ballroom shutters, cutting through the lead as easily as a knife through paper, lodging in the floor with a sound like no other, shuddering like a living thing.

Regan cried out in loss and in the next second covered her mouth.

This happened so swiftly that most of the dancers were not aware of it, and even those close at hand could not understand it. The screaming would not begin for several minutes. Nobody was injured, except for a curly-haired gentleman who was clutching his arm and gaping in amazement, backing off from the object that had grazed him and lodged, quivering, in the floor at his feet. He looked positively outraged.

"Let me through," Regan said, as blood began bubbling through his fingers. "He'll need a tourniquet."

"Wait a minute. Don't look." Bart was trying to hold her.

"I said let me through." She had forgotten that in her golden gown and the spidery slippers she looked like any other dancer. "I am a doctor."

She would not look back to see what her young man made of this. Right now only this patient was important.

"Something extraordinary has happened." The injured dancer looked down at the blood on his hand with an expression of outrage. "How could they, on a night like this? How could they?"

Their host was struggling to make his way to them. "Oh Mr. Ravenal, this is most unfortunate." He was ashen with distress.

"Here," Regan said to him. "Where can we go that's quiet?"

The old man looked tortured, as if it was he who had been injured. He gestured to a door behind the bandstand. "We can take him into the game room. Langston, believe me, I'm so very sorry . . ."

Bart's voice came from what seemed like a long way off. "What do you want me to do?"

"Just keep the party going."

Following the old man and the first casualty, Regan felt none of the things she had expected to feel. She was not afraid, and she was not even sorry the party had been interrupted. She was, rather, almost relieved to be lifted out of the lavish improbability of the ball and set down in grimmer circumstances. She had the sense that something important was beginning.

3

"Probably nothing serious," Ted Beckett said, and Bart wondered what made him so sure. He looked puffy and a little spoiled in the golden light of the Parkhurst library. "This kind of thing happens all the time here, and it doesn't mean anything."

Abel's voice trembled. "Inside the walls?"

Beckett shrugged. "Probably just a fluke."

They were sitting around a table at the far end of the grand library, discussing options while servants cleared and removed the banqueting tables as smoothly as if nothing had happened. On the other side of the fruitwood doors the orchestra played, according to instructions, and the dance went on as if indeed nothing had happened, people revolving in a kind of intent gaiety, as if their lives depended on the success of the dance. Bart had removed the projectile from the dance floor and brought it here. It was on the table in front of them now. Beckett touched it with an exquisitely manicured finger.

"A fluke," he repeated.

The colonel said, "You mean you think it was an accident."

"Yes," Beckett said. "After all, this is New York."

"Exactly."

Beckett's voice rose. "You mean you think we can't take care of our own?"

"I mean I think we're going to have to."

"Good old Iron Al," Beckett said. It was not necessarily a joke. "Born for glory."

The colonel bristled. "You don't think this is serious."

"I think the police can take care of it."

Brody snorted. Next to Bart, Abel put a hand to his breastbone. If he had a heart attack, who would take over? He was, as it turned out, collecting himself, as if he could put things back together with his right hand and still save the evening. "Please don't argue. We're here to discuss tactics."

"Tactically, we can't do anything until morning."

"I'd prefer that," Abel said quietly.

But the colonel overrode him. "The thing is, we have to be prepared."

"Prepared for what?" The bishop looked preposterous in his velvet knickers and his frock coat. There was a brocade vest stretching across his Santa Claus pot and a gold chain straining from one pocket to the other, but he had forgotten what he was wearing. He leaned forward with a commanding glare. "Colonel?"

"Whatever happens." The colonel's tone was deceptive. It was the even, bland voice the police had used when they told him about . . . Wait a minute, Bart thought and lost track of what was happening in the sudden rush of fragments: something returning. When he came to himself, Abel was speaking.

"I said what do you think?"

"I don't know." Bart shook his head, blinking rapidly. "It's your decision. It has to be your decision." He was too excited to stop. "People have to make their own decisions."

The bishop was looking at him curiously. "I don't see any point in upsetting the others until we know what we're up against. My guests went to a great deal of trouble and expense to come here, and I don't want it ruined because you're going off half-cocked."

"Somebody fired a harpoon into the ballroom." Brody tapped it with the tip of his pencil.

The bishop touched his glossy spade beard. "Rather a bizarre weapon, don't you think? Unique?"

"The point is, it's a weapon."

"And you think there are a hundred other harpoons out there."

The colonel spat the words like nails. "I don't know what's out there. We have to be prepared."

"Prepared for what?" The bishop's voice was silky. He had risen to episcopal heights for a reason.

"Whatever they throw at us."

"That, then, is the problem. Who do you imagine *they* are?"

Brody lost patience. "I don't know, but whoever they are, you can bet your ass they outnumber us."

The bishop put both hands on the table: point proved. "We don't even know there is anybody."

Bart surprised himself. "Well, there is."

They all turned to look at him.

"Mr. Parkhurst, tell them about the runner."

Instead, Abel said, "There may be more to this than you think. There was . . . There was some trouble before dinner."

"Whatever it is, I'm sure the police can handle it." The bishop spread his hands on his brocaded belly and stretched. "Hear those shots? They're probably dealing with it now."

Randolph had come in while the bishop and the colonel were arguing. He was silent, hovering in the shadows like an anxious ghost. For the life of him Bart could not read Randolph's expression.

Abel said, "Randolph, did you reach the police?"

"Sir, the phones are out." If there was more, he didn't offer it.

The colonel said, "You see?"

"Oh, that." The bishop consulted his plummy gold watch. "That happens all the time. If you want to know the truth, I'm more worried about the power. In another few hours my food will start to thaw and we'll have to have an orgy before it spoils."

"If we have to, we can rely on the house generator. Randolph?"

"There's been a little trouble, sir. We have people working on it now." Randolph seemed to be debating whether to go on. Bart thought, if he prompted him . . .

"The, ah. Runner."

Abel silenced him with a look.

"The generator." The bishop shook his head. "We need to solve our problems here at home. The rest will have to take care of itself."

Abel looked distressed. "I'm sure my men are doing all they can."

"I hope so." The bishop got up. "Now if you'll excuse me . . ."

"Shut up and sit down while we figure out what to do."

The bishop moved smoothly, as if the colonel hadn't even spoken. "I don't know what you're going to do, Colonel, but I'm going back to my guests. You're only a guest here, you're new to the city. You're just not used to the pace. This kind of thing happens all the time."

The colonel tilted his head significantly. "All of it?"

"Some of it." The bishop shrugged. "The police will take care of it. They always do. Ted?"

Beckett stood. "Al, are you coming back to the party or not?"

"Tell me about your defenses," Brody said to Abel, as if the other two were already gone. He was cool, but completely committed.

"Double shields on the windows. The gates are two stories high and strong enough to withstand anything." Abel touched the harpoon. "Almost anything."

The bishop looked concerned. "Mr. Parkhurst, your guests . . ."

"I'm thinking about my guests!" Abel matched the colonel's tone. "My great-great grandfather had the Bastille in mind when he designed this place, or Shark Island, I don't remember which. Either way, it's secure."

"Get your people to reinforce all the openings."

"I'll have Randolph send a crew. Randolph?"

Randolph began. "Sir . . ."

Ted Beckett cut him off. "You know you're being ridiculous."

"How well are you armed?"

"Ornamental cannon, on the parapets on the east wall and overlooking the north and southeast corners. They haven't been fired in years. I haven't been up there since the fiftieth. I'm not sure what else is available."

"Can you find out?"

"Look, Brody, you're a guest here, remember?" Ted Beckett came back into the group like a bull terrier, suddenly ugly. "If anybody's going to take charge here, I . . ."

Brody went on as if he hadn't spoken. "Get your men to make a count. We need to know what's here."

"Al, you're overstepping." Beckett could not budge him. "Let's go."

"Randolph will be in charge. Randolph?"

The majordomo dipped his head. Bart eased out of his chair, and into the shadows, where he could mutter and be heard. "Something else is going on, right?"

Randolph nodded. "Shh."

"In addition to whatever hand weapons Randolph turns up we have the gun rooms—hunting rifles, mostly; dueling pistols, that kind of thing. Naturally the guards are armed. And we have the Parkhurst militia—a hundred strong. Of course they double in a lot of other jobs."

"How soon could they be mobilized?"

"It would take a while." Abashed, Abel waved toward the busboys who were whipping cloths from the tables, folding them and stacking the spindly gold chairs. "As I said, they double in other roles. Say the word, and I . . ."

"Not yet." The colonel had found an abandoned seating chart and was making notes. "Tomorrow morning will be soon enough."

"You sound like a couple of ten-year-olds. You're going to feel like fools when the sun comes up." Still, the bishop lingered.

"Think what you want, Bishop. Mr. Parkhurst, what about food?"

"The basement freezer and food lockers are all filled. Mrs. Maddox brought in extras for the party and we have everything the tenants keep in their kitchens. There should be enough for weeks."

"If we're careful," Brody said.

"We have groceries delivered twice a week," the bishop said coldly. "Even in bad times the service is first-rate. Nobody can afford to lose an account this big . . ."

"Tomorrow we start provisioning."

"You ought to be in Bellevue, Al." Beckett's tone curdled with scorn. "You and your tinhorn tactics. You wouldn't even be here if . . ."

Abel said, "I'm afraid you two don't realize how serious this is."

Beckett looked at him angrily. "No. I'm afraid we don't."

Bart blurted, "The runner." Next to him, Randolph stirred; he shifted as if he bore the weight of something enormous, and in the brief silence that followed, Bart heard him breathing hard.

Abel sighed. "All right, Bart. I didn't want to bother you and Beckett with this, but . . . You might as well know, there's already been a death."

"Good lord!"

"Sit down, please. You don't look well. I don't know who he was, I . . ." The old man shook his head. "Randolph says he's from the next building, he'd been . . . stabbed in the throat."

"That's nothing. This is New York. Things like that happen all the time." Beckett was talking too fast now, flushed and twitchy.

"He was trying to tell us something. A warning? I don't know . . . It was apparent . . ." Abel's voice was shaking. "Things are pretty bad."

The colonel spoke to the problem at once. "How tall are the buildings on the side streets?" He was sketching on the seating plan.

"Tall enough to overlook us."

"If we get in trouble, we're going to have to bring them down."

This time it was Abel who protested. "We can't damage other people's property. We can't just destroy . . ."

The colonel made a chopping motion. "If we're going to defend, we have to clear the terrain."

"I'm sorry, I can't willfully . . ." Abel appealed to the others: the resident Anglican bishop, the feisty Ted Beckett, whom he did not even like. In the shadows next to Bart, Randolph stirred.

So the sentiment in the room was teetering, the colonel had gone too far and he was about to lose them. If he was right about this and they didn't arm, they were going to be destroyed—destroyed, Bart thought, and although he had not been able to see the runner while they were together in the archway he could see him clearly now, in memory: the tattered warmup suit, the stick in his throat, the blood; he could hear the mysterious screaming . . . His breath exploded and he gave Randolph a push into the circle of candlelight. "You have to tell them!"

"Oh, Randolph," Abel said distractedly, "I thought I told you to go."

"Sir, I . . ." Randolph waited for some sign to go on. He was not so much deferential as reserved; he was, after all, a servant.

"What do you think, Randolph, are we getting carried away?"

Beckett snapped, "We don't need to know what the help thinks."

Abel turned angrily. "He's much more than that."

The colonel was saying, "What we have is a bad situation here . . ."

"Shut up," Bart said unexpectedly. "He's trying to tell you something. You can't just ignore things and hope they'll go away," he said, to his own absolute stupefaction. He went on, his voice magnified by the force of his own discovery. "You have to make yourself look at things." He repeated, for them, for himself, "You have to make yourself look at things."

"Good man," the colonel said. "Good man."

So they had to turn to Randolph now. He looked from Bart to the rest with that same steadiness born of years of practice in patience and he said, "It's about the courtyard, sir."

"The courtyard! Has something . . ."

"I'm afraid it's filling up."

"What do you mean?"

"Refugees, from the other buildings. The city . . . Something extraordinary is happening."

Brody's voice was sharp. "That's a mistake. We can't afford . . ."

Abel turned on him. "They are our friends. We have to let them in."

"All right, Brody," the bishop said with great gravity. "We'll do whatever you say. What comes first?"

"I want a complete tally of supplies." The colonel ticked off his list as if they had never exchanged a harsh word. "Food, medical supplies, ammunition, arms. Get some people you can trust."

"I'll have to rely on my curates. I assume you want this kept quiet."

"For as long as possible," Brody said. "We're going to have to deal with whatever's out there, we can't afford to have anybody alarmed. Ted, if you're with us, you can go back and do your best to keep the party going. Keep them dancing until they keel over; I want them tucked in tonight, not wandering around. I don't want anybody on deck who isn't directly responsible."

Beckett's manner was not reluctant, exactly, but grudging. "Yes sir."

"We'll meet back here at six." Almost as an afterthought, he turned to Abel. "Is that all right?"

Bart was vibrating with good intentions. "What about me?"

Someone—was it Randolph? Abel? One of the others? Someone murmured, "Look after Sarah."

"Sarah," Bart murmured, looking at Abel. Of course he'd want her taken care of. She was his daughter after all.

"We're going to have to try to get a message to the police; check out the phones. If they aren't working, see if you can find a radio." The colonel was ticking off items. "Bring anything you can find; I want you all back here by six."

"Six!"

"By then we ought to know."

Abel spoke for all of them. "Know what?"

"Just how bad this thing is," the colonel said.

When the big black-haired guy that was nice to him came in with dumb old Sarah Parkhurst that used to be nice to him, they caught Archer in the act. He was hunkered in his quilts with about a ton of the Parkhurst anniversary cake. The remarkable truth was, it was the entire right-hand tower. He had just pulled it off and sneaked it onto a busboy's tray in the jumble after the lights went out. The elevators were all stalled between floors on account of the power failure but that didn't bother Archer, he just headed up the back way to his folks' apartment and walked into the foyer with his eyes wide open just like he owned the place. Didn't even notice his rotten tutor and whoever this girl was grappling on the sofa until she screamed and Granger cussed him out. He couldn't see worth diddley because it was like the inside of a mattress in there but he had this creepy feeling that it wasn't just any old girlfriend, it could even be . . . Oh no, he wasn't getting into that, and he guessed Granger wouldn't either, Granger just reared up in the darkness and his tone changed like a traffic light and instead of barking he was what, entreating Archer to go to bed and keep his mouth shut. Archer just said, Die, Granger, that will teach you to try and have a private life, after which Granger threatened him and he asked what would Granger give him to shut up. Granger promised no more algebra lessons and no more Latin either and then Archer just grinned and let him dangle a little, hanging by his guts and twisting in the wind, while the woman on the sofa tried to pretend she wasn't on the sofa and Archer tried to figure out why he didn't want to find out who it was. Then he said all right if Granger would throw in his next month's salary he'd think about it, and then he took the cake on into his room and locked them out.

He put it on his bed and got his old camp flashlight because he really hated eating in the dark, there was something obscene about it, and when he found the light and put it on his desk he sat down with the turret and started chomping on it, from the point on down. He kind of wished he could get something on the TV or radio because he hated eating alone but the best he could do was put a Beatles song on his cassette player and wonder what it used to be like in the old days when they were all alive, when there was a baby boom and the world was full of kids. Archer thought that would be great, there would be a ton of kids living in the Parkhurst and they would all be piled in here with him, divvying the cake. The very idea made him greedy and he hunched over the gumdrop-studded roof and ate.

Then dumb Sarah came banging. "Come on, open up, I'm your friend."

Like hell, he thought, she had swatted him for dropping gum wads off the balcony into Randolph's hair. He was down to the bottom row of gumdrops on the tower roof. Then this Bart was at the door, Archer recognized his voice, he would make Archer a lieutenant when the army formed.

"What army?"

"Never mind, we need your CB radio. I thought we were friends."

So Archer let them in. His friend that had been so wonky on the avenue, like catatonic, after the guy with the TV fell on them, was all business now. He was searching Archer's desk. "What do you want it for?"

"Something for the party," Sarah said with a fake laugh. She had stuffed a wrench in the space between her boobs; the handle stuck up out of the green evening gown. "We have to requisition it."

"Put it back or I'll tell my father."

Then Bart said, "I'll tell Granger where you went today."

"All right, all right. What do you want it for?"

"Exigencies of battle," Bart said.

"Ex-what?"

"Never mind," Sarah said, sounding like his mother, and they left.

Archer was down to the tower part, the next part was those things like teeth, crenellations, Granger told him when they did the unit on medieval life. He was stuffed with too many carbs and about to urp from too much sugar plus which he could not remember who his mom was dancing with when the lights went out. He picked up the tray with the cake and put it on his desk, noting with a grim smile that there was frosting all over his homework. He didn't care. There was frosting on his fingers and his hands were stained with food coloring, it made him want to puke.

Exigencies of battle.

What was going on?

Something, he was sure. Now that he thought about it there was a hell of a lot of racket outside, he could hear it through all the window coverings, shots and explosions, plus there was heavy traffic in the Parkhurst halls along with the no power, and why hadn't they turned the auxiliary generator on? When he went to watch TV before dinner all he got was colored snow, he'd had to put in one of Granger's porno cassettes to pass the time until his folks came in with glits in their hair and mouths and on her bare chest and told him it was time to go down to the banquet and eat. He looked at the partially devoured turret and thought it would be really neat to make it up there onto the real roof, he would pop up and peek through one of the crenellations and find out what was going on.

On the principle that ratty was the best disguise he got out his Halloween tramp costume and put it on. Then he smeared shoe polish on his face and sneaked out. At this level each apartment occupied a wing. The corner spaces were given over to the towers, which were sealed off from the rest of the building except on the top floor where the Parkhursts lived. Archer was afraid of running into his mother or Granger so he went down the narrow service stairs. There were a lot of people going up and down but they were too preoccupied to notice him. At ground level there was a locked door that Archer knew led to the private staircase, and the archway where there was a secret family door. There was also a door into the tower, and the key that led out might also let him go up. It just so happened that he had this key, which was why Bart found him outside.

In addition to the being spoiled and fat and mean, Archer was a thief.

He stole it from Sarah when he was little and she still thought he was cute. He just balled it up in a wad of bubble gum and swallowed it. She never found it and all he had to do was wait for it to come out in the poop. It was that simple. He could go places only the Parkhursts went. If he wanted he could go out onto the street. He waited until the service stairwell was empty and then turned on his flash and tried the lock. He would go across the arch and into the stairway leading up the tower.

The trouble was, there was a stiff lying in the arch. At first he thought it was only a heap of blankets, but then he shined his light and there was this white hand sticking out. He thought it might have moved. The damn thing was lying right in front of the tower door. For a minute he thought he would just drag it out of the way. He touched it with his foot. Then a low, moaning sound came out and he screamed. He was flattened against the far wall and peeing down his leg without ever realizing it was only a posthumous fart. The tower was out of the question now, but so was going home. The only other place to go was out. He had found the secret door one day when he came down here to hide from a family fight but he was too chicken to use it after dark. Now he heard voices in the service stairs, somebody coming to get the body, maybe, and a few feet away the corpse was just about to sit up; his back hairs were electrified and without thinking he had put the key into the lock and let himself out into the street.

It was like being skinned. There he was in the night air, all by himself. He wasn't even in a car. All hell was busting loose on Central Park West, there were craters up the block with the ends of cars sticking out. If there had been any traffic moving on the avenue, it was jammed right now, cars piled into each other with people running over the hoods and roofs and trucks trying to get things hauled out of the way and people using crowbars to pry the drivers out. Why were they trying to clear the avenue? Not for any honest reason, he could tell. There was a savage look to the people he saw, people in headbands and people in dreadlocks and people in slouch hats or tearing wild-looking hair, there were none of the carefully combed civilized friends and servants Archer knew; these people were something else entirely. On the side street, gangs were running around with flashlights or torches, and the top floors of the next building were on fire. Guys and women and strangers who were neither were yelling and carrying things out, two men were heaving TV sets at each other, they each had a stack of portables and they kept missing so the battle would go on and the sets could keep hitting the sidewalks with a tremendous crash. There were victims hanging out of the lower-story windows across the way and wild men throwing things out and throwing people out and letting valuables down on ropes: furniture and stereos. It sounded like there were thousands more over there in the park, Archer couldn't tell how many, but there were these huge columns of smoke everywhere, campfires, he supposed. He didn't know what to make of any of this and he stood there with spit piling up in his mouth. Only Archer could have survived outside that night, only Archer could have gone through the streets in safety, because he was a kid. One more dirty child excited no curiosity; he could have been invisible. He felt invisible, too, and if that was true then he must be invulnerable, so it was perfectly safe for him to go wherever he wanted. He could even go around the corner and down the side street.

They were piling up loot on the sidewalks, groups were wrangling over possession of a TV cassette player here, and there, an ornamental gilded clock with cherubs on the front. Nobody knew anybody else and everybody tore around getting away with everything they could lay hands on, doing as much damage as they could. Flames shot out of all the upstairs windows across the street; every once in a while, Archer imagined he saw somebody screaming for help and there was a terrible splat at the end of the street where somebody jumped. There were people dancing and waving their arms and yelling at the fire and halfway down the block some guys were doing something weird with a roll of cyclone fencing. He didn't know if it was going to be a barricade or a trap. It was dumb of him to be out here like this but he kept trying to figure out what was going on. These people didn't look like anybody Archer knew. It was as if every jail and fleabag hotel and insane asylum in the world had opened and spilled these people out.

There were really old guys and kids in rags and leather jackets and Army surplus and blankets with holes cut so the head went through, they all looked so crazed and hurried that Archer stuck to the hewn granite of the Parkhurst and tried to merge with it as clots of people scrambled in the streets. They were many, whoever they were, and so angry that he was terrified. It was like watching the passage of some enormous, rushing beast.

As it turned out they were all too busy running around and fighting among themselves to notice the presence of a filthy kid, and as a result Archer became overconfident. Maybe he was invisible. He could stay out here as long as he wanted. It was like being at the movies. You couldn't look but you couldn't look away either. A gang was beating up on some poor guy in a bathrobe and Archer could hear women screaming somewhere across the street. He made his way down the side street toward Columbus Avenue, heading for the little park that took up the last third of the block. There were people crammed in the park, all gesticulating and shouting, packed so tight that Archer could not worm his way in to find out what the guy was saying up there, waving his arms and talking from the top of a ruined car. Somebody had spray-painted KILL across the granite face of the windowless west wall and somebody else had written BARON in letters four feet high. Archer was trying to get closer when a huge, lurching shape passed too close with its claws bared and fiery jaws gaping; he could not tell whether it was an angry man or a grizzly bear. It didn't matter. He headed back up the side street, sprinting for Central Park West and the secret door.

He would have made it, too, except he was distracted by the sound of sirens heralding a flying wedge of motorcycles, wild-looking men and women screaming down the sidewalks with their hair flying behind. They were riding escort for a man who roared along, standing in the sidecar of the last bike. His head was wrapped in silver with silver material streaming behind him in the breeze. When the convoy stopped he put one hand on the shoulder of the squatty woman driver and stepped down. As soon as he did people stopped working on the barricade and came to listen to him, and the bikers nosed their machines into a protective circle. The guy in the silver head-wrapping was important, Archer could tell. He and the others looked like generals, parleying. It was like one of those Jap movies, Archer thought, the ones about the crazy warriors. He crept into earshot.

". . . going pretty well."

". . . let the factions wear each other down." The leader turned a profile like a silver blade. "Then we can make our move."

The squatty woman said, "Not until it's time."

A bunch of guys had dragged somebody into a gutter and they were doing something to him. The victim was screaming so loud that Archer couldn't make out much of the rest. ". . . good command post."

"Like Gibraltar." The squatty woman cleared her throat and spat. "Just as hard to get into."

There was a muffled crash as an upstairs window blew out and Archer could not be sure whether he heard the leader say the next thing or whether it was only the sound of falling glass. ". . . have inside help."

What? There was no time to think about it. Someone had thrown a firebomb against the wall of the Parkhurst, where it flared and then guttered feebly and went out. There was something about the . . . Archer crept out of the shadows, trying to see better, trying to hear.

". . . need to get around to the others and organize. Then we can wait our time." Who was this guy?

If he could just get a look at the leader. He thought he . . . One of the lieutenants was saying, ". . . move in and take over as we planned."

So there was something more than a riot going on. These people were organized and ready to move. Archer should have been scurrying away by that time, darting down the block and diving through the hidden door to warn his parents, Mr. Parkhurst, everybody else, but he was only ten years old and there was something here that he was just about to understand. At six, when he was still being taught by old-fashioned nuns in full habit, he had been shocked one day as a teacher leaned forward and between the temple and the starched linen he saw her natural hair. There was a similar prurience operating in him now, something about the turban, the silver turban, and this guy. What color was his hair anyway, and what did it mean?

He was never really going to know. If he almost found out in that last second, everything was erased by terror because a hand clamped on his head at that very moment with the force of a steam-shovel bucket and he forgot everything, even the unusually colored curl he may have seen just as the leader raised his hand unthinkingly and tucked it back. All memory was crowded out as someone yanked him up by the hair and smashed him against the Parkhurst wall with tremendous force. Flooded with adrenaline and nearly hysterical, he struggled helplessly, with his feet dangling and his vision eclipsed by the fiery moon of the squatty woman's face.

"Who are you?"

Archer strangled.

"Your name." She rattled his head against the wall. "Come on, york it up."

"Put him down, Madge."

"Little bastard could be a spy. What are you doing here?"

Archer wheezed. "Nothing."

"I said, put him down."

"What if he came from in there?"

"In those filthy clothes? Look at him. He's only a kid." The leader stepped closer.

She would not let go. "Who are you?"

"I'm only a kid." Archer was afraid to cry. If he did she would mash him flat and grind him out like a cigarette. Should he smile? It was beyond his power. Everything was going fast, including his scalp. The hair she was holding him up by was about to part from his skull in a single bloody patch.

"Put him down, Madge, we have fish to fry."

"Better safe than sorry," Madge said, giving him a vicious shake.

"I'll be quiet," Archer screamed.

"Damn right. I'm going to shut you up."

"I promise," he said, but it came out as a huge, formless wail, followed by something that surprised him as much as it did them. What followed was that Archer threw up. It all came out in spite of him: the candy bars he ate while they were having cocktails and the stuffed mushroom caps and hot hors d'oeuvres and the anniversary banquet, all six courses of it, up to and including the after-dinner mints and the man next to him's dessert, followed by the top of the right-hand turret on the birthday cake, down to the gumdrop tiles the baker had pressed into the frosting on the roof, it came out and spewed all over him and her too, all of it steaming into the open at last, along with his fear at this moment and his helplessness and the anger at his mother and rage at Granger for boffing her right there in his father's living room, where any innocent fool could walk in on top of them, it came piling up his throat and out and down his chest and cascading onto Madge, who leaped away and hurled him down in disgust. Something hit the sidewalk with a clink.

He could hear rough laughter. "See what you get, Madge. It serves you right."

"Poor little bastard," the leader said.

"Poor, hell. I'm going to get you," she hissed, in a rage.

Archer was more or less face down on it, raising his head so he wouldn't drown.

"Listen." She had her foot on his neck. "And listen hard."

He made a strangled sound.

"You never saw us. You never heard anything. Understand?

"Not one word. If you say one single word to anybody wherever I am I'm going to know it." She had lifted her foot from his neck and kicked him in the ribs as she made each point. "I am going to know it and come back and find you, no matter where you hide, I am going to find you and kill you like a yellow dog."

He thought she was going to kill him right there. He cringed, waiting for the final blow. Nothing. When he looked up they were all walking away from him and his vomit, leaving him empty and prostrate in the littered street.

By the time he was strong enough to sit up his key was gone. They must have shaken it out or else a dip got it along with his wallet or else it just fell into the vomit that he didn't want to touch. He would rather die than look for it, but he knew he had to get home before he was murdered or worse. After some thought he crawled back along the sidewalk to the wall and when he was able to stand he braced himself against the Parkhurst that had been his home all his life and backed along it slowly, miserable and scared and too weak and foul-smelling to be approached. He hardly noticed the packs of people clashing and popping off at each other just outside the park. On the side street, the remnants of a police squadron were fighting their way backward from the avenue. It took Archer an hour to make it halfway around the block to the Parkhurst gate. He still had the dry heaves and he was too weak and preoccupied with the intricacies of standing up to take much note of what was going on. He would not have made sense of it anyway: the sacking of the next building, the savage attack on the escaping limousine. The looters were too busy cracking open the limousine and pulling out the contents to notice the small boy plastered to the Parkhurst gates, and they would not see him reach out and pound the residents' emergency code on the Parkhurst bell.

To Archer's everlasting relief Dawson was manning the booth; he hit the switch to the speaker, challenging: "Who goes there?"

"Let me in."

"Identify yourself."

"You stupid son of a bitch, it's me." In spite of his weakness Archer managed his usual tone of command. His life depended on it.

"Oh, Master Archer."

"Open up."

"I have to check with the colonel, sir."

"What?"

"Orders, sir. I'm sorry but the colonel ordered me to seal the gates."

Archer was frightened, exhausted and desperate. He could not have considered what he did next, exactly; he simply opened his mouth and let his whole voice out in one tremendous scream that kept spilling out and spilling out like the vomit, all his pain and fear coming up from the bottom and bubbling out like the last of the birthday cake, he kept his throat open and the sound spilling until there was a commotion in the booth, somebody grappling with Dawson and pushing the button that opened the door, after which he felt somebody's hands dragging him in, Bart, maybe, but he was too spent to know. There was nothing left of him.

There was so much confusion in the courtyard that he managed to get into the building without being stopped. There were people lying around on the stones and moaning, Parkhurst staff making stretchers and carrying them away, everybody so engaged that nobody paid any attention to him. He was sick and filthy and disgusted, he hated this place and everybody in it, he hated his smelly clothes and the way everything had come pouring out of him. He could not sort out any of it, was freezing now, sliding into shock. Even on his good days he would be shaken and struck dumb by the vision of the terrible Madge, her murderous face, what she'd threatened to do. He could still feel her fingers in his scalp. He did not know what was going on outside or what was going to happen here; he only knew he had been shaken up and turned inside out and his life in here had been changed forever by the discovery in the dark living room; it was all too terrible to think about and he began sealing himself against it, building layers around himself like a determined caterpillar. Nobody must ever find out where he'd gone tonight, or what had happened to him; even he didn't want to know. When the servants in the courtyard clustered around Mr. Parkhurst and he began to speak, Archer slipped into the front door. He hid behind an urn until everybody was busy—they were preoccupied, setting up a command post behind the front desk under instructions from that colonel who made the shortest toast—at which point he whisked into the utility staircase and up the service stairs. He was almost home free. With any luck his folks were still at the party with that stupid Granger and he could get cleaned up and be in bed before they even started looking for him.

No such luck. When he came in his mother fell on him like Medea or one of those other babes out of a Greek play. She looked like a Halloween mask in the light from the Coleman lamp. Archer let her scold him and fuss as much as she wanted to, standing passively while she stripped his disgusting clothes and showered him with questions. His jaw was locked shut, frozen so tight that his molars hurt. Then when she set him in the bathtub he didn't say anything, and he didn't say anything when she handed him the towel, nor did he say anything when she tucked him into bed. She was still standing over him, her face a mask of loving remorse, when he rolled over and played dead. He knew she was still there; he could hear her crying quietly. Well tough. He pretended to snore. She should rot in hell before he would talk to her. If she found out where he'd gone she'd murder him and if she didn't murder him for that then she would kill him for walking in on her and Granger in the middle, well screw her, it was not his fault all the lights went out at once. If he never said another word to anyone he might be safe from that horrible woman Madge that was out to get him, and if anything happened to the dumb old Parkhurst, it would serve his mother right. It was not his fault this was happening.

Nor was it his fault that there was somebody in the tower at this very moment, using the last scraps of darkness to signal with a battery-powered flash. Off. On. Off. The light went on blinking until daylight diluted and washed it away, sending an incessant Morse message into the smoky turmoil of the park.

4

"It's time."

Bart woke to find Abel standing over him, looking anguished and as insubstantial as a paper doll. The colonel had sent them up here around three on the premise that they would be no good when it counted unless they slept. Bart had dropped like a felled tree on the leather sofa in the snug private library, but he had the idea that the old man had been pacing, considering, moving papers while he slept. It was clear that Abel was burning up from the inside out, being consumed by concern, and even though he knew ahead of time that it would not change anything, Bart had to try.

"Mr. Parkhurst . . ."

"You'd better call me Abel." He was considering a list.

"Mr. Parkhurst, you shouldn't take this so hard."

"If we're forced to defend here, we're going to need more weapons. The bishop's men have only counted . . ."

"Mr. Parkhurst . . ."

"Mr. Cavanaugh, we're too far along to be so formal." Abel went back to his list. "We have to figure out how to hang on."

"I mean, whatever is happening, it isn't your fault. If you waste yourself over this, it isn't going to matter whether we hang on."

"This is my responsibility. I brought these people here, and as long as they are here, they are my responsibility."

"They came because they wanted to." Bart felt his belly twisting. There was something about this dogged nobility that made him uncomfortable. How could anybody be so damn steady, he wondered, and so devoid of fear?

"They stayed because of me."

"You didn't force anybody."

The old man's jaw was set. "Tradition has its own peculiar power. The help are here because I employ them. It would not occur to them to go unless I told them to. The residents are here because I make them comfortable. They are still comfortable, and if they don't know . . . The guests are here because I invited them, and if they are all still here, it's because none of them know how bad things really are."

"We don't know either."

"If I had been less bent on my own design . . ." Abel turned briefly to the Sargent portrait of his grandmother, touching his lips in an unconscious salute. "We've always tried to do something very specific here. If we dwell on beauty, it is because outside . . ."

Bart dipped his head. Who wouldn't want to create his own world? Who wouldn't sacrifice everything to keep it intact?

"We all stayed because of the gala. Maybe we stayed too long. Maybe it was my fault, for wanting to make one last, beautiful thing . . ." There were tears in Abel's eyes but his voice was strong. "As you mature, you learn how important it is to follow through."

Bart buzzed as if he had been hot-wired. *Does he know about me?* All the connections in his head were jittering and sparking with fragments of a question he did not know how to frame. If he could begin, he . . .

"It's time to go," Abel said, pulling him back to the safety of the moment. He moved to the mahogany panel that concealed his grandfather's print collection. The arrangement unfolded like a clever advertising brochure, so that several panels opened into the room. They were hung from top to bottom with first states of work by artists whose work usually hung in museums, and as children Bart and Sarah had arranged them as carelessly as they would cardboard to make a tent, or a fort. Now Abel gave the inmost panel a tug and it too pulled away, revealing a door. How many times had Bart and Sarah scoured the Parkhurst, looking for secret doors? How many times had they played here without suspecting? "The colonel is waiting for us on the parapet."

The stone stairs that began at ground level and wound up and around the inside of the tower made another gradual curve from here to the top, where a heavy door gave on the parapet. Abel's key fitted easily into the lock. If he noticed how easily the door glided open, he did not remark on it. Bart assumed it was because of Maintenance. The staff had been working all night, reinforcing window coverings in the public rooms, making protected gun slits according to the colonel's specifications, while an entire crew worked over the generator. It seemed logical that they would have been here before the master, making certain the tower door was ready. He held the door for Abel and then stepped out.

As nearly as he could make out there were no lights burning in the city. The murk that hung over the city was heavier than a thundercloud and harder to penetrate. At least they had a good thirteen hours of daylight to work by. When night fell, they would probably have the generator working. He stood with his back to the conical slate roof of the turret, waiting for the colonel. Together, he and Abel looked out at the park.

What he saw confused him. Everything was quiet now; except for the occasional sound of a shot, there was no indication of movement. Nothing seemed much different. Those dark shapes could be rock formations or park buildings. Then Abel handed him the glasses. The dark patches were enemy encampments, isolated knots of people sleeping around dead fires. The Tavern on the Green had been occupied; someone had hoisted a crudely painted flag. He could not make out the emblem. It was hard to see anything at all because the air was charged with the smoke and fug of recent explosions, large and small, the spiraling traces of all those campfires, but as Bart made a half-turn he began to see gun emplacements camouflaged by bushes, and directly across from the building, some hundred or more feet into the park, there was what looked like a catapult.

"The harpoon," he murmured, handing the glasses back to Abel.

"It's worse than I thought."

"Whatever it is, the cops haven't . . ."

The old man was shaking his head. "I don't know how long it will take them. With no phones . . . Archer had the only CB radio."

"All the frequencies are jammed," the colonel said brusquely. He had come up the last steps and out onto the parapet so quietly that neither Bart nor Abel had noticed. "Somebody out there has set up some powerful interference."

"You mean we're completely out of touch?"

"Nothing's going in or out."

Abel said tentatively, "It may be temporary."

Brody said, "It may not."

"It may be just this neighborhood . . ." The old man seemed to be entreating him to say that this was so. "In which case . . ."

"I wouldn't count on it."

". . . we could have reinforcements by this evening."

The colonel made a sharp sound that Bart recognized: most men made it only in climax. "It may be the whole city."

What was interesting, Bart thought, was that they had spent much of the night counting weapons and provisions and fortifying the building, getting ready without even knowing what they were getting ready for. The park concealed most of the answers. From here there was no telling how many people were stirring there, or what kind of ammunition they were gathering. Across the side street vestigial fires flickered in the windows of the ruined building; it took him a minute to assimilate the information because it was the building where his family used to live, before his folks picked him up and ran away from the city. He was surprised by how angry this departure still made him. Just like them to run away and leave the place to whoever wanted to ruin it. But if they hadn't, would this have happened? If it had, if they were still living there, what would have become of them? What angered him most, he realized, was the connection between their departure and that disturbing gap in his recent past, the entire segment he was still missing. The holes were getting fewer and farther between. He still couldn't read, but, pretending to look over Abel's lists last night in the lobby, he had managed to isolate one or two broken letters, and here or there, even a word or two. What's more, moving the refugees into the building, he had found it possible to look into their faces in spite of the traces of the night's violence. It was only a matter of time, he thought, pounding on the stone balustrade because there was always the possibility that his parents' defection from the city had prepared and pointed to whatever it was he did, or did not do, when he lost Mardella. For better or worse, they had run out.

"Our neighbors," Abel said mournfully, looking into the windows of the gutted building. "Our friends."

"Just as well," the colonel said brusquely. "It's going to make it easier for us to clear the area."

"I used to go to parties in that building; there was a lovely lady I almost married after Sarah's mother left . . ."

Now he was wandering and it was Bart's turn to bring him back. "Mr. Parkhurst . . ."

"It was a very beautiful apartment, the penthouse, I believe . . ."

Bart started over. "Abel."

"To think that it should come to this. To think our best efforts should come to this." The old man faltered. "And now, she . . ."

"It isn't over yet," the colonel said.

"Abel." Bart took the old man's arm.

"Yes." He turned with a gracious smile and said, as if nothing else had intervened, not the horrors and disasters of the night, not the grim array of strangers in the park, "Yes Bart. So we will not be afraid to use each other's first names. We are all men here, all friends. Colonel?"

"Al."

"Bart?" His expression was almost boyish—just another kid.

"Yes, Abel."

"Very well." He seemed to get taller as he spoke. The misgivings and trials of the night fell away as he turned. He could have been the captain of a ship, preparing to go back on board. "It's time to inform the others."

Going quietly through the building, Bart perceived the Parkhurst as a sleeping vessel over which its owner had command, and so for the first time completely comprehended the weight and nature of Abel's responsibilities. Anything could happen here; he could get these people to do anything and he would risk anything to protect and keep them. Watching the white head bobbing on the stairs below, he wondered if his skipper was going to make it. The colonel was going ahead full steam when the old man missed a step and

Brody had to make a quick save, after which he and Bart contrived conferences on various landings so they could descend in slower stages. Except for the work crews and one or two oddly matched and brand-new couples making love in secluded corners of the Parkhurst, everybody seemed to be asleep. They had all eaten and drunk too much and danced until they were giddy, and at some point after two Ted Beckett had shepherded them out of the ballroom and hurried them along to their apartments, where they collapsed in silken nightclothes and slept the sleep of the sated.

Bart peeked into the game rooms in hopes of catching a glimpse of Regan, but here too the injured were disposed on pallets and on sofas, sleeping on whatever drugs Regan and Doc Millinger had found to ease their miseries. He would have tiptoed among them in search of her but the colonel snagged his elbow.

"It's almost time for our meeting."

The ballroom was empty now except for Abel's crews, who were busy making gun slits in the armored windows. Abel had come up from the courtyard after the last guest left to make a speech of gratitude to the staff, the caterer's people and the temps who had been brought in to work the party. In addition to their checks and commemorative medallions, he handed out cash bonuses as an expression of his thanks for all they had done under extraordinary pressure. They were all too tired to ask why they were being shuttled back to the servants' quarters before they were finished, and too pleased by the extra cash to ask why there were armed guards here and there to keep them from straying. They trooped down the hallway past the closed doors to the game room and traversed Mrs. Maddox's makeshift kitchen in the gymnasium like obedient children, and went through the door into the west wing as if grateful to be put to bed. In view of the dangers of city life, they would find the presence of the Parkhurst militia reassuring.

Now the only remaining traces of the party were the golden shroud which had been lifted to expose the cake and still hung from the ceiling, and a light dusting of confetti. The colonel stopped to inspect the gun slits and ask a few questions and then he and Bart and Abel went through the gap in the heavy fruitwood folding doors which were closed now, separating the ballroom from the library. In the library, the rotund bishop and his curates were dossed down like seasoned troopers; the bishop's snores were regular and thunderous. Ted Beckett was sleeping in a club chair, with his feet spread wide and his hands folded on his little belly. Some time in the night he had undertaken to arm himself and his clasped hands rose and fell on the handle of an antique dueling pistol.

Bart said, "Do you want me to wake them?"

"Not yet. Their reports are here." Abel sat down at the table. "It might be well for us to do a little figuring."

The colonel turned a profile like an American eagle's. "The first thing will be to get those cannon operational."

"In all the history of the building, they've never been fired in anger." Abel's voice was trembling.

"You forget, we're in trouble."

"We don't know what that trouble is."

"That doesn't keep us from being ready."

Bart tried to lighten the tone. "*Semper paratus,* or is it *semper fidelis?*"

The colonel ignored him. "Maybe we ought to get off a couple of warning shots. Show them we mean business."

"I don't think that's a very good idea."

"They fired on us, remember?"

"We don't know who fired on us," Abel said. "For all we know those people in the park are honest refugees."

"And Santa Claus brings chocolate Easter eggs." The colonel said, carefully, "If you haven't sealed the gates, I think it's time to do it. Your man is still letting people in."

"We can't just close our doors to refugees." Abel looked distraught now; the colonel was pushing him too hard and he seemed not to know how to stop him.

Bart looked from one to the other: two men used to command, tugging in opposite directions. "Abel, it might be like the lifeboat. If you bring too many people on board, you sink it."

Abel whirled angrily. "It's not our place to decide who does or who doesn't deserve to come in here."

"And how long do you think it will be before the enemy infiltrates?" The colonel was standing now, matching Abel's anger. "Man, let me do my job!"

"Who says it's your job?" Ted Beckett had risen. "Who put you in charge of what army?"

In a way, Bart thought, they should thank him. The minute he walked into their circle Abel and the colonel changed their stances slightly so that they were more or less shoulder to shoulder as they faced him. For the moment neither spoke, but Bart had the sense that they were both making subtle alterations in their positions.

"If there is going to be an army here," Beckett said, "as a former officer and one of the homeowners in this building, I should be the one in charge."

"Nobody's talking army, Ted."

"Old blood and guts Brody. You can't wait to go at it with those cannon. If anybody fires anything it's going to be me."

"I thought about it," Brody said. "Now I think we'd better lay back."

"Me," Beckett repeated. "After all I am an expert."

"Nobody. We don't want to attract attention."

"If we don't fight back, what are they going to think of us?"

"It's quiet right now," Brody said. "Let's just keep it quiet."

"And let them think they have us where they want us?"

"We don't even know who *they* are," Brody said.

Abel spoke. "At the moment we're safe, and we're protected."

Brody looked at him; the two men locked eyes for a moment and then the old man dipped his head slightly, in assent, so that the colonel said, "And we're going to be ready."

"Ready," Beckett snarled. "Mr. Parkhurst, are you going to let this outsider make our decisions?"

There was a long pause in which Abel considered. He spoke slowly. "Yes, Beckett. Yes, I am."

"But you don't know anything about him!"

"I know enough."

"What the idiot *did* . . ."

The colonel flushed.

"He told me. It doesn't matter. He is an excellent tactician."

"You're ready to trust . . ."

"That's enough, Beckett," Abel said in a tone that would admit no argument. "Now go and wake the bishop, so we can figure out how to break this to the others."

When Regan followed Doc Millinger into the billiard room with the injured guest, she imagined they would be through in just a few minutes. How could she guess he was only the first patient?

"This will only take a minute." She joshed with the patient, who was sitting on the edge of a billiard table, regarding the wound the harpoon had made with benign astonishment.

Langston Ravenal was still a little tipsy and confused. "A harpoon. Imagine."

"Better bled than dead." Doc Millinger covered his moustache with two fingers to hide his silly smile. He was drunk, she saw, and wondered whether this was what she looked like to others. Still, she envied him because right now all her nerves were jangling and she could feel her back hairs lifting. Scotch would ease . . . No.

"Think of everything you'll have to tell your friends." She swabbed the wound with antiseptic.

" 'Once more unto the breach, dear friends,' " he said unsteadily.

"Yes," she murmured, thinking of the dance. " 'Once more unto the breach.' "

The mood was light and the two doctors worked quickly so they could return to the party. It was a simple wound, and easily tidied. The patient seemed shaken and so they gave him a Nembutal and sent him back to his apartment to sleep it off. They were cleaning up at the sink in the whirlpool room, Regan had wiped a fleck of blood from the golden fabric on her thigh with a damp towel and was touching up her hair when they had the first indication that they were not finished here. Could she go back to the dance with the smell of antiseptic on her wrists? She put her hands to her face in confusion. She wanted to go on being Regan, dancing with that nice kid, pretending she was just a kid who could be silly and romantic, but here she was pulled back into real life: Dr. Millane, who had problems. She was swallowing water hastily, trying to deceive her thirst, when she became aware that there was a large figure standing in the doorway: somebody waiting.

It was Randolph.

With a deferential nod to Regan, he drew Doc Millinger aside, talking in an undertone. As she watched, the jolly doctor went from tipsy to sober in a series of stop-action frames. Shaken, he returned to Regan.

"My dear, something has happened. I wonder if you'd mind giving a little more of your time . . ."

"Doctor?"

"We have a few more patients. There's, ah. There's been a little trouble in the neighborhood."

"Whatever you need."

"Thank you." He took off his tuxedo jacket and rolled up his sleeves just like the doctor in a frontier movie. They could have been in a stockade, preparing for the long haul, uncertain but ready.

"What do you want me to do?" She wondered what was coming.

"We have to see to the wounded."

"How many?"

He sighed tremulously. "Just about everybody."

It was like being in the ER in the aftermath of a train wreck. Together, they treated a stream of people with head injuries, knife wounds, fractures and burns. Most were too upset to talk consecutively. In a way, she was grateful to them for keeping her so busy. She did not have much time to speculate on what was happening outside and had no time at all to stop and fortify herself. She had to keep her mind on the job at hand. It was safe in the Parkhurst, she thought, and if it wasn't, she had to proceed as if it was. Between them, Regan and Doc Millinger must have treated at least a hundred people, drawing on supplies that appeared as mysteriously as the patients, working without question or hesitation until finally they turned to greet the next patient and found that they were done. The rotund old doctor looked shrunken; he was shaking.

"Thank you, Doctor."

She said, "Thank *you.*"

"I've sent Randolph for some reinforcements." His tongue came out and circled his mouth in a way she recognized. "I think we've . . . both . . . earned a little brandy."

Regan swayed. "I can't."

"Just a touch, for medicinal purposes." He had the flask in hand now, and was pouring a shot into the cap. "I prescribe it."

"Thank you," Regan said, "but no thank you. If you don't need me here any more . . ."

"By all means."

"Thank you." She headed through the silent halls and into the Becketts' apartment. She didn't know what she had imagined she was going to do there —pack quickly, so she could put her things in a car and go—or catch a few hours' sleep before she got out of here. Whatever it was was going to have to wait because the apartment was filled with marijuana smoke and sweeter perfumes and as she let herself in she heard Billie moaning. She was by this time so exhausted that she wasn't thinking clearly and so she went into the darkened living room, expecting to find her friend injured or overdosed or something worse, writhing in the light of the guttering candle.

She was indeed writhing in the puddling candlelight, but it was clear that she was not in pain. What was not clear was who or how many people she was entwined with, and Regan gasped and backed out hastily, but not before Billie saw her.

Oh-oh, she thought, *maybe I need that drink after all.*

She was grateful to Billie for placing herself between her and the bar and she turned quickly and went into the kitchen, where, in a rush and without even thinking about it, she found and ate an entire pint of ice cream, after which, shivering, she snagged a warmup jacket from the hall closet and went back downstairs to the game rooms. It was clear that the party had gone on without her, that it was going on now at a certain level, and the events of the night had separated her from the frivolity. *All right, dammit,* she thought, *I am a doctor. At least I am a doctor.*

In the adjoining billiard rooms and card rooms and lounges, the injured were sleeping restlessly. Some cried out in their sleep; others seemed to rattle along in a muttered catalog of the horrors of the night. She stopped here and there to adjust a pillow or pull a blanket higher around a patient and then went into the last billiard room, which had been their makeshift surgery, with the sense of coming home. The old doctor was laid out on a sofa on the far side of the room, and with a facility she had picked up in internship, she curled up on the opposite sofa. She dropped into a sleep so profound that it would take Bart several minutes to wake her. Half-asleep, she responded to his hands with a sensuous murmur.

She stretched and lifted her arms without even opening her eyes, responding as she must have to Jake, on a dozen lost mornings, felt the luxury of his arms around her and in the next second gasped as she came to full consciousness. "Good lord!"

"It's me." He was grinning.

"What did I just do?"

"Nothing," he said, the cat choking on the yellow feathers. "Good morning."

"Is it morning?" She pretended to consult her watch, pushing up the sleeve of the jacket in an attempt to hide her embarrassment. Naturally she was not wearing a watch, had taken it off when she put on her costume for the evening, which left her even more embarrassed, because he was a kid, and looking at her, and because heaven help her she had wanted to continue. When was the last . . . ?

"About ten. Abel wants everybody in the courtyard at eleven. I think he's going to make an announcement."

"I'd better change." She wished he would stop staring.

"You look terrific." He considered. "Except for the jacket."

"This dress is like a straitjacket, and the stockings . . . Look, you don't have to wait for me." When they embraced, had she spoken?

"I'm not," he said, sitting on the end of the sofa.

"You can go." Damn her sleep-drugged state, his presumption.

"But I don't need to."

She knew this was impossible; he was, after all, only a kid and she had to put him in his place; all she could manage was, "Last time I saw you, we were dancing."

"Yes we were, weren't we?" His voice lifted with pleasure. He turned and caught her looking. He was occupying a lot of the sofa—more than his quota of physical space—and she was surprised by his expression. It made her aware of her power.

I thought Jake left me beyond it, she thought, and was embarrassed. She said, without knowing why, or what for, "I'm sorry."

"I didn't know you were a doctor."

"As it turns out, yes."

"Really." It was not a question.

"Why do you people always say that?"

"What people?"

"Kids. You say *really,* when you mean something else."

"I'm not a kid."

"That's not an answer."

Bart shrugged. "Lots of things you say to keep from saying something else. I learned that at my last college."

"I thought you went to Harvard."

"Another place." In the dim light, it was hard to tell whether he was blushing. "They didn't teach me much else, though, which was why I didn't stick around to wait for the diploma. My God, a doctor—how did you find out?"

"What?"

"That was what you wanted?"

"I didn't find out." She was surprised to discover this was true. "I just grew up knowing."

"I was going to be an architect. Now I can't read the lines in the damn renderings."

"Oh come on."

"Really."

"There you go. *Really.*" She laughed. What was she doing in the light of the kerosene lamp, flirting with this brash and sexy kid? What was she doing sitting here while in the next room the wounded groaned and stirred and in the streets outside forces she could not even guess at were bent on some end she could only imagine? Here they were threatened by some unknown crisis and still parrying like kids on a blind date. She was flirting—yes, flirting—without a thought except how dark his eyes were, how young he looked. To her amusement and gathering chagrin she realized she was aroused by the way his hair met the back of his neck, and touched his hand, wondering why and how it was that she could sit here and let this happen, when she was probably closer in age to his mother.

"Thursday I was on my rounds," she said in wonder.

"Thursday I had never met you."

"Don't," she said without conviction because she had been removed from the scene of her own daily misery and set down in a location she could not even have imagined. All bets were off now because this was not like being in her life, it was like being on vacation in a foreign country where nothing was quite real because it was so far from home and the daily exigencies; or like being in a movie. So she let him move closer and embrace her because right now the ordinary rules did not pertain; this was, after all, outside of real life. "Oh Bart, what do you think is going to happen?"

"I don't know," he said into her hair, pulling her even closer.

In the next second two things happened; on the other side of the room Doc Millinger began to stir and struggle to sit up, and on this side Bart unexpectedly released her with a sudden blank look, his face washed clean by an unwelcome discovery. "Lord," he said, going from white to red to white again.

"What's the matter?"

"It's even worse than I thought." Before she could assimilate this or figure out what had happened he was on his feet.

"What is?" She had just begun to imagine they were of an age.

"I'm sorry." He whirled in misery and bolted.

On the other side of the room Doc Millinger was sitting with his hands between his knees and his chin resting on his enormous front. "Dr. Millane," he said in a voice she recognized, "I need a little hair of the dog. Can you find me a little something?"

"Yes, Doctor." She located the half-empty flask so quickly that she realized it had been on her mind all the time, was on her mind even when she thought she was above it all, and she took the brandy to the aging doctor. He licked his lips and with a great effort offered her a swig; when she refused he upended it. Watching, she backed off from the puzzle Bart presented, but could not turn away from the spectacle of Doc Millinger: the unsteady hand, the stertorious breathing, the sagging face ruddy with broken capillaries. She put her hand to her face: *Is that what I look like?* At the moment, nothing could convince her otherwise, which meant that when the doctor proffered the flask in a last generous gesture before he killed it, she sprang away as if from a snake. "I'll be back in ten minutes."

"Take your time, young lady, take your time."

"I'll bring some food. Right now, I have to get a shower." What she meant was: *I have to check; I have to find a mirror.*

Archer didn't know whether he wanted to wake up. The bed was warm but his dreams were terrible. Still if he kept on dreaming the thing that was chasing him in the dream was going to catch up and he was scared to death to see it. He had spent the night burying everything that had happened to him because he knew that if he remembered and told somebody, she was going to find him and murder him. If he thought about last night at all he would remember that he'd eaten practically the whole anniversary cake on top of everything else, which was why he threw up all over himself. The rest of the cake was reproaching him right now, collapsing on his messy desk, and he sprang out of bed in wild haste to get rid of it, blundering into Granger without even recognizing him. All he wanted to do was scrape the damn cake into the toilet and flush it away.

"All right then, don't speak." The tutor sounded huffy.

Archer hugged the toilet because he had the dry heaves, stayed there even as Granger stood over him with his lantern.

"Get up. Stop that. You have to get dressed for the rally."

Archer retched and buried his face in a wet towel.

"We're expected in the courtyard at eleven."

If he didn't look at Granger, maybe Granger would go away.

"Of course nobody knows why."

If Archer knew, it was buried.

"Get dressed you little creep." Granger thwacked him with a towel. "I'm going to count to ten and if you aren't ready, I . . ." The tutor's voice hit an uncertain pitch. "All right, I'm counting."

To his humiliation, Archer farted.

"Little brute."

Probably this was what alcoholics felt like, the morning after. You woke up ashamed because you'd had too much and done things you could not remember. What did he do last night, that had left him feeling so horrible? All that sugar. But there was more involved than too much sugar. Still, if he was sick today, he would not acknowledge the real reasons that steamed his armpits and his crotch; the shame, what he had found out and was trying so hard to bury, would bury it, along with . . .

"Nine," Granger counted.

Something he had found out, last night, what was it?

"Ten. Now get your ass in those pants before I have to belt it."

Something about what was happening. Who was out there.

"Do you hear me, Archer?"

What was going to happen.

Granger was taking his belt out of the loops and doubling it. "Little toad."

If he could remember, it might help.

Granger let go with the belt. "Now."

Drop dead, Granger. Why should he help anybody?

"Cat got your tongue, Master Archer? Usually you squeal around now." Granger flicked him again and then gave up on the belting. "All right, don't talk, make motions. We'll expect you at breakfast in five minutes."

It was funny. He had started to say drop dead to Granger aloud, but the words hadn't come, and when he tried to holler at the belting, no sound came after all. In a funny way, he realized, the silence was driving Granger crazier than anything he had ever found to say to him and he thought he might be onto something. When Granger stopped in the doorway with a perplexed look, he smiled like a little cobra and gave him the finger.

Maybe that was why everybody made an extra fuss over him at breakfast. When he got his voice back, which he assumed he had lost because of throwing up so much, he just might keep it a secret. It was driving them crazy. He could see Mummy's pale smile: *Is it something I did?* She even put a little brandy in his coffee. His father came in late, looking pale and worn, and hugged Archer as if he were the only thing he had left. His father didn't say anything and Archer didn't say anything. It was better than most mornings.

He wouldn't say anything at the rally, either. He was only a kid, after all, nobody gave a damn about him and even if he did exercise himself to bring back all those ugly memories of last night, they didn't make any sense right now, and if he tried to tell anybody, nobody was going to believe him. As it turned out, he couldn't talk, even if he wanted to, and he did try when poor old Mr. Parkhurst took the microphone to plead for anybody with information to come forward. Archer tried his voice a couple of times and nothing came out, not even a squeak. If he could talk, what could he say anyway? Whatever they said last night, whatever it looked like, whatever the people outside were doing or threatening to do to them was locked deep inside him now, along with a dizzying flash of unexpected color in the middle . . . the middle of what? Did he know who . . . who what? *Not me. I don't know. Know what?*

Nothing, Archer thought, writhing in Granger's clutches as Mr. Parkhurst entreated them. *I don't know anything.*

So it isn't all women, Bart thought, with bile rising in his throat. *Maybe it's only women I care about.*

One minute he was hugging Regan and the next the void was opening. *Just when I thought I was getting better.*

Back in the Parkhurst apartment, where he had been sent to wake Sarah, he was surprised when she sprang out of a sound sleep with a surly growl and twisted herself around him, writhing like an alley cat. He was even more surprised by the way his body responded as they rolled in an embrace that was not so much an expression of passion or even rage as, what, dislike, fast and dirty and so intense that he disengaged himself with an enormous effort because it was as seductive as it was ugly. The worst part, he realized, was that he could get it on with Sarah right now with no problem, while with Regan . . .

"Too good for a quick bang?"

"You don't even like me." He was trying to reassemble himself.

"So what are you, Saint George?"

"I'm sorry. It's complicated." His voice dropped to an unhappy rumble. "I thought you were in love with Lawrence."

"It doesn't matter who I'm in love with. You're so holy, what have you been doing?"

"If you hate me, there are better ways to show it." That was part of it; Sarah was using her body like a weapon. The other part was all bound up with Regan, with the damnable vacancies in his memory, that caused all these other vacancies in places he cared most about. He backed off, into the safety of the task at hand. "Your father wants you in the courtyard."

"You can both rot in hell."

"We used to be friends."

"Things used to be different."

He said, desperately, "He wants you there when he announces his plans."

She hung back but in the end he got her dressed and moving, and dragged her down the several flights of stairs to the second floor, where he hesitated outside the billiard rooms. There were festive little knots of people moving along by candlelight, chattering with excitement because the picnic brunch was an unscheduled extra and everybody loved parties. Busboys working for Mrs. Imelda Maddox shuttled back and forth from the gym, carrying trays of box brunches, and the atmosphere was one of genial festivity. Still Bart could not quite get past the billiard room, although Sarah tugged impatiently. He pushed the door open a crack and looked inside, but all he saw was old Doc Millinger, who had changed into a white coat and was overseeing the distribution of brunches to the wounded. He had ringed Sarah's wrist with thumb and forefinger and she was tugging against him, so he did not try to ask after Regan. In a way, after what had happened, he was a little afraid to see her. Instead he closed the door on the wounded and led Sarah down the grand staircase to the lobby, delivering her to her father with relief because she stirred up bad feelings in him like little clouds of ink and at the moment he was troubled enough; Abel was used to being master; maybe he could deal with her.

He was bent over the counter at the main desk, making last-minute alterations in the speech he planned to deliver, and he turned to greet his daughter with a look of such loving vulnerability that Bart had to wonder whether the old man could survive.

"Sarah, I'm so glad you came."

"What else could I do? You said I had to. What's that?"

"My address, I . . ." He saw Bart lingering and said, pointedly, "We'll see you in the courtyard."

So Bart had to walk out on them even though it made him uneasy—On Abel's account? On his own? He did not know exactly.

The carnival atmosphere in the courtyard distracted him. Every group had its own idea of costume for the occasion, from morning coats and bourkas with golden masks in the sheikh's entourage to jeans and sweaters and shakers of Bloody Marys more appropriate to a tailgate picnic, Billie Beckett's approach to the occasion. Mrs. Turnesley Woot's crowd were monumentally dowdy as usual in printed crepe dresses and orthopedic shoes and in some cases hats; her gentlemen friends had dressed informally in flannels and country tweeds. The Ransom Hickox groupies were all turned out in the dancing costumes they had slept in; boys and girls alike stifled yawns and turned smudged faces to the platform. The box brunches included cold chicken and fruit and cake and little plastic containers of tossed salad along with a split of champagne for each and, in a gesture toward informality, a plastic champagne glass to go with it. There was a bright awning over the bandstand, where the brass ensemble plus volunteers from last night's orchestra were playing Mozart, so that this seemed less like an assembly than a party.

Bart supposed this was precisely what Abel intended. As he watched, Abel and the colonel climbed the bandstand, dismissing the musicians. Behind them, Ted Beckett and the bishop and his men waited to take their seats, and Bart knew that if he wanted, he could go up and take his place with them. For assorted reasons he did not. One was his failure with Regan, and the fear he had now that he might fail in other ways, always when it seemed most to matter. This had left him shaken; he would do anything Abel asked, but he could not go up there now and pretend to be one of the leaders. He was tough and he was willing, but unless or until he could sort out his life he could not pretend to be in command of anything.

In addition to which, he had spotted Regan standing on the steps next to a muddled-looking Billie Beckett. The pants and heavy sweater she had put on instead of the evening gown made him want to hug her. What would happen if he went over there now and tried to talk to her? Would it be OK, the way it was last night when they were dancing, or would she start to shimmer, the way she did this morning, and slip out of his consciousness and into the void where he had lost Mardella?

He was distracted by a little scene unfolding in front of him. There was Granger, the Livingstons' tutor, knuckling Archer in the back of the neck and holding him in place while he gave him a little kick in the ankles.

"I said, hold still!"

Archer writhed silently.

Bart tapped Granger on the shoulder. "Let go."

"This is none of your business."

"You're hurting him."

"He deserves it."

Bart grabbed Granger by the back of the neck and forced him around until they were facing. He made black Brillo out of his brows. "I said, let go!"

Granger yelped and dropped Archer, after which Bart released him. The tutor hissed and disappeared amid the opening of box brunches and the popping of champagne corks. It was only when Bart took his own box and couldn't get into it that he realized Archer was holding on to him. "It's OK, Arch. You can let go now."

Archer glued himself to Bart's side and didn't say anything.

"If he gives you any more trouble I'll take care of it. Would you let go, please? I'm starving."

Archer shook his head like a baby's rattle.

"OK, well, you're going to have to hold still so I can do this." Bart put the box brunch on the child's head, opening it with his free hand so he could stuff the bread and the champagne bottle into various pockets. He managed to pull out the chicken quarter while Archer stood patiently, steadying the box on his head with the hand that wasn't clamped to Bart's. "Thanks," he said, removing the box and setting it on an ornamental urn. Then he squatted to look into the child's face. "So what do they call you, Archie?"

Archer only grinned.

"Oh well, I guess it doesn't matter." Bart started on the chicken.

It was time to face front. Abel was at the edge of the platform, tapping the microphone.

"My friends," he said, and his voice quavered with his years and the effort of supporting all that which he had been carrying.

Guests and servants alike stirred and turned to listen.

"My friends," he said in a stronger voice. The colonel had taken the dead mike and handed him a bullhorn. "I want to welcome you all here and thank you for the success of this, the Parkhurst's hundredth anniversary. This has been . . ." He faltered. "This has been one of the happiest times of my life . . . and one of the most difficult."

If the guests had been drowsing in the murky morning air, sipping their drinks and waiting for him to propose a toast, this last statement roused them. Now they were riveted.

"As some of you may already know, these times are not the safest, or the quietest, and now . . ."

Ted Beckett sputtered with impatience and made as if to take the bullhorn and finish it, but as he did so Abel went white and rigid with determination, fixing Beckett with a look so fierce that he took a step backward.

"Now, it seems that there has been a little trouble. Trouble in the neighborhood. We are not yet certain of the scope of the difficulty or the extent of the damages. In fact if there are any of you here with information that would help us determine more, I would be more than grateful if you would step forward."

Archer writhed as if he had been stricken. "Are you all right?" Archer only grimaced and would not answer Bart's question.

"As you all know," Abel was saying, "there has been a citywide power failure, certainly not the first time in the history of Manhattan. We don't know when we can expect power to be restored but we will certainly have the house generator working by tonight at the latest, and we beg your pardon for this temporary inconvenience."

He took a deep breath and let it into the bullhorn by accident; the sound stirred in the courtyard like an ill wind. "It would seem that the phones are out, and we've had a little . . ." His voice went and he took another breath and began again. "We've had a little trouble with communications."

His audience began to rustle and twitter but any complaints were cut off by the urgency with which he continued. "I think that may be the least of our problems. You might as well know there has been a disruption in the streets outside, there is a disturbance in the park and at the moment we cannot say how widespread the trouble is, or how long it will last. I hope you will bear with us here until the difficulty is settled, and I would advise you that for your own safety you should expect to stay here with us at the Parkhurst until we are certain the trouble is over. I and my staff . . ." He raised his hands to silence those who were already muttering. "I and my staff will do our utmost to make your stay here pleasant and comfortable.

"For those of you who wish to cast your lot here, and may want to contribute your services, there will be an organizational meeting in the ballroom as soon as Colonel Brody dismisses us. For practical purposes, the colonel is in charge of operations. If any of you wish to leave, and we do advise you strongly *not* to leave . . ." Abel seemed to fail for a moment; he fell silent while several hundred uneasy voices filled the empty moment. At a word from Brody, he pulled himself together. "Excuse me.

"Excuse me," he said again, this time in a tone that silenced them. "Those who wish to leave will be given the opportunity to do so. The gates will be opened for half an hour at fifteen hundred, and all those who wish to go will be allowed to do so under cover supplied by our militia. I should like you to know, however, that we cannot guarantee your safety once you cross Columbus Avenue." Brody muttered something; Abel shook his head sadly and then shrugged, as if accepting the inevitable. "But at fifteen-thirty they will be closed and . . . *sealed* for the duration for the common good and in the interest of general safety." Pale as he was, diminished by shock and exhaustion, Abel looked out over the assemblage and his voice shook as he concluded, "My dear friends, I shall do everything within my power to protect and defend you."

Without another word he handed the bullhorn to the colonel.

There was something reassuring about the way Brody introduced himself and took over. He laid out the plan for the day simply and clearly, setting out the choices in such a way that the listeners were presented with two options, both determined by the colonel. It was simple enough: they could go or they could stay and fight. If they fought, it was under his direction.

Bart was surprised to find that this suited him fine. He was confused by everything that had happened to him; right now he would like nothing better than to have everything clear-cut. He would be happy to follow orders. Watching the others on the platform, Bart was interested to see what this had made of them. Beckett's genial mask had dropped, leaving him with a sour look; the bishop, who had dressed like a fool for the gala, was in simple black clericals now, looking monumental and as if he could be trusted to the grave. Even Brewster and Dexter, his weedy assistants, had a new toughness. It was as if the crisis had made different people of them. He hoped it would make a different person of him. Dragging Archer perforce, he stepped forward to join them. What this new entity would be called upon to do, he could not know, but he knew he wanted to be part of it. It had been a long time since he had felt this way about anything, had chosen a given direction with this kind of certainty. Looking for Regan, he saw she had left the steps to make her way to the platform, and he zigzagged through the crowd to join her. If they could work together, if they could carry this thing off and survive it one piece, maybe the rest would follow. He was going to separate the business of the next few hours into tasks and tick them off one by one; if he did what he had to do, one thing at a time, then maybe when he'd done all that he could just keep going until he was able to do some of the things he wanted. He would sneak up on them, one at a time, until he was just as good as anybody. Regan heard him call and turned to wait for him with a beginning smile. Matching her smile, he took her hand, only half-noticing that Archer was still attached to his other one. Without speaking, he and Regan turned to stand side by side while Abel made a little closing speech and the band struck up a martial air. Then they followed the platform party into the building.

Those who stayed in the Parkhurst would do so for any number of reasons—it would be hard to decide what to pack, it would be inconvenient, they might miss something interesting. If they left now and this turned out to be a false alarm, they would have to straggle back in the morning, feeling silly. There was the natural reluctance to leave the comfort and safety of the Parkhurst; *It's a jungle out there,* someone said at least once an hour, as Bart went around with his clipboard. It was hard for anybody to think about leaving the luxury; why should they? They were all safe in the embrace of the great stone building. Some were held by inertia and some by loyalty, some by a sense of duty; others stayed to continue love affairs begun in the night and others were fixed by greed. Who knew who was going to fall heir to abandoned treasures? Most people stayed for the simple reason that they could not believe this was serious. How could anything happen here, in the wake of this epic celebration? This was, after all, the Parkhurst. It had stood for a hundred years, in which nothing untoward had ever happened. Most of the people Bart talked to had no sense of danger. The ones who did declare said they were afraid for their lives or, like Rose, the maid who had taken Regan's coat, wanted to leave because there was nothing here to hold them.

When the gate opened at three that afternoon, everybody was in the courtyard to watch the departure. Bart stood on the steps under the porte cochere with Archer still more or less glued to his side. On his other side, the colonel ticked off the names on Bart's clipboard.

"What are they going to do after they leave here?"

"Head for the river. If they make it, they may be able to get over the bridge. There may be boats. If you want to know the truth, I think they may be committing suicide."

Bart turned quickly to study the colonel. No, he was not kidding. His expression was grim and his eyes were slitted as if fixed on some inner vision: the boats leaving Saigon, or something worse? Bart spoke hurriedly, more to reassure himself than the colonel. "We don't know what's going on out there. For all we know, it's nothing." Archer sputtered and Bart gave him a little shake.

The colonel slapped the clipboard against his thigh. "We're going to find out soon enough."

"Sir?"

"I need you for a mission."

"Whatever you say." Bart had to speak fast because the prospect made him giddy. "What . . . Ah."

"Foraging. We're going out in vans at four. There will be two armed parties of six. We don't know what the streets are like so I've got Maintenance building sledges for the supplies."

"I thought we had enough stuff in here to last for days."

"Days," the colonel said. "We don't know how long this is going to take or what we're in for."

"You don't seem too cut up about it."

"Something happened to me when I was a kid younger than you are." For the first time all day, Brody was grinning. "Uncle Sam picked me up and turned me into a soldier. By the time he put me down again, fighting was the only thing I was good for."

"You mean you'd rather . . ."

"I'd rather have you shut up until we get these good people out of here." Brody handed Bart the clipboard and lifted the bullhorn. "All right, people, it's time now. Assume your positions."

For one disturbing second Bart thought everybody was leaving. Then at Abel's signal the band began to play the slow movement from *The New World Symphony* and the crowd parted like the Red Sea to disclose the number who were actually leaving. There were fewer than a hundred, led by Mr. Langston Ravenal, who had tied a yellow scarf around his arm to indicate the precise spot where the harpoon had nicked him. The group he had marshaled looked alternately doughty and excited—and marginally sheepish, as if caught in a lack of faith that was slightly embarrassing.

They made a ragtag assemblage, festive in an amazing variety of costumes, from the uniforms of the temps, which were still visible under hastily donned jackets, to the striped burnooses of a handful of the sheikh's guests, to the splendor of Ravenal's mother, Mrs. Florine Ravenal of the Calhoun family of Charleston and Beaufort, who had put on a soft gray silk frock with matching shoes and bag and kid gloves and even though it was a little late in the season, her ankle-length chinchilla coat. Other women looked like stuffed grizzlies, waddling along in layered furpieces or two or three fur coats, while those who were a little more canny chose to look like bag ladies in costumes borrowed from the servants, all of them more or less voluminous because they concealed the layered Kenzos and Halstons and St. Laurents, which they had put on all at once because it made some sense to get out with the cream of their wardrobes, as they had no idea what was going to become of the items they abandoned. Others eschewed costume and took light suitcases containing their jewels, or in some cases, unwieldy bundles containing candlesticks and flat silver. Bart surmised that all these would be dropped at the first sign of danger; none of the people going looked capable of fighting to the death for possessions, or anything else, for that matter. The men were armed with hunting rifles or scuba gear or improvised spears; one Ravenal cousin had armed the end of a billiard cue with what looked like a Cuisinart chopping blade and the other spears looked just as improbable. It was apparent that these people had gotten ready in a spirit of frivolity and adventure, because they were also wearing a variety of hats and one or two had bright kerchiefs knotted on their biceps in the same place as Ravenal's. They all proceeded with lifted heads and high spirits, as if headed out on any other Saturday adventure in the city. They were smiling as if they were going window shopping on Columbus Avenue, and the only indication that this expedition meant business came from the handful of Parkhurst militia that Abel had given permission to make the departure. They were armed, grim and professional-looking.

There was a hush as the band finished its piece and at Abel's signal the huge bronze gates swung open. Outside the street was deserted; the city itself seemed to be completely still. There was no sound, in fact, except for the multiple snick as the colonel's men opened the new gun slits on the second floor, cocking their rifles and preparing to cover the departure.

"You will tell them we are all in here," Abel said to Ravenal.

Ravenal drew himself up, pale but gallant; his great-grandfather had fought for the Confederacy. "I'll give a complete report to the authorities."

Brody spoke. "You can tell them the situation is well in hand."

"But we would appreciate some assurance that we are not alone here," Abel said passionately. "We are, after all, taxpayers."

"And soldiers."

Abel turned to the colonel. "Some of us."

"You can tell them we are standing fast here."

Ravenal looked at Brody sharply and there was electricity in the looks they exchanged, each man standing for something more than his own interests. Ravenal grinned at the colonel in the brash assurance that this was an easy afternoon's outing, while Brody wore a stony, stubborn look, his feet set wide in the stance of the defender. The emotions of the people in the courtyard ebbed and flowed perceptibly as the defending group stepped back: Abel, Brody, Bart separating themselves from the folly of the departure.

Then, with the same dashing grin his great-grandfather had given as he led the charge at Antietam, Langston Ravenal raised a gold-headed cane and with a single bold gesture started the group moving. The two violins and the trumpet that had joined the van struck up "The Battle Hymn of the Republic," and the departing company began to sing, their voices surprisingly strong in the open air. They set out then, with brave shouts and a ripple of careless laughter, and long after the gates had closed behind them and they headed across Columbus Avenue, Bart could still hear them. Whether the music was unnaturally cut off or whether the little band simply marched out of his hearing, he could not know, any more than he could predict what was going to happen here, or outside, when he and the others went provisioning.

If all went well, Ravenal and his group would make it to the river, where of course they would find some way off the island. If there was a problem with the bridge up at this end, they could march downtown and leave through the Lincoln or Holland tunnels. In any case they should be in New Jersey by nightfall and the National Guard, or federal troops, or whoever happened to be handling this would take information from Ravenal and his party. It would be over soon, he thought, with a surprising twist of regret because he had come to the Parkhurst in a desperate attempt to change his life for the better, and did not want to leave until he found some way to redeem himself.

He realized he was standing with his knees locked and his jaw so wide it was about to crack at the joints, because he was—good lord, he was listening. Everybody in the courtyard was listening. The hush was profound, the vacuum created by some three hundred souls all straining to hear. Whether they were listening for shots or screams or the dwindling strains of the song or sounds of life in city streets gradually returning to normal, nobody could have said; they knew only that they were waiting. If Bart thought about this later it was as the moment of suspension, the astounding pause before the wave rolled in and broke over him.

5

It was Regan's job to write death certificates for the man in running clothes, who had been moved into a cool subcellar, and one of the refugees, who had slipped away during the half hour she and the others were in the courtyard, watching the Ravenal group's departure. When she returned to the billiard room to check on her patients, she almost overlooked the old gentleman, who was propped in a howdah in his ascot and his Thai silk dressing gown. When she did come upon him he looked so well-groomed, his expression was so pleasant, that at first she wondered what he was doing here. It took her a moment to remember what she had treated him for: tachycardia and an ugly spreading bruise on the flank—lord, they weren't equipped to cope with internal injuries—but it appeared his heart had quite simply stopped. It seemed appropriate for her to send word to Mr. Parkhurst, but she was surprised when he hurried in.

"Where is he?"

"Here. We'll have him moved to the subcellar as soon as I fill out these papers."

He stood over the old gentleman with his head bent and his face drawn not in grief but something much more complicated. When he spoke, it was inadvertently. "How very nice it would be."

"I beg your pardon."

"Just to go to sleep."

"Mr. Parkhurst, he's dead."

He turned slowly. "I know that. He looks so completely at peace, doesn't he? If you want to know the truth, I envy him."

She was aware of Randolph at his master's back, shifting uncomfortably, and looked up into that great square face to find the majordomo scowling significantly. She acknowledged this with a dip of the head and began. "You don't mean that, Mr. Parkhurst."

He looked from her to Randolph, whose face was a mask of entreaty. After a long pause, he sighed. "I suppose I don't. It's just . . . not to have to carry on . . ." He collected himself and finished the thought. "It would be so restful."

Randolph said, urgently, "We'll have the generators going in another hour or two, sir, and I spoke to the people in the ballroom and they're all cheerful. They're looking forward to the cocktail hour."

The old man's face twisted. "The cocktail hour."

Randolph reminded him. "You said it would be good for everybody. You said it was important to . . ."

"Carry on."

Regan said, "If you need something to help you cope . . ."

The old man shook his head; she admired the swiftness with which he refused her. "It's difficult, but . . ."

"Please, sir." Randolph flushed and covered his mouth.

The old man drew himself up. "Of course I will carry on. After all, I am a Parkhurst. Now about this gentleman, and the other . . ."

The two, man and master, seemed to have struck an unspoken agreement. "I'll take care of it."

"Some quiet solution," Abel said.

"Of course, sir."

"We don't want to alarm the others."

"Certainly not, sir."

"A few prayers might be appropriate . . ." The old man was wavering like a paper cutout, exhausted and almost translucent.

"Mr. Parkhurst, I think you'd better get some rest."

"I can't, my people . . ."

"You won't be any good to them unless you get some rest. If the party is at seven . . ."

"I'll be fine, I . . ." He sagged against Randolph. "Oh dear. Excuse me."

"I'll take you upstairs, sir. And I'll see that you are waked in time."

"The generator, the—deceased."

"I'll take care of everything, sir."

"And I'll take care of everything here," Regan said. "Rest now. Doctor's orders."

The look Randolph gave her as he took his master out of the infirmary was one of such gravity that she found herself wanting to run after him and press him to take care of himself. They seemed to support each other, master and man, and if either was strong it was because the other expected it. *It's funny,* she thought, *what you can do because people expect it.* In Cambridge, drunk as she had been much of the time in the past few months, she was always on deck at the hospital and always ready to work with a clear head no matter how much coffee it took for her to achieve it, would do it against all odds and no matter how great the effort because she was Dr. Millane, and people expected it. If she was on her feet now, steady if exhausted, it was because she had patients to see to here, people who depended on her, and she was grateful for the imperative. She was not certain what kind of complex tug of souls she and Bart were engaged in, or why he fled her one minute and sought her out the next, but she would look to Abel and Randolph for a clue, doing what seemed necessary—because it was expected.

It was quiet in the makeshift infirmary; she had retreated from the other game rooms to the billiard room she and Doc Millinger had converted to a surgery, partly because her patients in the other rooms were restless now, some of them crying out in their sleep and others getting anxious, plying her with questions. Except for the most badly injured, the refugees would go to the ballroom in time for the evening's party, at which Abel would introduce them to the residents with the idea that they could be given shelter in guest rooms and empty maid's rooms in the various apartments. The most badly injured were grouped on beds in the game room nearest the elevators and at the moment one of the Hickox groupies, who turned out to be a graduate nurse, was keeping tabs on them. It was these patients who worried Regan; they ought to be in a hospital. She was not certain how many of them would survive until they could be transferred, or whether some were going to need surgery, and if they did, whether she and the drunken old doctor were skillful enough to do what was needed. She could only sit tight and hope. She curled up on the leather sofa where she had slept an hour or two this morning and looked at the flask Doc Millinger had abandoned without even a flicker of regret. Whatever else came out of this, she thought she was free—not of the craving, but of the necessity.

"Regan?"

She started out of a doze. "What is it?"

"Nothing but a scratch. Would you mind?"

"Bart!" He shucked the heavy sweater as if taking off a buckler. "Up here. You can sit on the edge of the table. I thought you were . . ." Injured or not, she thought he looked wonderful.

"I was. It's crazy out there." His voice lifted. "Fantastic. You can go anywhere, as long as you stay clear of the park." He looked down at the nicked shoulder Regan was tending and then into her eyes. There was something new in his manner. "Hey, I did it."

She inspected the cut. "Of course you did it."

"Lady, with me, that kind of thing is an open question." After a little silence in which he seemed to be picking his words, one at a time, he said, "I've been trying to tell you, I have this problem. I . . ."

"Shh," she said. "This is going to hurt."

"You should see it out there, it's like the Deadly Desert. We brought back enough stuff to hold us for a year from Thursday. We even got into an armory."

"Nobody got in the way?"

"Nobody but squatters." If the alcohol stung, he was too excited to notice. "We cleaned out a couple of drugstores, too. More supplies than you can use in a dozen days like this one."

Her heart lurched. "You think we're going to be here that long?"

"No telling. I wouldn't mind, would you?"

"Be quiet and let me take care of this."

Bart hardly heard her. "We got a lot of electronics stuff—perfect for demolitions."

"Demolitions!"

"Al says you never know what's going to come in handy."

"You make it sound like you're getting ready for a war."

He was blazing like a Christmas tree. "I don't know what we're getting ready for, but we're getting ready."

"Hold still," she said, and applied the dressing.

She could feel the electricity in her fingertips and she had to make a conscious effort to keep her hands from lingering. What was the matter with her, anyway? His vitality drew her like a magnet and she found herself looking at this wild boy with all the fever of adolescence, when everything was for the first time, and brand-new. At the same time she was strongly aware of her own unsteady state; she was like a recovering burn victim, afraid to make any abrupt movements for fear of tearing the parts of herself that were healing. It had taken her this long to recover from the divorce, she might spend the rest of her life recovering from it, and the last thing she needed now or ever was to be in another fire. She was wavering, swept by heat and cold and desire and anxiety. Frightened, she stepped back.

"Finished?" His look told her that he was aware of the tension.

"For the time being." She gave the arm a professional tap even as she swallowed the familiar, sweet-and-sour taste of anticipation. Remembering the morning, she thought if she could just figure out how to do this, if he would just meet her halfway, then maybe it would be all right after all.

But he was getting down from the table, and if he had been changed by his expedition, somehow improved and emboldened by the fact that he'd brought it off without any trouble, he was still torn; when he spoke even his voice was ragged. "Thanks a lot."

"Keep it clean and stay out of trouble." She was holding her breath now, which puzzled her until she realized he was holding his breath too, looking at her with an expression that would not stay in one place; even his irises seemed to be whirling. *Passengers, this is only a temporary disturbance.* Temporary, she thought; this will be over in a few days and I'll be back at Mass. General, telling my chief about the funny thing that happened to me at the . . . Was this going to be part of it?

But Bart drew on his heavy sweater and took a black ski mask from his back pocket, slipping it on with a gesture that reminded her of warriors, in certain movies; when he spoke it was in a new, valedictory tone that spoke of generations of partings. He was only going out on another foraging run, they expected to meet at Abel's party at seven, but he said, gravely, "There are some things I'd like to tell you, but I can't, at least not yet. The thing is . . . If this comes out all right I'll be back for you."

Dear baby, she thought, as he went out, but it was not what she meant.

Getting it done, Bart thought, bringing in the munitions and food, electronic gear, explosives they had liberated from the Mismaloya Wrecking Company; *having a finite task,* he thought, unloading and storing food and pharmaceuticals; *at least you have one thing you can point to and say: I did it. Me.*

It made him feel good—not, perhaps, the answer to all his problems, but one part of the solution. In all his time in the Institute he had been turned this way and that in the light by the good doctors, who had arranged various make-work schemes for him, but they were make-work only, which he knew almost before they did, one more reason for him to pull the chain on the whole experience. In Cambridge a job was a job. Now, for as long as it lasted, he was engaged in something that mattered, and when he went back to Cambridge he was going to go back to learning to be an architect. He was fairly certain that his problems were his own doing, which meant he was going to have to find some way to undo them alone; if he could not figure out how to close the black holes, he was, by God, going to work around them. It was in this context that he went to the subbasement to help Randolph cremate the unidentified old gentleman and the dead runner, whose suffering in the archway had threatened to undo him. He helped Randolph get the bodies on planks, one at a time, and slide them into the incinerator, even though its mouth shimmered like the outlines of another black hole, just about to engulf him. He had managed; from what the colonel told them they were going to be put to much harder tasks before this was over, and he would find a way to manage. If he got it done, one thing at a time, then pretty soon he might be able to do anything. Anything.

The problem now was an emerging conflict over what they should be doing. He came into the courtyard to discover Abel and the colonel locked in argument over a family of four who were huddled inside the gates, exhausted and defeated-looking in bulky layers of disreputable clothing.

Abel was saying, "We have a responsibility to these people."

Brody knuckled his brush cut, perplexed. "We can't afford any mistakes, Mr. Parkhurst."

"Look at them." The woman was trying to put her arms around both children and her husband, who was so weedy-looking that he might have been a large child; they all looked pinched and desperate and their faces were smeared with blood and recent tears. "What can they do to hurt us?"

"For all you know, they're infiltrators."

"Look at them! Bart, do they look dangerous to you?"

He answered reluctantly. "Not really."

"Mr. Parkhurst, in Nam I was almost killed by a woman no bigger than that one. You can't tell who they are, or what they're hiding."

"And how many died who were not hiding anything?"

Bart looked from one to the other; they both wanted the same thing, the safety of the Parkhurst and everybody in it, but they were already engaged in a clash over the means.

"If you're going to protect what you stand for, you have to do it no matter what the cost." The colonel fixed them with a yellow glare.

Abel shook his head. "Maybe it isn't worth it."

"Maybe you'd just like me to have what's-his-name there open the gate and put up a sign: 'Come and get it.' "

"You know that's not what I want," Abel said wearily.

"Then please bear with me."

"I cannot turn away innocent people."

"Even if it's suicide?"

Abel colored because the colonel had hit his mark, but when he spoke it was with a stiff determination: "I have my responsibilities."

"Then for everybody's good, I'm going to have to confine you to quarters."

Bart caught his breath and stepped forward to intervene, but both men turned on him at the same moment, silencing him.

"If that's what you intend to do, then do it," Abel said to the colonel, holding his wrists out, as if for handcuffs. "But you'll have to do it at a public assembly."

Brody kept knuckling his hair with an expression that went from anger to grudging admiration. "Oh look, Mr. Parkhurst, I don't want to hurt you any more than you want to get in my way."

"Then let's not discuss it any farther."

"If that's the way you want it. But you won't throw any of these things in my face when I'm trying to do my job here."

"And you won't defy me publicly."

They neither nodded nor shook hands; instead they turned and went back into the building. So it was left unresolved and Bart was troubled by the way in which they could both be right and still be in such opposition, by the conflict between ideals and expediency and the increasing difficulty of knowing which was which. Who was right in this case, Abel or Al Brody? If these people turned out to be harmless, then he supposed the old man was, but if they weren't, then that must mean the colonel was. Did this mean these things were determined not by ideals or honor but by outside events? It was perplexing. They looked innocent enough, still huddled in their rags and blinking at him appealingly. "Oh come on," he said, and led them into the building. Which did not prevent him assigning one of the Parkhurst guard to see them upstairs and into the infirmary, even though he felt like a damn fool for doing it.

When he caught up with Abel and the colonel they were in the ballroom. To his surprise, it had not been much changed by its conversion. Granted, the lanterns had made it smoky and there was an armed man stationed at each of the gun slits, but the golden draperies still hung from the windows and Abel had ordered lounge chairs moved from the library to accommodate the men on duty. The candles in the chandeliers had been replenished and the atmosphere was quite festive. The small tables and chairs from the gala had been replaced by a long bar and two side tables already being stocked by Mrs. Imelda Maddox, who had people running back and forth with trays of ham and turkey, smoked salmon and hot *hors d'oeuvres.* She slapped Bart on the back with a big grin and said, "When you go home I want you to spread it far and wide that Imelda Maddox provides quality service even in a crisis."

"Yes ma'am."

"This might make my reputation. You don't happen to have a camera . . ."

"When they put you up for the Nobel prize, I'll vote for you."

On the bandstand a small chamber orchestra was tuning up, while at the gun slits the riflemen were in high spirits.

"Nothing to report, Colonel." Bart recognized Abel's houseboy, who looked like a kid at a costume party in his idea of what to wear while guarding the master's building.

One of the regular guard was at the next gun slit and he snapped to, looking a little embarrassed. "I got off a couple of shots but I guess I was blasting shadows."

The houseboy began laughing, a little too hard. "He hit a couple of them too, sir."

"My son." Abel raised his hand like a priest conferring a blessing, but the correct gesture eluded him and he let it fall.

"Good men," the colonel said.

"Whatever happens . . ." Abel's face was a mask of concern; he was a little like the Old Woman in the Shoe, trying to take care of everybody at once. "Whatever happens, please take care of yourselves."

"Do what you have to," the colonel said crisply. "How long have you been on duty?"

"Since this morning."

"Very well. At 20:00 the second shift will relieve you. Bart, will you round them up?" He proffered a clipboard.

Bart took it eagerly. "Yes sir."

"Good man." The colonel tapped him with the heel of his hand; Bart would have done anything for him.

The party was better than it had any right to be. When the guests came in, it was with high spirits and a celebratory air, as if they were living the adventure of the century and they could hardly wait for it to be over so they could go on TV to talk about it. Some were rehearsing speeches to give the folks back home and others had begun journals. They came from all corners of the building and each group had its own idea of costume, which ranged from guerrilla clothes—the young smarts, and Sarah, who was rather dirtier—to the fifties cocktail dresses resurrected by Mrs. Turnesley Woot and the other dowagers. They were in a variety of printed crepes and exhausted taffetas, frumpy but grand in their best jewels and, in some cases, shoes with diamond buckles. Abel himself had gone upstairs to don a velvet smoking jacket; he returned freshly shaved, with his white hair brushed until it shimmered. His face, when he saw Sarah, was sadly altered, his expression undone by disappointment. *What does he care what she looks like?* The answer eluded Bart; he saw them exchange words, Abel tentative, Sarah swift and bitter: ". . . not anybody's windup toy," she said angrily just before she told him what he could do to himself. But here came Ted Beckett with the bishop's men, Dexter and Brewster, and, trapped or guided by convention, the old man turned smoothly and greeted them cordially. Looking at them, Bart felt something click in the back of his mind: a warning *clunk*, as of tumblers engaging. For whatever reasons they were all dressed alike in surplus khaki shirts and black trousers; naturally the bishop's people would have priest pants, but if Beckett had tried to approximate them with his tuxedo trousers, was it accidental? But here came the sheikh with his entourage, the women magnificent in black bourkas with masks of gold, paper thin, and here were the entourage people preceding Ransom Hickox with—good grief—finger cymbals and a tambourine or two; they hadn't exactly conferred on what they were going to wear, but they cohered; the effect fell somewhere between astronaut and gypsy.

As the room filled, conversation quickened; thanks to Abel's careful preparations the atmosphere was not one of crisis but rather of camaraderie. The guests would swap stories with an amused air that came with the knowledge of security. Yes it was annoying to do without electricity for a day or two and losing phone service was inconvenient, but the Centrex was going to be working soon and their petty hardships would make for better stories later.

Abel had orchestrated this event as carefully as he had the anniversary gala, arranging for double shots at the bar and a rich variety of food, waiting until the party sound reached just the right pitch before he stepped to the bandstand.

"Friends, I'd like to make an announcement."

In the second before he picked up the bullhorn the room pulsed with a fevered gaiety, a joyful hum that was probably enhanced by the partygoers' sense of their position. They alone in the city were celebrating now; they alone were privileged. They were wealthy and blessed by good fortune, so fortunate as to be singular. Bart felt it too: lucky to be here and protected. In contrast to the ruined city outside, the terror that had emptied it, the order and brilliance created here was a marvel.

Abel repeated: "My friends."

The silence was so immediate that Bart understood how close the danger really was: without knowing, they had all been aware of it. At a signal from their host, the chamber music group slipped into "The Battle Hymn of the Republic," a choice which had been carefully considered. If it reminded everyone of the Ravenal group, this was intentional. Raising his voice, Abel said a few words of welcome and then introduced the refugees, who had been waiting in the hallway, with Regan and Doc Millinger. All the ambulatory cases had been tidied up and they came into the ballroom to a round of applause—life's unfortunates, who would be plied with food and drink and made welcome. It went just as Abel had intended. The refugees were surrounded by well-meaning residents and guests, taken up and cared for. If they needed further medical treatment they could drop in at the game rooms for medication or fresh dressings, but they were being absorbed into the life of the building. The people of the Parkhurst quickly opened their hearts and offered temporary homes to them. They would go home to hot dinners and freshly changed sheets in various guest rooms, and Bart could see that Abel was moved by the speed with which they were accepted. He made an affecting little thank-you speech which was followed by thank-yous from various of the refugees and at that very moment the maintenance crew that had been working on the generators below threw a final switch and the lights came on to such a volley of cheers that Bart heard his own voice joining the others.

In the ballroom and elsewhere, the building shuddered to life. Lights that had been turned on Friday and then forgotten shone with exaggerated brilliance, each one a tiny celebration, a reminder that this part of the difficulty, at least, was at an end. People's private machinery resumed doing what it had been doing before the blackout, tended or untended: vibrating, brushing, vacuuming, cooling, heating. The rooms were filled with music as stereos and cassette players spoke, and a cheer filtered in from the courtyard as the dazzling anniversary display flashed its happy message to the skies.

"My God," the colonel said, and dragged Bart and the owner out of the ballroom.

"What's the matter?" Abel tried to dig in his feet but Brody was pulling them both, pell-mell, down the lobby stairs and out, under the porte cochere.

"My God, we've got to stop it."

"I beg your pardon?"

"Turn it off!" The colonel was waving his arms in a frenzy.

"But we just got it going!" Abel looked up, and Bart followed his eyes; he imagined that the light generated here cut a straight shaft through the murky air of the city. "Look at it. It's beautiful!"

"Idiot. Don't you know what you're doing?" To their surprise Brody lunged forward and grabbed the old man by the shoulders and began shaking him. "It's like a red flag. It's just like a red flag."

Bart saw this a second before Abel did. Abel was saying, "It will show them we cannot be vanquished."

"Abel, he's right."

The old man was shaking his head. "I have to give them *something.*"

"God knows what you're calling down."

"But I'm responsible."

The colonel's voice was grim. "Precisely."

"My God." Abel put his hands to his face. When he lowered them again his aspect was changed. "What do you want me to do?"

"Douse this damn display and cover the windows." The colonel was having a hard time controlling himself, but he managed to bring his voice down to dead level. "Enforce blackout conditions and hope to God it's not too late."

"Oh lord. You don't . . ."

"What?"

"What do you think? Don't try to spare me."

"I think we've probably already blown it. They know we're here."

In the public rooms and corridors and bedrooms and kitchens and dozens of exquisitely appointed drawing rooms, people had begun to laugh and embrace and congratulate each other on the return to normal life. Now that the lights were on, the rest would naturally follow. The halls rang with talk and a dozen different kinds of music, and in some places people danced, everybody rejoicing as if life itself had been restored. Within minutes they would be busily covering their windows, but they would all do so with good feelings and light hearts, unaware of the sussurration that began in the park at the precise second at which the courtyard began to blaze, and flowed across it as the outsiders assembled there began to mutter and move and sway in a single common direction like wheat under a beginning wind. The masses in the park would turn as one at the flare of this beacon.

Another group was also drawn by the light: the last police battalion, which fought its way backward to the gates in the minutes that followed. There was no dispute over whether they would be admitted: they were armed, they could be helpful. It was only when they had come inside that anyone realized that most of them were desperately injured. The game rooms were filled almost as quickly as they had been emptied and Bart hardly caught sight of Regan in the hours that followed. When there was no more for him to do he went to the main library and, surrounded as he was by the second shift of riflemen, worried as he was by the implications of this last wave of refugees, he fell on a leather sofa and slept like a stone until morning.

When the sun came up and they went to the roof to reconnoiter, everything had changed. The old man may have anticipated this because he closed his eyes for a minute and stood with his back to the outside door as if he could still keep out any evil forces. Bart stood with his hand on the rail and Al Brody cleared his throat tactfully, ducking his head as if he wished he could hasten this progress. Abel acknowledged this with a sound that was like the rumble of an old dog, stiff but willing, and then opened the door and led them onto the parapet. When Bart looked into the park, his heart contracted. Instead of isolated groups spotted here and there, as they had been yesterday morning, there was a single massed force on the other side of the avenue, people without number. There must be thousands of them standing directly opposite the Parkhurst, not moving, simply waiting, and everything in his head jolted to a stop at the sight of them, all his elaborate formulations, his ways to be good, his attempts to separate right from wrong and choose between were shelved for the moment, in the face of this assembly. They stood like rocks, or blind statues massed there in front of the Parkhurst, held back by a barrier no more substantial than the curbing between them and the empty avenue.

"We are in it now," said the colonel, with joy at something begun.

"Yes we are," the old man said.

Transfixed, Bart did not even try to speak, only looked down at the clustered faces like different colored beads in the moment before they threatened to blur and he would begin to . . .

He turned quickly to escape the vision, but one element was fixed in his mind forever, would flash in his brain again and again for as long as he lived, even if it was only until tomorrow. They were many in the process of becoming one, the enemy. The sunlight on their spears was terrible.

The colonel was saying, in a low tone, "Cavanaugh, I'm going to need you."

6

"Your blood pressure is very high," Regan said to the bishop. She was catnapping in the billiard room when his assistants brought him in. The lanky, sepulchral one looked worried, the skinny, epicene one terrified.

The Most Reverend Bertram Rumsey was more florid than ever, and breathing hard. "I don't know what happened, I just blacked out."

"Up here, on the table." What did Dr. Millinger have in his bag of tricks, she wondered. Probably everything known to man. The foraging party had emptied the trophy case and stocked it with their plunder, willy-nilly. She would locate one of the standards, with the fewest known side effects, and start the bishop on it. Meanwhile she wanted to stall him so she could take his blood pressure again before she released him. "It wouldn't hurt if you got a little rest."

"Just give me something to keep me going." The bishop had climbed up on a stool with help, and from there to the edge of the table, where he sat now, dangling his feet.

Regan kicked the stool away so she could keep him. "You need more than that." Up close, the man looked twenty years younger; there were no lines in the face; he couldn't be much more than forty but here he was trapped inside this huge body that would not stop collecting fat and fluid. "You need . . ." Never mind. This was not the moment to try to change the habits of a lifetime.

"We all need . . ." He shook his head. "These are terrible times."

"What do you think is going to happen?" Regan had been too busy and too tired to speculate. The survivors of the last police battalion had brought in scattered fragments of news, all bad. As nearly as she could make out, Manhattan was almost completely in the hands of some huge unknown power; building by building, it had fallen to a murderous rabble. There was supposed to be an enclave holding out in Wall Street, and another up near Columbia, but this was only rumored. If the people here could join forces with one of those groups . . . The bishop had not answered her question.

"Your excellency?"

"I suppose government troops will be coming in."

"Troops!"

"To restore order. We don't know what this is, whether it's just a riot that's gotten out of control or something more organized, but it's beyond us now. The government is going to have to take care of it."

This gave her the dry swallows. "What do we do in the meantime?"

"Hold out. The colonel thinks we're good for several weeks."

"Weeks!"

The bishop flashed the reassuring smile that had seen him through a great many tight political situations. "Nobody imagines it will take that long. By this time the whole world knows we're here; it's only a matter of time before we're rescued."

This seemed likely to Regan. There was the occasional plane passing over —at a great height, granted—but yesterday she thought she had heard one or two helicopters. If, from above, the Parkhurst looked not much different from the surrounding buildings, she would have no way of knowing. "How long do you think?"

"A day at the most," the bishop said smoothly. "Meanwhile, we're extremely grateful for your efforts here."

"It's my pleasure."

"If that's all you're going to do to me, Doctor, I'd like to get going."

"Not yet."

She saw the bishop weighing the idea of jumping from the edge of the table, but his bulk was so great that even he realized he might sprain an ankle. "Doctor, I'm all right now."

"I need to triangulate from a more normal reading."

"I feel fine."

"It would help if you'd lie down." Her tone let him know she was in charge here. "We'll take it again in five minutes and then we'll see."

"But I'm needed."

"And I'm the doctor."

The bishop lay back on the billiard table with his belly crouched on top of him like a huge, predatory beast. "I don't know what is going to happen," he confessed. "I don't know why they haven't tried to rescue us. To tell the truth, I don't even know what we're going to do."

"Hang on, I suppose." Regan did not like his color. "I think you'd better loosen your collar and undo your belt."

The bishop undid a snap and the white clerical band flapped like a loosened spring. He let out the belt with a groan of relief. "We looked out this morning and they were all there. Thousands of them."

Regan tried the pulse. "That's better."

"I don't know how they zeroed in. I suppose it was the lights."

"And we thought it was so wonderful when Mr. Parkhurst got them working."

"When we do things, we don't always know what we're accomplishing." The bishop stirred impatiently. "I have to hurry. I have things to do."

"If you don't wait until I finish, you won't be doing anything. You're not in very good . . ."

"I know. Eating is one of my few vices."

"You ought to do a little less of it," Regan said judiciously. "Or exercise a lot more."

The bishop said, "I think that may be coming."

"What do you think they want?"

"Everything we have."

"There. That's better."

"If we're lucky, that's all they want."

"Your pulse is a little slower."

The bishop said, "They'll do anything they can to get it."

She tried for another reading on the sphygmomanometer.

The bishop went on talking quietly, as if he could bring down his blood pressure by thinking about something else. "The colonel thinks they're going to attack tonight."

"What are we going to do?"

"He thinks we're strong enough to withstand anything." He looked at the instrument attached to his arm, and then into Regan's eyes. "It's not much better, is it?"

"I can give you something that may help, but you're going to have to try and take it easy."

He gave her a helpless look. "I'll do what I can. Right now . . ."

"I know."

"There are people depending on me." With an effort, the bishop sat up, splendid in clericals with a large gold chain hitched across his magenta front. He refastened the collar with some effort, rolled down his sleeve and tightened the belt as if he could make himself thinner. He looked positively preposterous, with his big belly and his heavy, handsome face with the spade beard, but Regan knew he had been working heroically ever since the incident in the ballroom. He had run around without a thought for himself, marshaling all the organizing qualities and worldly, political gifts that had paved his way to the bishopric, to help prepare the defense.

"Maybe if you got into something a little looser . . ."

"People need to know." He touched his magenta front. He looked at the ring. He put on the black coat. "We fulfill a certain eschatological function."

"These are strange times."

"The outward signs . . ."

"Everybody knows who you are. I think you ought to get comfortable."

The epicene curate and the sepulchral one helped him get down from the table and steadied him until he was composed. Regan took the keys Doc Millinger had given her and rummaged through the trophy cabinet, making a mental note to have the glass replaced with something more solid. The cabinet was filled with antibiotics in every spectrum, anesthetics, barbiturates, drugs to ease pain and drugs to erase the knowledge of pain. She found what she was looking for. It was, perhaps, a dramatic choice, but he needed something that would provide dramatic action.

"Start on these. Three times a day should be right for your weight. Try to cut down on what you eat and watch out for salt. Don't expect results right away. Check back tomorrow, and if you get a reaction come back immediately."

The bishop shook one of the capsules into his hand. The epicene curate was at his elbow with a paper cup before he could close the bottle. He took his medicine dutifully and turned to Regan with a courtly bow. "Thank you, Doctor."

Her tone was not altogether serious. "Thank you, your excellency."

"Oh hell, call me Bert."

"Take care of yourself."

Now Regan was alone again, threatened as she always was when she stopped to catch her breath, threatened even now when she thought she was beyond it. The game rooms were empty now, and she half-hoped for more patients to take her mind off the bar, which she would continue to avoid, and to keep her from checking into the trophy case for a little something to tide her over. No. She put the keys into her pocket and jammed a handkerchief in on top of them. She was sorry now that she had sent Doc Millinger off to his apartment to get some sleep. He was too old for this, all nerves and brittle bones and thirst, but he would take her mind off it. The refugees were all taken care of. The bed cases had been moved. With Abel, she had gone to inspect the great, vaulted attic of the west wing, where Randolph was overseeing the operation. The place was airy and in daytime lighted by a huge glass skylight in the angle where the roof pitched toward Columbus Avenue. The garret was cluttered with crates and sofas, pieces of machinery, and while Randolph cleared spaces for the bedridden at one end, Ted Beckett strutted and turned at the other, talking to the remnants of the last police battalion like Patton at the front. Regan was surprised by a wave of dislike that rose like nausea; whether because of his officiousness or the edge of cruelty in his manner, he was disconcertingly familiar. Jake, she thought. In this circumstance he would be just like Ted Beckett.

When she returned to the game room it was with her mouth tight and her stomach sour—because of Jake? Because of the thirst that was going to cost her a conscious, daily effort? Because of *them,* in part, the blind, powerful army of the unknown, massing in the park, like some monstrous, slow-moving animal gathering itself to strike. *If I'm going to die anyway,* she thought, *I might as well have a little something to ease the pain.*

"Regan?"

She was disproportionately glad to see him. "Bart!"

He was in black, with a holster slung on one hip and one shoulder weighted by a heavy canvas bag. She noted with alarm that there were black smears across his forehead and under the eyes. "I never explained what's the matter with me."

Yesterday, when they almost . . . Regan looked around the billiard room, at the signs of change and beginning deterioration: the bits and pieces left by dozens of patients, abandoned clothes and small objects, discarded shoes, and at the new stains on the rug. In this context, whatever shadow had fallen between them was not going to matter. She just shrugged and smiled. "No time or place for explanations."

"I guess we're beyond it anyway." There was a new urgency in his tone.

"You mean the old rules?"

"The old things."

"What's the matter?"

"Nothing." His look said otherwise.

"You're not going out."

"I have a job."

"You can't go out. We're surrounded. The colonel has locked the gates."

"It's OK. He has a diversion planned. I just thought I'd drop in and say goodbye. Oh Regan."

She rose and lifted her arms, and as she did Archer Livingston pushed between them with a stifled growl. He was flushed and chipmunk-cheeked and looking stuffed in a pink reindeer sweater with the design in blue stretched to bursting across his belly.

Bart groaned. "You remember Archer."

"Yes. Yes I do." Regan made as if to shake hands but the furious little boy wasn't having any; he glowered at her in naked jealousy.

"So I just thought I would say goodbye." He tried to push Archer out of the way, but he was attached like a bear trap to one hand. "I just have to do this, and then I'll be back." He said, over the child's head, "The thing is, I have to work fast, before . . . We have proof they've infiltrated. Somebody in here is a spy."

Between them, Archer was writhing and buzzing at the same time; the buzz matched the hum in her ears and it may have been anxiety or simple fatigue, but she did something she had never done in all her years in pediatrics; she gave him a spontaneous, angry push, shouting, "Archer, will you go *away?*"

He gave her a nasty punch and Bart turned without thinking and cuffed him; Archer wheeled in astonishment and fled like a scorched cat as Bart said, "Our friends out there knew Ravenal was going, when and how. They even knew which route he was going to take."

When Archer slammed the door, they were too engrossed to notice. "How do you know?"

"Because of what happened." His voice shook. "You don't need to know."

"Good lord, who do you think I am?" She did not have to add: *I am a doctor.*

The mask of bravado dropped, exposing vulnerability, grief. "It's Ravenal. I . . . Ah." He drew a ragged breath and let it out all at once. "They got him. They're parading him out there in the park."

"Good lord, we have to go and . . ."

He shook his head. "We don't have to do anything. He's beyond it. He's . . . Ah. He's already dead."

"Oh Bart."

He put his arms around her. "Don't say anything. Let's just be alone."

She nodded and they stood close, embracing not so much in passion as in a complex of needs and emotions that would not sort themselves out or even be articulated for quite some time. Regan rested her forehead against his chest, welcoming the warmth. Even as Bart took in his breath, preparing to speak, she knew they were about to be interrupted; she could already hear hurried footsteps approaching and locked her arms around him, wishing they would never have to move.

Archer knew what they were going to do as soon as he ran out on them, they were going to get down on the rug just like his mother and Granger, and start grunting and rolling around. Well they couldn't treat him that way, together they had shoved him out, well they could go to hell. If Bart couldn't catch the spy it would serve them right. All he was trying to do was get their attention so he could write them a note, and all they could think to do was kick him out. He would show them, he thought, picking at the edges of his tightly sealed memory. There was something in there, something about the silver turban, what it hid, and if he could just . . . Good grief. He felt like he was going to throw up and fled the memory that upset him. If they couldn't treat him any better he was not going to make himself sick on their account, trying to dig up all that bad stuff. All they had to be was nice. He ground his fists in his pockets and cursed them both.

BART IS GOING OUT TO BLOW UP THINGS, he wrote on the wall opposite the elevators, using a lipstick of his mother's and spitting in gobs when it broke.

He knew this because in a passion of loyalty he had stuck with Bart like a faithful dog ever since the beginning, which was why he was around when the colonel told Bart what he had to do. Poor old Mr. Parkhurst didn't like it much, he was practically crying himself, but like it or not they were going to plant charges in the buildings on the two side streets and when it got bad the colonel was going to set them off. Well he had gone everywhere with Bart, when Luigi the plumber loaded Bart down Archer was right there, holding open the pack and look at them, this is what he got, kicked out like an unwanted rat.

He stood back and looked at the message. The letters were tall and ugly and when the spy came along and read them Archer was going to, what, spring out from behind the sofa and catch him? Or offer to help spy? What would happen to Bart if the enemy found out? Serve him right for boffing that floozy. Let them parade his body in the park.

The trouble was when he looked at what he had written it did not make him feel better; he felt worse, like he was going to throw up anyway. So he had to try and scrub it off with the front of his sweater and when that didn't work he moved some high-backed chairs in front of it and hoped for the best. His stomach twisted with remorse, which he mistook for hunger, and he headed down the hall to the gym. Mrs. Imelda Maddox was everywhere, overseeing preparations for the next meal for the members of the guard, the bedridden refugees and the temps. Archer attached himself to her, knowing from experience that she would give him a box of Scooter Pies, just to get rid of him. He happened to know she lived on Scooter Pies and Wild Turkey, stuffing herself with alcohol and marshmallow while she oversaw exquisite French dishes, and crumpled chefs' caps in righteous rage at the sight of a truffle that had gotten rubbery or a piece of parsley that was out of place. Today's food was not up to her usual: the chefs were making vats of brown gunk with a few scallions thrown on top.

"Maybe the garnish will help," she said, as if she and Archer were already in the middle of a conversation. "How can you make *boeuf* Bourguignon out of cold roast? Well, in hard times you have to make do, I suppose."

Archer managed to get between her and one of the vats, so that she tripped and almost fell.

"I mean, we don't know how long we're going to have to make our supplies last." He had managed to knee her leg from behind so that it almost buckled and upset her and she turned in a flurry of irritation. "All you care about is food. Take these and get out of my hair."

So Archer had his Scooter Pies, and as he settled under a heap of coats hanging from one of the exercise bars, he ate six Scooter Pies in a rush, thinking it served her right for being cross, it served his mother right, and Bart right, and ate four more; then in the shadow of the coats he imagined the guy in the silver turban was right behind him, which scared him so much that he ate the eleventh too fast, and to make himself feel better, bit into the twelfth.

This turned out to be a mistake. It made him want to die, which seemed like a pretty good idea now that he thought of it. He could go to the tower and throw himself off, which would settle everything. The trouble was, he couldn't get to the tower because he had lost his stupid key the night he went outside. He could blow his brains out with one of Daddy's dueling pistols, but by this time the bishop and his people had rounded up all the privately owned firearms with the possible exception of the tiny automatic his mother kept in her favorite purse, which she always carried because it was also jammed with her pills. By this time, he was knotted by cramps. Maybe he could poop himself to death. Pills. No, that bitch doctor had locked them all up in the trophy case. He couldn't throw himself out into the courtyard because his place was only on the third floor and there were bushes underneath it, and he couldn't go over to the park and get shot because the guards wouldn't let anybody out the gates.

Counting the ways, he came to the marbled lobby, which was looking like those places people used to go for air raids. Randolph and Mr. Parkhurst were talking in the curve of the banister, with Randolph looking weary and for the first time slightly dumb because his teeth were out. Worse yet Mr. Parkhurst, *Mr. Parkhurst*—was crying, for the other buildings that they were going to blow up, he supposed, or for everything. Right now Archer would not mind crying over everything, but boys were supposed to be brave, so he fished in his pocket instead, coming up with the best he had to give. With a sense of doing something right for once, he darted in and gave Mr. Parkhurst the mangled half of the last Scooter Pie. Something about this cheered Archer right up—doing something for somebody else, maybe, or making Mr. Parkhurst smile, which he did as he put the gift in his pocket and promised to eat it as soon as he got time. Archer, who was not used to this much emotion all at once, fled into the courtyard with the light step of the redeemed, and ran headfirst into Bart.

It was like the end of *Gunga Din:* loyal water carrier and long-lost master, Archer felt positively great. There was Bart laughing and brushing him off; Archer writhing in an orgy of reconciliation: father, son, father, it was just like the movies for sure. Bart was wearing a watch cap and carrying a canvas bag, and he set Archer on his feet with a smile.

"Hey, it's good I ran into you. I just wanted to say—I'm sorry I got mad at you."

Archer's eyes flooded and he opened his heart. He took his pocket notepad and began scribbling his own apologetic note, which he tried to hand to Bart, who glanced down with a dizzy grin and then simply kissed him on the head and started for the gate. By this time, Archer was grinning too; he couldn't stop. Forgiven. Forgiving. It was wonderful. He would dig up what he knew even if it killed him, and the minute it came to him he would write a note and save them all. The only trouble was, now that he wanted most to remember, it was all gone; he had lost even the little bits he'd had left. He was never going to be any good to them. He groaned.

All right, Bart thought. *Now we've made it up.* In a strange moment of double vision, he imagined the little boy needed him in some of the same ways he needed Regan and he thought, *Oh God, what if she's only doing it to be nice?*

He could not afford to dwell on this. What he had to do right now was slip into the building across the street and wait. If he was undisturbed for thirty minutes, then they could assume it was safe for him to begin planting charges. Brody had wanted him to wait an hour and Bart didn't know whether it was the waning daylight or his agitation that had made Brody let him chisel it down to half an hour. He had to plant charges in all the buildings on both sides of the Parkhurst and make it back inside in one piece and hope to God the remote would work. What if they already knew he was coming out? What if they were lying in wait? He realized that Archer knew. A flicker of suspicion broke the surface of his thoughts like an unwanted silver fish. Oh come off it, he's just a kid. Everybody in here wants the same thing. Still everybody in the courtyard looked—not bad, exactly, but newly sinister. He supposed Ravenal got it because somebody in here was a spy; until he was identified, everybody could be a spy. Even good old Randolph looked alarming now; he looked only slightly better as he put in his teeth and touched Bart's arm.

"I came to see if you needed anything."

"I don't think so, thanks."

"I mean, out there."

"This is supposed to be a secret."

Randolph said, gravely, "Not from me."

Bart said, "You sent the invitation."

Without answering, Randolph handed Bart something wrapped in a handkerchief; it felt like a small pistol. "Mr. Abel wanted you to have this."

"It was you. Why did you send for me?"

"It's already loaded and there are two extra clips."

"Randolph, hold still. Look at me. Did you know this was coming?"

The venerable majordomo blinked. "What makes you think that?"

"Randolph, why did you . . ."

"I'm sorry, sir, I'm not at liberty to say."

The spy, Bart thought. *He knows something about the spy.* "Hey wait a minute. Wait."

"It's already loaded," Randolph said over his shoulder. "There are two extra clips."

Uneasy now, Bart looked around the courtyard: at Dawson, who kept popping in and out of his wicket; at the random temps and lower echelon, who were under Ted Beckett's direction, making a baffle of sandbags this side of the inner gates. Why should the help care what happened to them? And what about the Ransom Hickox groupies, who had spilled into the courtyard to watch? They were rattle-ass teenagers, gaga on dope. What did they care which secrets were kept, and what about Beckett? Smooth bastard, in his ersatz uniform, what did he want? Bart even cast a wary eye at the bishop, who was standing by the entrance to the underground garage, waiting for the sheikh's car to emerge.

When there is a spy, everybody looks like a spy, Bart thought, squatting on his heels and waiting for the sheikh's progress to begin.

The sheikh was indeed leaving, and Bart would use the limousine to cover his own exit. He was a jumble of jagged edges now, slit-eyed and jumpy with suspicion, compounded by anxiety; could he do it, or would one of those black holes open and swallow him up? He was spooked by the last flash of Ravenal he'd caught from a gun slit in the ballroom; they had raised him and were carrying him impaled on a stick like a disemboweled scarecrow. Who had told them Ravenal was leaving? Was it Dawson or Brewster, that creepy curate of the bishop's, or his man Dexter, who was even creepier? Maybe it was the Sikh, who was waving the sheikh's limousine up the ramp, or the sheikh himself, or one of his entourage, in which case the problem would leave when the armor-plated limousine with the gold fittings glided out. Bart did not know whether they were going to make it, but nobody had a better chance because the limo would be surrounded by an escort of armored compacts, which would be protected by runners with repeating rifles. The sheikh had convinced Abel that he would break through to safety and tell the world the Parkhurst inhabitants were stranded here, which was one reason Abel and the colonel had allowed the departure. Soon the authorities would know there were some three hundred of them in siege here, cut off from safety and under imminent threat. There was the added matter of Bart's mission: if they didn't make it, at least he would get out under cover.

The atmosphere in the courtyard was one of hope, as it had been when Ravenal set out. The huge bulletproof Rolls nosed out of the underground garage, followed by four armored compacts; the convoy curved around the baffle of sandbags and one car slipped into lead position, nosing the inner gates. Leaving the motors humming, the drivers stepped out and signaled to the people clustered under the porte cochere. Clattering, chattering, heavily veiled and highly perfumed, the sheikh and the pick of his zenana and his most valued servants crossed the courtyard under heavy guard, along with Ransom Hickox's best beloved, who would not be missed for hours because she had stolen a bourka and mingled with the rest. The guard moved with its back to the little knot of Arabs and Bart understood that the guns were trained on the rest—anybody who might prevent the departure. The passage was marked by the chinking of hidden weapons and jewelry stacked on shrouded arms and legs. Everybody but the sheikh was laden with their leader's necessities, bundled in camel bags and bits of Persian carpeting; one by one his people ducked into the limousine and when that was filled, the compacts, in a miracle of compression.

The sheikh was last. He would ride next to his trusted driver in the Rolls. As instructed by Brody, Bart ducked into the shadow of the limousine. As soon as the sheikh finished his farewells and slammed the door, Bart would attach himself to the handle; he would go out with the convoy, running low. As the limo turned right toward Columbus Avenue it would swing wide and hesitate, so Bart could cross in front and sprint the last few feet. The building had better be deserted. He was ordered to shoot on sight, but could he?

As the sheikh raised his arms in a valedictory gesture, the colonel clapped a hand on Bart's shoulder. "They won't make it two blocks."

"Maybe you ought to stop them."

"We went over that. Necessary diversion."

"If it's murder?"

"We don't know that for sure. We have to do what we have to do."

Bart wondered if this was true. But the sheikh had begun his valedictory speech. "My friends, I will send help."

Abel called, "Thank you. This is a fine thing you are doing."

"I will tell the world of your plight."

The inner gates were opening.

"You're just going to let them get murdered?"

"Farewell."

"Thirty minutes," Brody growled. "Then plant your charges and get out fast."

"If this is murder . . ."

"Shut up and get out."

Oh hell, Bart thought, running along in the shadow of the Rolls. Maybe they really will make it. Maybe I can too. He turned as the driver took the limo onto the sidewalk to bring him closer to the door. He thumped the fender as the huge car hesitated and threw himself the last few feet into the opening. He lay in the rubble for a long time and to his astonishment his body imagined Regan's body, and so he saw the relationship between fear and danger and certain moments in love. The insides of his eyelids were studded with fireworks and his head was charged with blood. Only thirty seconds had passed, according to his watch; he was pledged to wait thirty minutes, facedown without stirring, and his body and Regan's fused in some portion of his consciousness in a powerful expression of need. Then the rest came back.

He could have made two of Mardella; she was skinny and passionate, looking up at him through long, pale hair. He did not realize her vulnerability until he took her to live with him in his basement room that he didn't even think of as dangerous because he was a man and too big to feel threatened. He took this fragile sick girl away from the sheltering faculty family against everyone's advice and made her his responsibility. Even when he saw her body marked by the daily shots he didn't see how precarious her life was, how delicate the chemical balance and how chancy the emotional life she led, did not see it even when she turned on him after a fight, threatening: *You know, all I have to do is quit taking the shots.* He loved her and thought he could take care of her. In the basement room they made love and then Bart would tuck her in with extra covers and new magazines and go off to class, and if she hadn't been to a class in weeks, if she stopped going out altogether, it was her privilege, she was his now and they would love and be happy. Mardella was safe with him. So it was probably his own stupidity that began her slide, his not knowing where she kept the insulin, or when it ran out, or what she was supposed to eat or not eat in what quantity, or when; he knew only that he loved Mardella, loved her too much, knew that when he came home one night and found her stiff and cold he had no idea what was the matter, saw her sprawling in her vulnerability and, God help him, he thought she was dead. He had never seen anything like it, went crazy, did not pick up the phone, but ran out and left the door open, fetched up at the locked door to the health service, pounding and sobbing because he did not know what to do.

By the time they got back, she was gone, not exactly without a trace; there was blood on the doorjamb where her arm had brushed it; there was blood on the sheets. When they found the body, which was dumped days later, when they finished doing all the tests, they had to tell Bart that she was still alive when most of the things that had been done to her were done to her. They told him this at a time when he was already grappling with the rest—the coma that looked like death, that he might have found some way to bring her out of—that she had been taken and it was his responsibility; it was all his responsibility. If he had left her living with those steady people, eating the right things by the measured ounce, none of this would ever have—God, when they called him to identify the body, he reached for the dead hand, knowing it was Mardella's, and he had never admitted to anyone that the first black hole opened at the precise moment that he was supposed to look into her dead face. *God, Mardella. God.* Alone in the ruined building, he was rocked with this, weeping silently with his face on his folded arm, gnawing his wrist because he had to stop. If he could not do anything for Mardella, then, it was twice as important for him to do this for the rest of them.

When he looked at his watch the thirty minutes were gone. It was time. With his mouth cracked wide open in an attempt to hear, he tried to identify the sounds in the building—the creak of damaged walls, the rolling chitter of plaster, the slither of rats, or was that something or somebody else?

"Stop it," he said aloud, and got up.

He thought he heard a cough.

When the sound did not repeat itself, he turned on the hooded light. The ruin that surrounded him was complete. The lobby was thick with shifting rubble, and floating here and there on the surface of the debris were spindly chairs, prized bits of statuary, gaping suitcases and over there a cut-crystal punch bowl, intact, all these things monuments to the people who had dropped them in their haste to escape. He half-expected to see the bodies of the stragglers, but found no sign. The evacuation had been successful in that respect, at least. Next to the elevator he found traces of a campfire, so somebody had followed the residents, but so far as he could tell the building was not occupied. Observers at the gun slits in the Parkhurst library had reported no signs of movement, and those stationed on the third floor on the uptown side and the squadron on the roof were convinced all the action was in the park.

In the early days of the city's decline, abandoned buildings were occupied as soon as they fell; they became havens for marauders and scavengers, who holed up to divide spoils and feast on whatever was left in the larders; they would use up a building and then move on. Now there were too many buildings, so much abandoned junk, or treasure, that it would take looters years to go through all of it. If this building was deserted, there was another, he knew. Something or somebody had drawn all the outlaw forces to the park. All those desperate, angry people, all the killers and thieves and deadbeats and punks and psychopaths had been gathered, but who had managed it, and how, and why? Bart could feel his back hairs crawling and he shook his head. Then he dipped into the canvas bag and began the job.

There were six of these intricate little things, whose workings were mysterious to Bart. They had been assembled by Luigi, the crazy-looking plumber at the Parkhurst; he did not talk much and his face always looked slightly off-kilter, as if the features had been smeared out of place by his experiences in Nam. When they brought in the stuff from the electronics firm, along with the plunder from the demolitions company, he simply turned up. What had his crazed genius created, how volatile was it, and would it work? Bart planted the first device without knowing. Gingerly, he armed it, as instructed, and, according to orders, set the auto-destruct. Nobody could get near it now. Cautiously, he backed out, praying to God that he had done it right. If the power in the park could jam the airwaves, could they interfere with this electronic device? Not even Luigi knew for sure. His Army training told him it was their best bet. They could not risk laying telltale fuses, or putting down wires. If they couldn't trigger it electronically they were going to have to find some way to fire into the buildings and hope for the best.

He had five more to plant. With any luck he could finish the buildings on this street without interference. Abel's men were covering him from the library. When he reached the uptown side of the Parkhurst, he would be covered again, but he had to make his own way along the blind west wall. Damn the founder anyway, for designing a west wall without windows, and damn him for donating that indefensible little park that faced Columbus Avenue. Anything could happen to him on the west side, and nobody would know. It was twilight as he came out and made his way along the wall like creeping moss. If he faltered, if his nerve failed him, he had the renewed image of Mardella to fuel his resolve; he could almost see her now, and if he never could make out her face, he had at least confronted their sad love and his own fault in the matter, and he would do anything to make it up. He went into the next building swiftly and did his job without caring whether they caught him; if he did this and they got him, then he would have made it up. As he came out of the last building on the south side, the violet light settled around him like a protective shroud. Swatched in shadows, he moved along.

If he was being followed the shadows also swathed the alien shadow, so that guards watching from the gun slits in the library would not be precisely sure when Bart left the side street to begin his perilous progress along the blank granite of the west wall, or when to expect him at the secret family entrance on the northeast corner, where he would use Abel Parkhurst's treasured key, or indeed whether he could accomplish this and return before dark, when the army in the park would swarm over the wall that bordered it and begin the attack. Nobody would know whether he was being followed—least of all, Bart.

7

Al Brody was a good friend, Regan realized; without talking much, they knew each other in the easy way of people who are more or less of an age. They had certain things in common—his hopeless love for the general's daughter, her growing attraction to Bart, who was twenty-three, at best, which might be why Al came to the infirmary to invite her to join them on the parapet. The game rooms were empty; Doc Millinger was going to the west garret to look in on the bed patients.

"Things are slow, it won't hurt you to bug out for a while." He meant: *Let's try and take your mind off it.*

She was disproportionately grateful. When this was over, maybe she could help Al win the general's daughter after all. She couldn't see Bart, but he was down there in the shadows that puddled between the buildings, filling the space from the bottom up, like ink. It was right for her to keep this vigil; all her muscles had tightened when he left, would not relax until he was safe. It was a matter of concentration, she thought: the power of her will fused with his, she didn't know what good it would do, but if she did not . . . She had gotten a look at that self-styled demolitions expert and could not for the life of her tell whether he was crazy, and if he was, whether he was good at the one thing he claimed to know. Would his devices go off or was Bart risking his life for nothing? What if one of the things blew up in his face? If he set them without being blown to oblivion, could he do it without being seen or would the blind monster in the park reach out and snatch him? Her ears filled with noise. He should be here by now, she thought, and tensed, fearing the rumbling flash. Nothing had happened so far, which she took to be a good sign. If nothing happened in the next five minutes maybe he was home free.

Behind her Al paced the tower walk with his head bent; he and the old man who owned the building passed without speaking, both burdened, intent on the enterprise. Al's face was drawn with anxiety and Mr. Parkhurst seemed to be in mourning, whether for his own people or the past that would be demolished with the buildings across the street, she could not say.

Regan said into the silence, "What time do you think they'll attack?"

"Another hour, probably." When Al approached, she saw that there was more to his expression than she had imagined; if he carried the weight of certain decisions, he was also electrified, wired by all this and ready to blaze.

She said, "And our chances?"

"Good, I think. This time."

She whirled. "This time!"

"We aren't going to kill very many of them. Look."

She followed his eyes, saw the thousands of strangers spread like a living carpet in the park. It made her light-headed and strangely frivolous. Maybe this was what Marie Antoinette felt like, twirling her fingers in the face of death. There were streaks of light cross-hatching the park—runners going through the twilight with torches. It was only a matter of time.

As darkness moved up the sky, she became aware of work lights being switched off here and there, and knew Al's men would be covering the windows, giving the building a black face. To her right, the colonel's men were positioned along the parapets overlooking the avenue. They stood with heaps of Molotov cocktails assembled from bottles and rags and gasoline from the building's pumps. Below, the men at the gun slits were armed and waiting, she knew. The ornamental cannon in this tower had been armed and the colonel's gunners had donned their flak helmets, waiting for the attack. Everybody was ready here, but where was Bart? Next to her, Mr. Parkhurst was resting his forehead on his fists in an attitude of prayer. She bent her head likewise, hoping his God would look down and see.

"He'll be back, don't worry."

"Oh, Al!" She wished she could do something for him, say something that would lift his heart in the same way. "You really think we're going to make it through this one."

"This wave, yes. We're in good shape."

Looking into the growing darkness, she said, "That's all we need to do, get through one thing at a time."

He swallowed his words, so Mr. Parkhurst wouldn't hear. "I hope so."

"By this time tomorrow the place will be crawling with federal troops."

"I wouldn't count on it."

"But somebody's bound to come."

The face he turned to her was drawn in exaggerated lines, like one of the building's stone gargoyles, but when he spoke he tried to keep his tone light. "Never underestimate the sticking power of red tape."

"Wait." She touched his arm, did not know how to frame the question and was spared the necessity by Randolph, who appeared on the parapet like an enormous ghost.

"Mr. Abel. Colonel Brody. I came to tell you . . ."

Regan covered her ears.

"Mr. Cavanaugh is back."

"Oh Randolph!" She hugged the aging majordomo in a gesture that surprised her most of all. "Where is he?"

"They're in the wine cellar."

Al's tone alarmed her. "They?"

"I'm afraid he's taken a captive, sir." Randolph grimaced apologetically. "Somebody followed him. He ambushed her just outside the secret door."

"Her?" Brody was already heading for the tower door.

"Well, I think it's a her."

"Regan, you don't need to . . ."

Randolph said, "I'm afraid a doctor is indicated, sir. It got a little rough."

They took the Parkhurst family elevator to the main floor, where Randolph led them across the lobby to the service elevator. For whatever reasons, he and Bart had chosen to stash the captive in the wine cellar. They had locked her in with the cabernet sauvignon and Bart was standing just outside the padlocked grate, dabbing at the torn ear with a rag soaked in wine. It had indeed been rough. The woman—if that was a woman—had taken a chunk out of Bart's ear and the side of his neck was streaming blood; there was blood clotting in his sweater, which Regan guessed might be hers, and the side of the captive's head was badly scraped where Bart had bashed it against a wall. When she saw Bart their eyes clashed, but there would be no time to bring out the things they had stored up to say to each other. Instead she took care of the ear while he made his report.

"I had to mash her. She was going to bring the whole mob down on me."

"Who is she?" Brody was looking through the bars. She was laid out on the stones like a side of beef and from here there was no telling how badly she was hurt or how many layers she was wearing or what they concealed.

"I don't know. I was almost home free when I caught her. She must have followed me from the start."

Al was quick. "The devices . . ."

"Auto-destruct. If she'd touched one, we'd know."

"Then what was she . . ."

"I think she was trying to find the secret door."

"You'd better let me examine her."

"No ma'am." Brody was pacing again, glaring at the inert captive. "Why would she be looking for the door?"

Bart said, quietly, "Because she knew. I shook her down and found this."

Mr. Parkhurst's voice escaped him in a groan. "A key."

But the woman was sitting up; it was a woman, her eyes blind and empty for the moment, her face blunt as a shark's. She was growling, a sound that was not quite speech, and in the next moment her eyes had cleared. She got to her feet and bunched herself like a rhinoceros; she charged the grate headfirst.

"My God!" She might have hit Mr. Parkhurst head-on; he gasped with pain.

Her own voice came out in a sodden whump. "Muh!"

"What are you doing?" The old man was wild.

She shook her bloody head and squared off and charged the grate again.

"Oh please don't!"

The sound as she collided was sickening.

Abel was pleading. "Please don't do that!"

"Bart, will you take Mr. Parkhurst upstairs?"

She had backed off to run at the grate a third time; Bart had Abel by the arm but he was pulling away, crying out to their captive to stop hurting herself, so that she hesitated before making this third run, saying, cannily, "Want me to stop?"

"In the name of heaven, please!"

"Abel, we'd better go . . ." Bart could not draw him away.

"Bad enough to let me out?"

"Anything," the old man said. "Anything. Colonel, the key . . ."

"On one condition. Bart, on your way up with Mr. Parkhurst, tell Dawson to come down with the cuffs." Al watched them out of sight. Randolph followed like an anxious ghost.

"Not later." Their terrible little captive charged the grate again. "Now." The sound was moist and gruesome; she looked at them through a veil of blood. She was staggering slightly, reeling.

"Al, who is she?"

"We'll find out after we get the cuffs."

Their furious, stubby adversary was grappling with empty air; she looked more or less used up and Regan said, "You'd better let me see to her."

"Not yet."

"I assume you want to ask her a few things."

"She's going to tell us quite a few things."

"Not unless I see to her." She said this with such authority that he turned. "She's dead on her feet, Al. You can see that."

As if on cue their strange little enemy collapsed.

"You'd better give me the key."

He grimaced.

"Al!"

"All right. But I'd better keep you covered."

"Look at her. I can handle anything that comes up."

"Still . . ."

They had the key in the grate when there was a sudden din, the sound of hundreds of shots, the roar of a thousand throats opening at once.

"It's starting!" Brody shoved his service revolver at Regan; in the next second the corridor filled with Brody's men and in the clamor he must have assumed he had placed a guard and she must have assumed she was covered as she knelt over the captive in the grotto. The woman lay on her back in her own blood, with slitted eyes that were not swollen shut as Regan first thought but, rather, fixed on her in such hatred that it made her belly quake.

As the first wave massed, Bart gave the cuffs to one of Brody's people and headed for his post in the ballroom, taking aim as best he could in the darkness that shrouded the avenue. At first he could pick out nothing, but eventually he fixed on the glint of metal, the outline of dark, advancing shapes, and in a confusion of motives discovered he could not fire. On either side of him the riflemen and Thompson gunners were letting go and re-arming so fast that the ballroom was already getting hot and filling rapidly with smoke. Still the attackers came on and kept on coming, racing into the fusillade, careless of what might come down on them from above, and as Bart watched they reached the façade, the fit climbing on the backs of the fallen, and began to batter at it with poles, axes, picks, and yet Bart had not yet gotten off a shot and meanwhile, where was the fire from the roof? To his shock a face appeared directly in the sights of his rifle, some shaggy bastard baring his teeth in the light of the rising moon, and protected as he was by the armored gun slit, Bart saw the enemy's face shimmer, the black hole opening and then my God he fired and blew the whole thing apart.

He was transfixed then, aroused and angry and vindicated all at once, and having fired at last he was himself on fire, running on adrenaline and triumphant, as if he had fought through to some former, stronger self who would take control now, screaming like a cougar and firing again and again, howling with grief for Mardella and lashing out in the name of everything he had lost.

There was a stir on the avenue, the rumbling approach of some large engine, or battery of machines, and in the first wash of moonlight Bart saw the ranks of the attackers part. Several heavily armored trucks rolled onto the avenue, fitted with boilerplate and armed with homemade bazookas, crude barrels hacked from pipe. Protected by makeshift armor and surrounded by support troops, the things lined up across the street. It was only a matter of seconds before they opened fire and Bart gnawed at his knuckles to keep from screaming at Brody and his roof batteries, still silent all those floors above.

Al, he thought. What was the colonel doing up there in the tower? *The bastard bastards, hit them now.*

In the next second there was an outcry from the roof; it was audible even here, and as the enemy swarmed within range the air was filled with fire, all those Molotov cocktails raining on them as Bart and the others in the ballroom opened fire again and the Parkhurst cannon began to fire into the masses of enemy hidden in the park. The avenue was lighted by a dozen different conflagrations, flaming bodies lighting up the scene like living torches and here was Bart, who had never even gotten in schoolyard fights, who had twisted himself in knots over the right and wrong of what they were doing here, Bart screaming blue murder and firing again and again until there was nothing left to fire at.

Somebody shouted, "It's over."

"We got them."

A woman: "Oh, no!"

Did he recognize the voice? He wouldn't know because they were all shouting now, making a sound that fell somewhere between prayer and laughter: "They're gone."

At the far end of the ballroom, where a large shell of some kind had turned a gun slit into a flower of dim light from the outside, Bart thought he heard somebody moaning, but the sound was drowned out by a rising cheer. If Bart was surprised to find himself sobbing with joy and exhaustion he would not admit it; he simply stood with tears streaking his cheeks and his face splitting in a crazy grin, as light filled the ballroom. Every sconce and chandelier was ablaze. The defenders were all blinking as if at an unexpected sunrise, gasping, screaming, cheering, and if Bart was already aware that this was a mistake he would not admit it, any more than he would examine the contents of his head right now. Instead he left himself go with it, kissing Billie Beckett, who responded with alarming passion, dropping her to grab Mrs. Imelda Maddox and twirl her in a waltz of relief; he set her down and patted her, but he was trembling with so many conflicting needs that he was grateful to Ted Beckett for drawing his attention to the bandstand, where he had begun a little speech. He took the mike like an emcee making his debut in Vegas, a world-class group leader streaked by sweat and smut and blood, and then in one of those strange panoramic sweeps of vision that alternated with his black holes Bart was aware of Brody, swooping down on Beckett, and his assistants preparing to douse the lights, and Sarah sobbing by one of the gun slits and at the far end the Most Reverend Bertram Rumsey on his knees in the spot he had been defending, oblivious to his surroundings, and, God. Praying. Whether he was struck by gratitude or deep in supplication or engaged in a more complicated and mysterious transaction, Bart could not know; he only knew that it was not over after all, it was not anywhere near over. On the bandstand, Brody and Beckett were engaged in a furious pantomime and the look Beckett gave the colonel as he relinquished the microphone was one of hatred fueled by this public defeat.

"Friends," Brody said, and the crowd in the ballroom was silenced by his tone. He signaled to the men standing by the wall switches and they doused the lights.

"Sorry about that," he said almost apologetically. "We're not done yet. Pick up your flashlights and get back to your places. I'm afraid it's 'Once more unto the breach.' "

"Mr. Cavanaugh." In the darkness Bart recognized Randolph's voice. "You're needed on the tower."

The scene from the parapet was jumbled and hard to read. Even in the new moonlight, Bart could not make out what had happened until two of Brody's men dropped flares. The enemy had withdrawn all right, but only to the far side of the avenue. It was clear they were regrouping. The ruined armored trucks were being removed and replaced by what looked like heavy artillery. Bart had no way of knowing how much equipment they had to replace what they had lost but it was clear that anybody who fell could be replaced ten times over. He and the others had fought to the point of exhaustion and they hadn't even made a dent in the thousands in the park. It was like being at the beach and watching a wave gather itself. It was only a matter of time before it broke.

The other buildings along the avenue were black and empty, no more than deserted hulks, and so far as he could see, except for the campfires in the park no lights shone anywhere. Across the side street and a little above him were the shattered windows of the building that used to be his home. They gaped at him like dead eyes. Except for the enemy, they were alone on the island now.

Brody was at his elbow. "A word about Beckett. We're going to have to keep an eye on it."

"If that's what you want, what am I doing up here?"

"A couple of things. I thought you might like to be on deck for the fireworks." He was studying Bart.

"I hope that guy knew what he was doing."

"If he didn't, we're going to find out soon enough. The other thing is, ah . . . It's going to be hard on the old man."

"He's stronger than you think."

"He thinks we're destroying private property. I thought, maybe if you could get him down to his apartment?" The colonel knuckled his hair. "Everybody has to do things they don't want to."

"But they don't all have to see it," Bart said ruefully. "If you don't see it, you don't have to deal with it."

"Something like that. Now would you hurry it up?"

Abel was at the parapet, fixed on some distant point Bart could not see. "There's a point when you have to decide whether the end justifies the means. I had many happy times in that building, the people in those buildings were our friends."

"Everybody we care about is gone now, OK?" Bart gulped. "The colonel thought you might want to go below."

"I don't run away."

Does he know about me? "It wouldn't be . . ."

"This is my responsibility." He might have been lighted from within. Bart looked at Brody over Abel's head and shrugged.

"OK. When they charge, we're going to do it. Which means we'd better get under cover." The colonel said patiently, "Mr. Parkhurst, it's also your responsibility to stay in one piece."

When Bart put his hand on Abel's arm, he was surprised by how insubstantial it was; most of the flesh had burned away and he could not shake the suspicion that his bones were hollow. He managed to turn him, but Abel insisted on standing back until the cannon crews and all the men stationed along the parapet filed toward the towers and into the protection of the stairs. When Bart looked along the roof walks, he saw that the heaps of Molotov cocktails had been expended and he wondered whether the roof batteries had used everything they had. Then there was a howl from below, a fresh round of firing, and Bart and Abel ducked into the tower immediately before the colonel, who closed the door on them, just as the new wave broke.

"Do what you have to," the old man said in a strained voice. "Do it now."

Crouched at the top of the tower stairs, Brody was doubled over the detonator. "Something's the matter with it."

"What's . . ."

"Bart. Hold the light." There was a terrible, concentrated silence in which Bart held his breath and Brody worked over the device. The men on the stairs below shifted in the darkness, but did not speak. They could already hear the sound of heavy fire beginning in the park.

Bart began. "What if . . ."

"It has to work."

"Electronic. Jammed?" *What if I did it wrong? At least I . . .*

"Should be all . . ."

"All right!" Bart found himself lifted straight up, hurled down. Socked into the angle of the stairway, Bart felt the linked concussions in his guts and listened to the thunder in his head as the damn things went off. If his mouth was filled with blood, it was because he had bitten the inside of his cheek without even knowing it, replaying his tapes, retracing every step he had taken and numbering every move and wondering: Had he done it right, would the detonator work and if it did, would the buildings go straight up in the air the way they were supposed to or topple like giant logs, collapsing on the Parkhurst? Once on television he had seen an office block blown off its

foundations by a fail-safe demolitions company; it lifted a foot in the air and collapsed on itself in layers without even ruffling the flags next door. Would it work? Crazy Luigi had promised. In a minute they would know.

The emptiness was awful. Then the tower shook as the Parkhurst rattled to its foundations; somewhere below a chandelier fell and there was the chatter of hundreds of small objects as the buildings that had gone up with the explosion began to come down not on them but around them. The Parkhurst was intact.

Above him, Brody was shouting: "It worked!"

"Mr. Parkhurst, are you all right?"

The old man's voice came from deep inside him; it might have been his body that had been threatened by the explosions, his body that was spared. "Yes. Yes I'm all right."

All right, Bart thought. *All right.* It hummed in his ears. *All right.*

Above them, Brody said, in a voice so tremulous that it surprised him: "Sit tight for a minute. Then let's go see what we've got."

By the time they got the tower door open and filed out, by the time the dust settled, the enemy was gone. The enemy was gone and the buildings were gone. There was nothing out there but postatomic-looking rubble and a heavy, sifting dust.

Al said, "It's done."

"Yes," Abel said, and fell against Bart like a tree.

"We've bought another day," Brody said, helping Bart lift him with surprising gentleness and restoring him to his feet. "I think we'd better go downstairs and crash."

They made it as far as the family apartments, and if Bart did not go looking for Regan then, it was because he was completely raw now, scored from the inside out by his renewed memories; he could blow the entire island of Manhattan to blazes and not make up for what he had done, or failed to do; he could kill everybody out there and not make up for it, which meant he had no right to go looking for her, he had destroyed one woman, if he had any brains he would wear a warning label, or run around ringing a bell; the least he could do was stay away. Miserable, he rolled himself in a blanket in Abel's library, and slept.

Brody woke him. Both he and the old man had bathed and changed. Bart stripped his bloody sweater and put on something Abel handed him: part of an old shooting costume from Abercrombie's; the shoulders were reenforced with canvas to keep some long-dead Parkhurst's rifle from catching on the wool.

The mood was one of guarded optimism. Abel was trying to get the colonel to say they had bought enough time to allow their rescuers to get here; all Brody would say was that they had bought themselves some time. Some time in the night the enemy had removed its dead and dragged away most of its ruined vehicles, which meant the Parkhurst lookouts had permitted it. Looking at Abel, Bart knew this must be on his orders. What did they call the DMZ in the old days? No-man's-land. Central Park West had become a no-man's-land. Everything was still and looked freshly washed in the silver morning light. All the dust had settled and even the outlines of the rubble his bombs had created looked serene. Because it was morning, Bart allowed himself to think it might be all right. They had bought time, they had fought off the enemy not once but twice, by the time those jokers regrouped the Army and the Red Cross would be here. The only hard thing he would have left to do would be getting out without seeing Regan—unless he decided he owed it to her to explain.

Next to him Abel stiffened.

"What's the matter?"

"Shh."

"Listen," Brody said.

Now Bart heard it—a faint sound coming from a long way off. It was unfamiliar, disturbing, strange—the sound of many motorcycles approaching, he thought, but did not know why this was the worst thing he'd heard since this began. He followed the others to the parapet and looked up the avenue. Something made him slip a hand under Mr. Parkhurst's elbow. There was a convoy of motorcycles coming down the avenue, some fifteen of them grouped around a bike with a sidecar, and there was a guy standing in the sidecar: somebody tall and skinny, with his face more or less hidden by mirrored goggles and his hair hidden by a swath of silver cloth that was wrapped around and knotted, with a tail of silver streaming behind.

Abel said, "Look."

"Al!"

The figure raised its fist.

"I see."

The rabble in the park began to cheer.

They could not see much, only that the procession took its sweet time until it reached the Parkhurst, passing directly underneath their tower. Bart hung out to watch as it sped up suddenly, making an unexpected swerve as the first bike reached the southeast corner. They kept moving in tight formation, with the guy in the silver headpiece shaking his fist one minute and in the next picking something out of a pouch as the bike with the sidecar reached the point nearest to the curb. He lifted it high and in the next second leaned out to send it rolling down the side street in the direction of the main gate. They would not see it roll down the street with the accuracy of a bowling ball, or land just outside the double gate. What they did see was the man in the silver headgear turning, almost as if he knew where they were standing. He shook his fist at them. Then the convoy picked up speed and roared on down the avenue.

"What was that?"

Brody's voice was strained. "Nothing good."

Abel, who had seemed close to collapse, pulled away from Bart with the determination of a trouper who has been told there will be a second show after all. "I think we'd better go and see."

They waited in the study while Brody sent a man down. He came back with Dawson, who had already retrieved the thing. Dawson stood in the doorway for a long moment before he came in. His expression was sketched in anguish. At a nod from Abel he came in and dumped the thing out of the wastebasket he had used to scoop it up. It was clear why he hadn't wanted to touch it. The object was hard to identify at first, bloodstained as it was, encased in canvas that had been sewn shut with heavy twine. Abel motioned to Randolph, who cut the twine with a kitchen knife, revealing the object inside. He had come a long way, Bart realized, from going blank on muggings to this moment when, without flinching and without any shimmering outlines to spare him, he looked this dead thing in the eyes. He was not at all certain whose head it was. The face had been badly mutilated; someone had run a curved needle and string through the lips in several places, stitching the mouth closed, and it was the fact that something protruded from the lips that made Bart, who felt he would never again be shocked by anything, reach for Abel's scissors and cut the string.

With the lips undone and the foreign object removed from the mouth so it was no longer dragged out of shape, it was a little easier to identify the sheikh.

The foreign object was a plastic bag. Inside they found a newspaper, folded carefully into a wad small enough to fit.

It was a front page, yesterday's, from the Newark *Star Ledger*, and if Bart could look at death now he still could not read; when he fixed on the headlines he saw only the blur, one or two isolated letters. Abel was spelling them out for the others, who crowded around Bart, waiting.

> "CITY ABANDONED TO CRIMINAL ELEMENT," Abel read.
> "RIOTERS' HEYDAY AS GOVERNMENT STALLS."

Brody snapped, "The bastards."

"Wait," Abel said. "The rest:

IS DESERTED CITY
WORTH SAVING?
CONGRESS DEBATES."

"See if there's something about us."

"Nothing." Abel's voice was so low now that Bart and the others had to strain to hear the last few words. "There is another story.

STATE, FEDERAL GOVERNMENTS
LOCKED IN JURISDICTIONAL DISPUTE
AS EMPTY CITY WAITS."

8

Regan lay where the concussions had thrown her. Pebbles and sand were sifting down so fast that she thought the ceiling would come next. At the far end of the grotto her adversary howled in fury and then fell into a profound silence as the reverberations spent themselves. If they were trapped here it was Regan's fault, for grappling the gate shut when the ugly little captive attacked. It had stopped the fight but left her trapped here in the wine cellar. *The wine cellar,* she thought with a certain sense of irony. On either side the rows of cabernet sauvignon chattered in their racks. *The buildings,* she thought. *They've blown the buildings. Maybe now they will come back for me.*

"I hope you're satisfied." The ugly little woman's voice was almost conversational. After hours of silence it came as a shock.

"I didn't know you still talked." Regan sat up.

"I didn't have anything to say." The captive shrugged. "You've got what you want now, you know?"

"If you want to call it that." Regan was near the end of her strength and yet this stubby woman who had, in the early stages, tried to open her face with the jagged rim of a wine bottle, was trying to make friends. "What makes you think so?"

"If we'd won it, you'd know. Baron would be gutting you like a Connecticut River shad and I . . ." She touched her hair. "Let's say I would not be here."

Regan looked at her warily. "I see."

"So this is it for now." She took a comb out of her back pocket and began yanking at the steel wool that passed for hair. "Want to use my comb?"

"I don't think so." Regan regarded her. "Want to tell me who you are?" She meant: *Want to tell me why you're trying to make friends?*

"Might as well make ourselves decent, you know?" She looked into a scrap of mirror, then at Regan. "It doesn't matter what my name is."

"I'm Regan Millane."

"Madge."

"Madge what?"

"Madge never mind. What's a nice girl like you doing in a place like this?"

"I'm hardly a girl."

"You know what I mean."

"I'm a doctor."

"I got into it because to tell the truth I got tired of living without men, but you . . ."

Regan was surprised by her candor, found herself matching it. "Let's say I was trying to get away from myself. But here I am."

Madge sighed. "Me too."

"Look, what do you want from me?"

"When they get here you're going to tell them I'm an OK person, right?"

"After you tried to kill me?"

"Didn't I just loan you my comb?"

"Look, you're making me tired." Regan unfolded slowly, letting herself down on the stones. If Madge thought she was asleep, she might shut up. "If it's really over, we might as well get some sleep."

"Not me. Might as well get loaded while we wait."

"You're not afraid I'll bop you or tie you up?"

"Not any more. It's over. I don't suppose you have a corkscrew."

"No."

"It figures." Madge had been knocking at the necks of various bottles with a rock, broke two before she managed to shear the head off one without shattering it. "Have a snort?"

"No thanks. What makes you think it's over?"

"Not a sound up there. Have you heard a sound?"

"Not for a while."

"So it's only a matter of time."

"I hope so," Regan said, and rolled over on her side. When the attack began Al and his men swarmed out of the wine cellar without a thought for her; what made her imagine they would be back? It might be days before she was missed. Doc, tending the wounded in one part of the building, would assume she was in the other, and Bart? The last time she saw him he was so wired he hardly knew who she was. So, she thought, with a little shrug of resignation, once more around the block alone.

It was her own fault, she thought, for caring about her job, for caring too much to cut her work day short because Jake expected her to be waiting when he came home, to make with the warm body and the hot casserole and all the extra obsequies doctors seemed to expect—she corrected herself—male doctors seemed to expect from the women they were married to, which Jake explained in the white night of their marriage, when everything stopped, even the abuse, and he turned to ice. *What have I done wrong?* Bereft, she had pleaded with him. *Just tell me what to do.* What had he said? *If you don't know what's the matter, I'm certainly not going to spell it out.* He had already lined up Mrs. Right. No wonder she drank.

The contents of the smashed bottles filled the grotto with a delirious smell; she was surrounded by the stuff and if she wanted to escape her misery all she had to do was roll over and sit up, but it occurred to her that she had come all this way and gotten herself into this for a specific reason, and she had not come this distance to revert. She was miles from Boston, light-years from her old life, which she realized she'd thought of as essentially over even as she trudged through the days. What surprised her now was how long life turned out to be, and how various. For the past two years she had been dying by degrees, getting ready for death because she did not really want to live. Why should she? Her marriage was over and Jake had made it clear this was all her fault. Why shouldn't she pollute her blood and threaten her liver and risk the terminal car wreck, the accidental departure because she'd mixed alcohol and pills? Lying on the floor of the wine grotto, cold sober and chilled by the stones, she realized that she had not managed to kill herself, all she'd done was ruin her life, and as she lay in a state that was not sleep but was not waking she considered this. She played all her old tapes one more time and in this suspended state she studied them with a new clarity.

What if she had done everything Jake said she had failed to do? What if they'd had the baby, if she'd cut back on her hours; she had brought it up, over and over, but they needed the money, their lives were too full, it was always the wrong time; these were not her decisions but his, she realized, it had all been his doing, it was . . . *Lord, it would have happened anyway.*

She started; she must have slipped out of consciousness. Now she heard Madge tinkering with the grate. She was cold and stiff by this time, knew she ought to get up and start moving, but she was also fixed by the chain of discoveries. *It wouldn't have mattered what I said or did. He had already lined up Mrs. Right.*

Madge was still fooling with the lock, reeling slightly and beginning to hum under her breath. She muttered, "Where are they?"

It was not my fault it happened. His cruelty was pretending it was.

"Where are they?" Madge fumed and bumped against the bars. "If he loved me he'd be here by now. He said he loved me, but . . ."

It was his. With an enormous effort, Regan rolled over and sat up, shrugging off the old burden. *His fault. His.*

Madge was pounding on the bars in a boozy rage. "Men rot!"

Regan's response was spontaneous and liberating. "Damn right!"

"What? Oh. There you are." Madge turned unsteadily. Even her mouth made a wavy line. "I told you not to lie on those damn stones."

"What time is it?" She was finding it hard to get up.

"Late. You'd better flap your arms a little."

"I can hardly move."

"Should of tanked up. Try running in place." Madge addressed herself to the bars. "Oh you son of a bitch."

"Right. Who's a son of a bitch?"

"Baron. Where is he, where is he anyway?"

Regan was just beginning to warm up. Her voice still shivered. "Where are any of them?"

"Bastard. After what I gave up, for him. I was highly placed in the city government, and then that bastard . . . All I had to do was this one little thing, and now look at me." She whirled angrily. "Me, that stole him all the plans."

"Wait." Regan was listening.

"It was me that helped him cut the city off."

"They are all selfish bastards," Regan said in a tone so reasonable that even she was surprised. "All they want is what they want. Now hush."

"Now he's out there playing Castro, while I . . ."

"The main thing is, you can't let them do it to you." Regan was so busy trying to identify the new sound that she hardly heard herself speaking the truth, only fleetingly recognized it as the truth. "Won't let Jake do that to me."

"Who's Jake?"

"Somebody that doesn't matter any more. That's water. Look Madge, it's water." It was moving lazily down the underground hallway to the grate; it crept along the cracks between the stones and now it was sending fingers under the bars.

"You're right," Madge said grimly, without even noticing. "We've got to save ourselves."

"This place is filling up with water," Regan said.

"I wish I could do something for you."

"Just be kind to Sarah when you see her."

This made Bart uncomfortable. He hadn't seen her since last night, and he would have to admit he hadn't given her a thought. At the moment he could hardly remember what she looked like, or why they had been friends. His head was filled with everything he had seen and done and remembered and what he wanted right now was to be left alone here for a few minutes so he could open one or more of Abel's books. But Abel was sitting at his desk, which was stained now by the sheikh's blood, and he had been Bart's father in so many ways for so many years that it was Bart's turn now—time to try to find some way to help. "If you wanted, I could do whatever the next thing is. You look like you could use some sleep."

"I can't afford to."

"Just for a couple of hours."

"There are too many factions now. It's important for me to be seen."

"All we're going to be doing is lugging stuff around, moving people, donkey work. You're . . ."

Abel smiled. "I'm no good at that. I know. But I fulfill a certain function just by being visible."

"You look just about used up."

"As long as they see me . . . ." He stopped and began again. "Sometimes you can help people to be a little better than they really are."

Bart knew this old lesson. "What One Does."

"Precisely. Now . . ." Abel got up, but instead of amplifying or giving instructions he said, in an altered tone, "You know, I've always thought of you as my son. I always hoped you'd marry Sarah and come to live here."

"I couldn't," Bart said.

"Then she took up with this terrible man . . ."

"I mean I couldn't live here. I'm not good for people. I . . ."

"Now it's too late," Abel said.

"The thing is, there was something I did, or didn't do." Bart looked at Abel now, saw that he was suffering and because he did not want to burden him any farther shifted his shoulders as if adjusting the weight of a burden he expected to carry for a long time.

Abel walked around the desk and stood over him. "If you think you're atoning, you've already done more than your share."

Bart sprang up. "Sir?"

"Everybody knew what happened, nobody thought it was your fault."

"You knew about Mardella?"

"We all did. Then, later, when you tried to do what you tried to do."

"What?"

The old man considered for a minute. "You don't remember, do you? You don't remember what you tried to do. I'm sorry, I shouldn't have brought it up. You have enough to worry about now, I think it's time we went to the lobby. The colonel is expecting us."

"Wait a minute. Wait."

"It wasn't so bad."

"Please. I did all that to Mardella, I stole her," he said, in an orgy of confession. It was a relief to be able to talk about it. He never remembered when the doctors tried; now he could. "Stole."

"No. She wanted to go with you."

"Then I ran out."

"You didn't make it happen."

Bart groaned. "But it happened."

"You didn't make it happen, you let it happen. It's a very delicate line to cut but you will cut it if you're going to survive." The old man took Bart's arm and now it was he who was strong. "You couldn't have stopped it if you'd tried, and I . . ." His voice shuddered "I could not have stopped this if I'd tried."

"Nobody expected you to stop it," Bart said in dawning discovery. "Things that happen, happen."

"Yes. One of the most important things about life is learning to tell the difference between things you can help and things you can't help," Abel said, "and the other is facing up to what you have to do. In the long run, living is a matter of doing everything you're called upon to do."

"I see." The old man had placed his hands on Bart's shoulders and Bart raised his own hands so that they stood for a moment in a double brace, sometime father and would-be son. If he counted on Abel, then Abel was counting on him.

"It's particularly important in terrible times. You have to keep going. Have to."

"I will."

"Now the colonel is waiting in the lobby. I don't need you right now," he said unexpectedly. "I think it would be well if you went somewhere and tried to forgive yourself."

Damn his mother and damn Granger, Archer thought, waking up. Damn being little and having to do everything they said, including drinking that funny milk, and damn whichever one had opened the reds and stirred the powder into it, they both stood over him until he finished every drop, and meanwhile, where was Daddy anyway? Why did they want him out of the picture and what was he doing folded up here in the Turkish corner right where he had collapsed? He remembered feeling this way on other mornings, now that he thought about it, when Daddy was out of town and he was alone with them, but it had never been quite so bad, so did they want him on ice or out of the picture permanently, and where was Daddy now? The spies. Granger, maybe. If Archer could prove it, he could get him fired. The business about the spy was supposed to be a secret but he knew that, along with a lot of other things that he could not get to come clear because his head was filled with feathers and his mouth was fluffed up from the pills; it was all he could do to sit up straight.

When he did, he found Daddy. He was sitting in the big wing chair facing the fireplace, so all Archer saw from here was the arm in the smoking jacket, dangling, and hanging from the hand, the gun. The gun! When he went around front Daddy looked so peaceful that he might have dropped off after a hard night guarding the house. Archer gave him a push.

Daddy?

He slipped sideways a little, that was all. Archer righted him carefully.

Please don't do that.

He began to slip the other way. Maybe he was only doped, if he could get him up then they could walk it off.

Oh please.

He was heavy, cold and stiff.

Oh Daddy.

He wasn't there at all.

Next to him on the table, along with the glass and the empty bottle of reds, Archer found the note. They had set Daddy up so it looked like he'd spent the night trying to decide between the pills and the gun. If there was a problem with this, it was that Archer knew Daddy would rather die than kill himself; any fool could see they'd put it in his brandy and then Granger typed the note.

Damn spies. Right, it was both of them. They had not been rolling around after all, they had been making terrible plots. When he told on them they would be hanged or shot. All he had to do was get the news to Bart.

The trouble was, he still couldn't talk. All that came out was breath. "Hhhhh. Mmmmm . . ." He finally made a noise but it wasn't words, it was only helpless sobbing that would not stop.

So he stood there in front of Daddy bawling like a fool until he figured out he had to cover him up so he could stop. Knowing this and doing it were two different things. It was a long time before he wrenched himself loose and went out and put his head under the tap, after which he went to Granger's typewriter and typed the telltale note. Finally he went back in and arranged Daddy so he looked dignified instead of dopey, after which he took the paisley throw from the Turkish corner and put it over him.

When he could not find Bart he went to the lobby, where Colonel Brody was set up in the manager's office. There were gangs of people waiting outside, so wrapped up in what they wanted to say to the colonel that they didn't see him slip by and sneak in. The colonel didn't notice him either; he just went on arguing with the bishop, who was looking like a giant panda in his huge black sweatpants and layers of sweaters. Over in the big leather chair Mr. Parkhurst was sitting like an ivory carving, turned in on himself so tightly that he didn't pay any mind to the rest of them. Archer could already see this was not the time.

The bishop was saying, "If you don't tell them, I will."

"You know I can prevent that."

The bishop never raised his voice but the words came out at full force. "My people won't let you."

"Your people." The colonel snorted. "You might be surprised."

The bishop said, "They have a right to know the truth."

"So they can panic and surrender? Forget it. Right now they think they've won it, which means they think the next time and the next time they can go on winning it, which happens not to be the case. If it helps them fight, why not help them fight?"

"You're not being fair."

"It doesn't hurt to let them think there is some hope." Colonel Brody leaned over the desk. "The less they know, the easier my job is. It's as simple as that."

"Maybe not."

The bishop turned away and Archer thought the interview was over. Now was the time to get in there and turn in stupid Granger and his damn mother, who . . . But the bishop was pacing, looking large and untidy and upset. He was sweeping back and forth in front of the desk. It crossed Archer's mind that maybe he should just give his note to Mr. Parkhurst but Mr. Parkhurst would never do anything to them, he was too much of a gentleman, while this colonel looked mad enough to do almost anything. He was growling at the bishop now. "Why shouldn't they think help is on the way?"

So the bishop turned and rested his hands on the desk, nose to nose with Colonel Brody. The two big men, the fat one and the tough, muscular one, faced off and the bishop began. "When a patient is dying, he needs time to make his peace. Nobody likes to see us coming but we fulfill an eschatological function when we administer the Last Rites."

Unlike Archer, the colonel knew what this meant. "If you happen to believe that crap."

"Even if you don't."

"We're talking about a military situation here."

"We're talking about an absolute situation," the bishop said. "If you don't have much time at least you have the right to know it, so you can prepare."

"You sound like a sea lawyer."

"It's a simple matter of free will. These people have the right to know."

"So they can surrender and be killed anyway?"

"So they will know." The bishop's voice was strong. "What makes you so sure they would surrender?"

"I've been in the business a long time."

"Well so have I." The bishop's tone made Archer think maybe there was a hell that people could go to. "What gives you the right to decide for them?"

So it was the colonel who fell back, looking not scared of the bishop or hell or anything else but, OK, thoughtful. "Let's just say I've taken the responsibility. Now are you going to keep your mouth shut or am I going to have to lock you up?"

The bishop did not answer, exactly. "Will you think about it?"

The colonel did not answer the bishop, either. "You're not going to be any good to anybody locked up."

After a long silence in which nothing was resolved the bishop said, "You get what you want, don't you? Maybe you get what you deserve." Then he turned quickly and went out.

Archer thought his moment had come and he sprang for the desk, but suddenly Mr. Parkhurst was in his way. He hated being a little kid and not being able to talk. He hated being stuck here, waiting for the right moment to get this guy's attention so he could deliver his note. Mr. Parkhurst was shaking all over and talking, loud.

"You're taking too much on yourself."

But whatever the colonel was about to say to him was drowned out by Mrs. Turnesley Woot and about eight other old ladies who had made it through the door when the bishop opened it to go out. They were all swarming around the desk and complaining about the noise and the discomfort and the no water, Mr. Parkhurst was going from one to another saying there there and instead of shooing them all out like a bunch of hens the colonel turned into a completely different person as he watched, saying tisk tisk yes it was completely terrible and he would have his people get on it just as soon as he could pass the word, after which he came around the desk and took Mrs. Turnesley Woot's elbow with a Marie Osmond smile and ushered her out of the office so smoothly that the other old ladies just followed without ever realizing he had given them the bum's rush in the nicest possible way.

Mr. Parkhurst was saying, "Thank you for being good with them."

"We need their cooperation too. You know we are going to have to fortify the west wall."

"There's not a window in it."

"They'll be all over it as soon as it gets dark."

"I thought they were all in the park."

"Not for long. I've made some drawings. Look here."

So Brody laid out the plan while Archer hung on the corner of the desk and waited for the right moment, which came and went too fast. Three things happened right in a row. First Randolph came in and said the water pressure had dropped to zero, damage from the explosions, he supposed, and the colonel said after the west wall was taken care of, first things first.

The second was that Archer finally got the colonel to read the note he had typed. He sprang up on a chair and unfurled it in front of the colonel's face, sobbing because he had it out at last.

PIERCE GRANGER, CLAUDIA LIVINGSTON
MURDERERS . . . SPIES

The third thing was not what Archer expected. It didn't even come close. Brody just went on talking to Mr. Parkhurst.

"Who is this Granger?"

"Archer's tutor, I'm afraid. He and Mrs. Livingston have . . ."

"Poor kid." The colonel's hand fell on Archer's head.

Not what he expected. Why wasn't the colonel sending for his guards, why didn't they just go up there and drag the two of them out? He wanted him to swing until he yorked and turned purple and died. Archer gagged on a sob. He wanted her to swing.

"Easy, kid. Easy." The colonel was making these terrible faces and grabbing around for things on his desk.

Archer growled and jabbed his finger at the note. After what . . .

"The situation is under control, all right? Just a minute while I . . . Here. Take this." The colonel settled his cap on Archer's head. "And this." He thrust a clipboard and pencil on Archer, who writhed and sputtered and could not speak. "I want you to go out and make me some lists."

After what they did? He took the clipboard in both hands and smashed it on his own head.

"What's the matter with him?"

"He's been under a strain lately," Mr. Parkhurst said. "We all have."

"For Pete's sake don't cry. This is an important job and I'm counting on you." The colonel waited a couple of minutes while Archer pulled himself together, which he was going to have to do because he was counting on him; the colonel was counting on him. "That's better. I want you to go down and count all the rolling stock and come back with a tally. Cars. Service vehicles. Everything that moves. Pronto."

But Daddy is . . . He could not cry now; he could not afford to think about it, even, because this guy was really counting on him. *But.* Something in his head kept stuttering, but the colonel had him halfway out the door. *But.* He rocked on the sill. *B . . .*

"Good man. Now go do your job."

Bart spent the better part of an hour with Abel's books, grabbing volumes like a gunfighter going for his six-shooter, sneaking up on them in agonizing slow motion, trying to make words hold still so he could pounce on them. Once he caught an *ng* in the lower right-hand corner of a page, and later a *th ng* that flickered like a candle and went out. He picked up an entire entry from the DAB and then forgot it as soon as he put down the book. The best he could do was some big type from the Yellow Pages: *Roto-Rooter* in one place, and in another, *FunKing East.* The Chinese characters, he could see fine. Maybe if he took Chinese . . . It was amazing. All this and he still couldn't read. He had just naturally thought when the bad parts came back, so would all the rest. Before I couldn't remember anything and I couldn't read anything. Now I can't read anything and I remember everything. Well, almost everything. There was whatever it was Abel was trying to spare him. *Did I do something worse?*

What he wasn't going to do was let another one slip by. Before the attack he had tried to say certain things to Regan which he had not been able to finish because of these black holes which it seemed clear were in his head. The least he could do was find her and explain. He sprang on one last book: Abel's desk diary. "Hah. May. Monday, Tuesday. Gotcha." He quit while he was ahead.

When he didn't find her at the Becketts' he was certain she would be in the billiard room, but the hallway outside was lined with people who didn't seem to be wounded but who were in bad shape. Setsu, who had turned an unpleasant color, was first in line outside the examining room.

"I'm looking for the lady doctor. What's the *matter* with everybody?"

"Food poisoning. I blame that damn Mrs. Maddox." The houseboy gripped his side as if it would keep his heart from falling out. "Look in the servants' quarters, everyone is sick."

This was not precisely the case, but it was clear there were quite a few and it was also clear Regan was not there. The pointy-faced temp he had met the night of the party tottered to the door of her room and said she thought she'd been here, but somebody was having a heart attack in the gym. When he doubled back he found Mrs. Imelda Maddox lying on a pile of coats with her right hand clenched on her chest. "It's my tachycardia. Get me the young doctor, not that old drunk. I think she went up to look after that candy-faced boy, you know, overdose."

She was not in the Hickox apartment either. The groupies were all either ricocheting off the mirrored walls or lying in stoned bliss while Hickox himself asked would he like to snort a line. Bart shook his head.

"Later."

"Later," Hickox said.

In the billiard room Doc Millinger was cross. "Hell no I don't know where she is, I haven't seen her for hours."

"But you have seen her today."

The little doctor was unsteady, not from booze but from fatigue. "I don't even know when today began. But look, I can't be in two places at once. We still have all those bed patients in the garret, if you would help me carry these things . . ." His smile slid.

"I'm looking for . . ."

"And these dressings too. Who knows," the old doctor said craftily. "You may just find what you're looking for up there."

Of course she wasn't in the garret, but it was apparent Doc Millinger could not have made it without his help. He came wheezing into the garret on Bart's arm, already muttering in distress because there did not seem to be any patients in the garret.

"Oh dear," he said. "Where are they? Oh dear."

The skylight had been knocked out of the slanting roof and Ted Beckett's detachment had turned over the beds and shoved them against the angle where the roof slanted into the floor. The skylight was sited so low that with the panes all broken and removed, a tall man could put his head out. At evenly spaced intervals workmen were cutting through layers of building material and insulation and lead roofing to make slits for the ornamental cannon that had been stored here since the first world war. In other locations they were creating gun emplacements of the weapons Brody had liberated from the armory. Some had dragged ancient steamer trunks and movers' barrels out of storage and were heaping them so the police sharpshooters would have a place to stand. The long-range weapons were heaped here, including a stack of rifles with telescopic sights.

Bisecting the garret was a bizarre, makeshift apparatus that Bart took to be a catapult, a huge arrangement with gigantic springs and what looked like a construction workers' pallet on the business end. What were they going to do, loft furniture at the enemy or put explosives in the drums and sail them out? Beckett was not about to tell him anything, not even where he'd moved the doctor's convalescents.

Beckett had tied a scarf around his bicep—red against the dark shirt. He was pacing from one gun emplacement to another, barking orders in a tone that made Bart bristle. When he wouldn't stop to answer their questions Bart snagged his elbow and jerked him to a stop.

"The doctor was asking you a question."

"Well make it quick."

The old doctor was blinking in confusion. "I can't seem to find my patients."

"Everything had to be moved."

"What's happened to my convalescents?" Doc's head was shaking on his plump neck; it would take more than a pull from his silver flask to fix him up.

"So if you'll just let go of my arm . . ."

"But they're *gone.*"

Beckett snapped, "They all got well, all right?"

Doc Millinger was shaking his head.

"If you look around, you'll see half of them." Beckett pointed to men with bandaged legs and heads all lugging barrels and pushing trunks. A woman with an arm in a sling and another with her arm in a cast braced bottles of gasoline against their bodies and stuffed in wicks. "Everybody pulls their own weight here."

"You haven't told the doctor what he wants to know."

Doc's lips quivered. "What happened to the rest?"

"If you'll excuse me, I have to see to the sharpshooters."

"Wait a minute." Bart snagged his arm again, would not let go even though Beckett pulled silently. "What about Dr. Millane?"

"What about her? Haven't seen her."

"Is she with the wounded or what?" She wasn't, he realized.

"How the hell am I supposed to know? Now let go of me," Beckett said through his teeth. "Let go or I am going to have my men remove you bodily."

"Your men?" But what would keep her from doing her job?

"Up here, I'm in charge." Beckett had him. "Now let go."

Bart became aware of Beckett's men, all wearing dark shirts like Beckett's, all armed and, as it turned out, all watching closely. Beckett flicked his head and four approached. He turned back to Bart with a maddening smile, which Bart would not erase. He thought he knew where Regan was. If she wasn't working, she was trapped somewhere. He wanted to knock Beckett down and kick him into chunks, but the quartet was still advancing and he was putting the pieces together now, so Bart turned and led the old doctor out of the garret before they reached him. He hurried Doc downstairs and into the service elevator.

"Later," Bart said.

The old doctor blinked like a turtle. "What?"

"We've got to do this now. When it's over, I'm going back for him."

At the second floor he let the old doctor out and pressed the DOWN button. To his surprise, the elevator did not move. All right, he thought; things are slow. He pushed the button again. The damn thing still wouldn't move. He hit the OPEN button; the stairs would be faster anyway. When he stepped out somebody caught him with a crooked arm across the windpipe. He felt steel under his chin. "Quiet. Don't move. This is a knife."

"Who . . ."

"You have something I want." The knife point forced his head up.

"Granger!"

The tweedy tutor raised his voice, calling to somebody just out of sight. "It's all right, dear. I have him now."

The next face Bart saw was a surprise: not one of the enemy; by now it had crossed his mind that Granger must be the spy. This pretty, aging face did not belong to an outsider. Mrs. Livingston was flustered and anxious and pointing a gun at him.

"Now," Granger said silkily, pulling him into the elevator. They started down. "If you'll just be so kind as to give us the key . . ."

"What key?"

"You know perfectly well. You also know where the exit is, I believe. So if you'll be kind enough to show us out . . ."

"So you can quote chapter and verse?"

Mrs. Livingston's hand wavered. "I beg your pardon?"

"Please hold that thing still. I know you're working with them, and I'll be damned if I'm going to . . ."

"Pierce, this young man thinks we're . . . Well look, I assure you, we're not. All we want is safe conduct out."

Bart shook his head and felt the knife point break the skin. He was more afraid of Mrs. Livingston, who was obviously so bad at guns that she could let him have it without even meaning to.

"If you don't help us I'm going to kill you."

"If you kill me you'll never get out."

"Tell him where we're going, Pierce." Mrs. Livingston was flustered; her free hand flew at her hair, her breast, her belly.

"All right." They had reached the ground level and now Granger nodded to her and she put one hand on the CLOSED button. "We're going to elope."

"You're kidding. You'd be crazy to go out there."

There was a new edge to the tutor's voice. "We'd be insane to stay. Now you went outside yesterday. When you came in it was not by the main gate. You're going to show us how you got out."

"They'll kill you." Was Regan all right? He was fairly sure he knew where she was; he had wasted most of the day looking elsewhere and now that he did know he was stuck in this damn elevator wrangling with these two fools. "They'll put you out."

Granger said coolly, "That's a risk we're prepared to take."

"We go as friends. We're perfectly safe." Mrs. Livingston raised the hand with the gun so that her sleeve fell away. Her arm was stacked with jewelry to the elbow. "We have plenty to barter with."

"We can be in Jersey tonight. Now let's go."

Regan must be in the wine cellar because she wasn't anywhere else. "OK," he said. "It's your funeral."

Granger let go so he could reach the key. "We'll take the risk."

They were so eager to get away that Granger gave Bart his knife in earnest, and she handed over the gun. Still Bart pulled the key out of his left sneaker only after they reached the arch. It was dark when he came in yesterday;

when he cracked the door now he saw light, which meant he had to get them out and the door locked behind them before anybody saw the opening.

He felt honor bound to say: "It's suicide."

Granger only pushed him out of the way and pulled her out. He grappled the door shut and locked and hit the deck reflexively just as she cried, "Don't, we come as friends," and the machine guns on the far side of the avenue began to speak.

9

Bart and Brody collided at the entrance to the wine cellar; the colonel was coming up the last flight of stairs with a bulldog scowl. "Cavanaugh. I've been looking for you."

"Is she down there?" The machine gun chatter echoed in his ears.

"Who? Oh. No. She's upstairs. The doctor is putting her on ice for a while. Come with me. We've got something to do."

"Wait a minute, what happened to her?"

"She got locked in with that bitch you bagged. It's OK. Randolph came down to see about the water . . ."

"Water!"

". . . and he got her out. One of the pipes went in the aftershock. Pressure's at zero, which is how we found out. They're pumping it out now." Brody could see Bart was trying to get away from him and he kept talking, matching his moves like an experienced cutting horse. "Believe me, it's the least of our problems at the moment."

"Will you let me *by?*"

"Can't. I need your help. Look, on my honor as a Marine, she's up there, she's fine. She's also out cold. Let's do this and when we're done she may be ready to come around." Brody's voice dropped. "You know we're cut off. There's one more thing I want to try."

"Like . . ."

"Later. I'm trying to keep a low profile on this."

They met Abel in the courtyard. He seemed diminished, as if the scars on the building were duplicated in his hide. Workmen were extending the baffle of sandbags inside the gate. The fountain on the north side had died and the flowerbeds were being trampled by workmen who were siphoning water from the basin into plastic bottles. The courtyard was sadly altered, heaped with debris and stacks of supplies, crowded with equipment ranging from a fork lift to a small tractor embedded in the grass; it was littered with spent shells and small objects dropped by refugees, and shards. Abel's own maintenance people were ripping off ornamental ironwork, balconies and gratings, wrenching metal out of stone. It could have been coming out of Abel's flesh. He touched Bart's arm.

"The minute you agree to be helped, you begin to pay."

"What are the cars for?"

"Another of his plans," Abel said.

"Rampart," Brody said. "I need you to drive."

In the northwest corner, the first of a double row of cars, trucks, everything that moved, nosed out of the underground garage and made an arc around the baffle of sandbags and stopped with bumpers nudging the gates. The stream of vehicles was unbroken from gates to ramp to first tier of the underground garage, and Bart imagined the caterpillar winding around stanchions in the bowels of the Parkhurst, waiting to be released. At a signal from Brody the drivers cut their engines and workmen began to arm the cars with their pieces of ironwork, outsized gratings and bits of flashing, drainpipes, everything they had. They shoved the jagged pieces into luggage racks and trunks of cars and into windows, so that the procession began to bristle like a poisonous crawling thing.

"And you think this is going to work. More destruction." Abel winced.

"It's got to work. If it doesn't they swarm up your west wall as soon as it gets dark."

The old man said, sadly, "All those cars. I have a feeling we're burning our bridges. And we haven't even told them what's happening. They deserve to know what we're up against; they deserve a chance to decide for themselves."

The colonel's eyes were ringed with white. "Mr. Parkhurst, if you want to quit now, do it. I'll give you safe conduct, with as many as you want to take."

"You know I'm not going anywhere," Abel said in bitter pride.

"Then let me do my job."

"It seems such a waste." Abel seemed to be numbering the cars like snapshots in a family album. "The Bentley, for instance. The Cord."

"We need everything we've got."

"I just don't see what they can do against a solid granite wall."

"Honey, they are going to sneak up and blow a goddam hole in it." The colonel consulted his watch; inside his head invisible counters had begun to click. "Now you can let me do this, or you can kiss me goodbye."

"Bart, what do you think I should do?"

"Cavanaugh?"

It was a delicate business, the two of them sawing back and forth over something that was not his to settle. "I'll do whatever you both say."

Abel raked his fingers through his hair. "These lives are my responsibility . . ."

"I'm trying to save them for you."

"But if anything goes wrong."

"If anything goes wrong, I'll take it on myself." The colonel shoved his face into the old man's, glaring, filled to bursting with good intentions and growling urgently. "If anything goes wrong it's not your fault. It will be mine."

"But these are my people."

"Lay back. I told you, I'm taking this on myself."

Abel took a long breath. "All right. Get on with it."

Brody jumped to an overturned crate and signaled to Dawson to open the inner gates. He dropped his arm and, with the thunder of a small explosion, the drivers all started their motors at once. His voice rose over the roar. *"Now let's get these wagons in a circle."*

Bart and the colonel went out in the lead cars, Brody in, what, post position, with Bart on his left and the Parkhurst militia flanking them, ready to fire at anything that moved. Strangely, nothing did move. Where were they? Why weren't they out in force? This was too easy. Why? There was nobody stirring in the rubble across the street and when they made the wide turn onto Columbus Avenue he didn't see anybody or anything on the avenue or in the buildings on the far side. Bart drove with his belly tight and his shoulders high, so intent on making the swing around to the northwest corner of the building that when the colonel veered he veered automatically, and when the colonel jammed on the brakes and sprang out, screaming, Bart stopped short, electrified.

"Hold it," the colonel bellowed, standing in the road with his arms wide, but he was too late to stop the next pair of cars. "H . . ."

The explosion blotted out the rest. Both cars went up in a fiery cloud as Brody hit the asphalt, screaming, and Bart threw himself down.

"Son of a bitch. Son of a bitch!"

"What was that?"

"Land mine," Brody said violently.

"But who?"

"They planted it. Looked like a goddam manhole cover and it was a goddam mine. Should have scouted, but no, I didn't want to tip them off." Bits of debris had finally stopped falling on them and the colonel bunched himself and sat up. He crouched, keeping his head low. "If somebody blew, it should have been me."

Bart's belly twisted at the implication. "You tried to stop them."

"It was too late. Go get Luigi. We have to comb this place."

"You think there are more?"

"I know it." He shouted. "Know it!"

"Who?"

"Somebody inside. Somebody told them what we were going to do."

In all they found six others, all carefully camouflaged. Luigi disarmed them while Bart ran messages and the colonel paced. Then at Brody's signal the procession resumed, skirting the crater and forming an arc that embraced the west wall and the little park, and the side street all the way back to the gates. When all the cars were in place the drivers disabled them, pushing them over where they could, shoring up the metal barrier with the jagged scraps they had ripped out of the building, sandbagging the top so people could take shelter, resting their gun barrels on the top when the next attack came. Bart was glad the colonel had prevented Abel from coming out. The rampart was sound, all right, but the cars were irretrievable. Bart saw a twisted Duesenberg in the lineup, along with a ruined Isotta-Fraschini, vans that would never run again, dozens of family cars ranging from Mrs. Turnesley Woot's Olds to a couple of Silver Clouds, all wreckage now, part of the defense. Brody posted sentries and then motioned to Bart. They went the length of the rampart and into the double bronze gates. Brody went into Dawson's booth to push the lever that pulled them shut.

"So we have a bigger problem than I thought," he said under his breath. "Somebody in here tipped them off."

"You said you didn't tell anybody."

"Somebody did."

"Somebody did what?"

Bart bristled at the sound of the new voice. When he turned Beckett was standing in the entrance to Dawson's booth, filling it so they could not get past him without acknowledging him.

"Did what?"

"We have a security problem," Brody said, hitting Beckett with his shoulder. "Now get out of my way."

When he could speak Beckett said, "You needn't worry about it, Colonel. We're going to have an investigation." Brody was already halfway across the courtyard but Beckett finished anyway. "As a matter of fact, it's already under way."

At Beckett's back Bart could see Abel and the colonel talking soberly; he wanted to join them but here was this officious roadblock, a middle-aged parlor soldier determined to have the last word. "He doesn't care what you do. Now will you move?"

"He will."

It was fairly clear to Bart what he had to do. When he finally detached

Beckett, who was clinging like flypaper, he headed into the building and up in the private elevator to the Parkhurst apartment. What did he think he was going to do, catch her in the act? He didn't know. Randolph must have been thinking some of the same things. Bart found him shuffling in the hall outside Sarah's locked door like a worried father bear. He was huge in the damaged Parkhurst livery; his silver hair shone like a cap. "Mr. Bart."

"What's going on?"

"I'm so glad you're here." His voice was ragged with emotion.

"You're the one who sent for me."

"Yes." The lines in Randolph's face relaxed slightly. "I thought if anybody could prevent it . . ."

"Prevent what?"

"Whatever."

"You should have told me what it was."

"Mr. Bart, there are some things it's wrong to say, unless you have proof."

"You should have told me what to do."

The huge man swelled with pain. "I still don't know."

"Is she in there?"

"Yes, but she won't talk to me."

"Sarah. Say." Bart tried to do something special with his voice. "Say, open up. It's me."

He could hear her moving inside, but when he tried the knob the door was still locked. Randolph was still hovering. "Do you think we can break it down?"

"I don't think we're going to have to." Bart dropped his voice. "How did you know where I was?"

"Mr. Parkhurst keeps track of everyone he loves."

There was no time for Bart to address this; he was knocking and calling: "For Pete's sake, Say, I come in peace." They heard the snick of the latch. Bart wanted to snag Randolph and ask him what did he mean, kept track, what did he mean, love, but the door was opening and when he shot a quick look over his shoulder the old man had melted away.

"What do you want?"

The biggest thing was, she had cut off her hair. Trust her to do a neat job; she could have been a Spartan boy, getting ready for an ordeal. Behind her the room was straightened as if for a military inspection. She folded her arms and dared him to speak.

"Worried about you."

"I'm fine."

"What are you doing?"

"What do you mean?"

"You know."

"Me? Nothing. I'm not doing anything."

"You heard what happened."

"No." Her eyes were cold.

"On the avenue."

"I don't think so."

"You knew what we were doing with the cars. You knew ahead of time."

"Bart, I don't know what you're talking about."

"And you told them."

"And neither do you. Now if you will just say goodbye and go, I have some things to do."

"More secret messages? How do you send them? Mirror? Flash?"

"I don't know what you're talking about."

"Like hell you don't." He bore down on her.

"Leave me alone."

"That's enough." The voice came from behind him: Abel, enraged.

"Daddy, get him to leave me alone."

At Abel's touch, Bart whirled. "Look, we have a problem."

"I said, that's enough!"

"When you went crazy, you went all the way," Sarah said. "Daddy, would you get this freak away from me?"

"Wait a minute."

"He's gone for good this time."

"She's lying. She's lying to you."

"Out! Get out!" Exhausted as he was, drained by the pain and effort of the past few days, Abel Parkhurst was suffused by the power of his anger; he rushed Bart, pushing him out of the room with a steely strength. "Leave my daughter alone."

As soon as they cleared the sill Sarah slammed the door. In the hallway, breathing hard, Bart said, "I know you don't want to hear this but you're going to have to listen."

The old man simply rushed him, propelling him backward to the elevator. "Just go."

"It's about Sarah."

"She's my daughter."

"There's going to be trouble."

"There already is trouble," the old man cried in pain. "She has nothing to do with it."

"I think she does."

Abel reached past Bart to stab at the call button. "No!"

"If you would just have her *watched.*"

"No. Get out." The elevator door opened and the angry father lunged, catching Bart off balance and pushing him inside. The doors closed on the old man's angry face, his fury as he said, "I will not hear of it."

So there he was. What did he have to go on? What could he tell the colonel if he tried? That he had this feeling? That Randolph did? It was not enough. If Brody believed him he would have her executed at worst; at best he would lock her up. It might be all right if he was sure of his ground but he was hobbled by ignorance and slowed further by her accusation. Right, he had been crazy for a while. He might still be halfway round the bend. He didn't think he was, but he had no right to assent to the damage—the cost to Abel if he turned her in. He was mulling it: the obligation, as he saw it, the fact that he had no proof. What could he say to the colonel, anyway? Hey, I think . . . But he couldn't let go, either. When the elevator reached the lobby and the doors opened on Archer, it was like being presented with a gift.

"Arch. Hey, Arch!"

The kid was agitated, sputtering and fizzing. Bart heard the echo of machine gun chatter and he wondered: *Does he know what happened to them?* He looked for traces of tears in the crusted grime on Archer's face. *Maybe not.* The kid was cross-eyed with concentration, trying to give him, what? A note. A note? Hopelessly, Bart unfolded it. Looking into Archer's fierce, fat face, at the touching softness under the chin, Bart thought: *Maybe he doesn't know what happened to his mother.* For the moment, it was just as well. Later, when the worst was over and they had their systems working; later, when the kid's father was around to take over, Bart would break the news. Right now, he needed to be protected from any further discoveries; he could be particularly useful right now. Archer was squirming and fuming, waiting for Bart to read and digest the note. Which at the moment he could not. He nodded in a show of efficiency and folded it and tucked it in his pocket. "I'll take it to the colonel," he said. "Our men will take care of it. Meanwhile, there's something I want you to do."

Which was how he managed to post a guard on Sarah—somebody who would not be recognized as a guard. He managed to post a guard on Sarah and then, after checking in at the command post and finding he had no immediate instructions, discovered that for the moment he was free. He was free and Regan was in the billiard room. What kind of dope had the doctor given her, and had she slept it off? If not, he would just sit there and wait. All he wanted now was to be with her.

Slipping into the billiard room he touched her cheek with the back of his hand. She stirred and raised her arms to him without speaking and he buried his face in her. They rocked and clung for a moment until she put him away from her with gentle hands, pointing to the door; they could not be alone here for long. Putting her fingers to her lips, she scooped up as many pillows from the howdah as she could manage. Bart picked up the paisley throw, the small Oriental and a bolster from the sofa and followed her into the whirlpool room, where they threw the pillows into the empty tub. He turned to lock the door while Regan pulled the shade that covered the window overlooking the billiard room. He had not asked her what happened in the wine cellar and she hadn't asked him where he'd been or what happened in the attack; they weren't going to ask whether they were going to do this, or why; they simply slipped into the stainless steel basin and began. As they embraced and sighed everything became the one thing, and either at or immediately after the moment, when they were both crying out, a white light exploded in Bart's head, a complete vision of himself flying, as if from a great height; the sky was brilliant, he was a dazzling blur heading into the unknown, would have made it, too; he had rushed up the last flight and was halfway out the window when they grabbed his feet and carried him away; what he did, after he lost Mardella: tried to kill himself. At the time he thought he was going to fly.

"Regan," he said in the half-light, as she sobbed and stirred and tried to recover her breathing and Bart thought they were going to coalesce and become something new, "I have to talk to you."

10

The luxury, Regan thought as they settled into the cushioned whirlpool; after all I've been through, after so many years alone, just having somebody here to love me. The luxury! She was still groggy from Doc's sedative and everything had begun to run together until there was only one certainty, the warmth of their bodies, his against hers, which she met with cries she did not immediately recognize as her own.

But Bart rolled away from her; he was propped on one elbow, fixing her with an intent look. Even in this light she was afraid of what he might see: the first marks of age, the skull beneath the skin. When he began to talk it became clear that he didn't see any of these things. He was too preoccupied by what he had to tell her, about what had happened that he took to be his fault. He kept rehearsing it: what he should have been doing for this girl he'd loved, how she'd still be alive if he'd left her where she belonged. He did not want to hear Regan on childhood diabetics, the death wish, or on diabetic comas—as described, Mardella was probably as good as dead by the time he came home. No, Regan said, she would not have regained consciousness when they took her; if Bart had dragged her to the emergency room, she would not have come back; there would have been brain damage. She had slipped from sleep into a state where there was no memory, and if anybody had suffered at the abductors' hands, it was not Mardella, but Bart. This did not prevent him from saying:

"But it was my fault."

"You didn't make it happen."

"I let it happen."

"I'm not so sure." Regan looked at the rough black hair, the black brows that almost met, the tough face rendered completely vulnerable by trust, and in a new consciousness forged on her own forced march through memory, she said, "This sounds hard, but in a funny way, most people get what they want."

"She wanted to die?"

"Something like it would have happened, no matter who took care of her."

"But if I had known . . ."

"Exactly. You didn't. There was nothing you could do because you didn't know."

"Oh." His face was suffused. "Oh, Regan!"

"Oh, Bart."

She was aware of somebody trying the doorknob, rattling it gently and calling her name but she put her hand to his lips and they both fell silent, waiting until whoever it was gave up trying and went away. Lying together with their arms locked they plummeted into sleep.

When she woke she had no idea what time it was. Was it night outside or was it still late afternoon? Had she and Bart slept an hour or a lifetime? It was crazy to be happy now, when she had no idea. Still, lying next to him, she had slept like a stone. When we get out of this place, she thought, we are going to have to . . . But she did not want to finish. It was wiser to back off from the future and be grateful for what she had. This is enough, she told herself carefully. It has to be. Next to her, Bart stretched and opened his eyes. "Regan?"

"Don't. I'm a mess."

"I'm just looking."

Lord, she thought, looking at him. *He's just a kid.* "Maybe you'd better not."

"Whatever happens after this, let's find a way to be together."

She begged the question. "If we can." So for a moment at least she let herself become part of the story he was creating, but it took an effort to shut off the part of her mind that remembered the world as it was. That part of her mind was already considering what it would be like to go off to Mass. General every day, wondering whether he would still be there when she came home. She could not address the real question, which was whether she could really be herself, a tough, capable doctor just this side of middle age, and come home tired at night and still have this boy look at her this way. *Let's be in love for now,* she thought, moving against him. *For now we'll be in love.* The tears slipped out in spite of her and tracked her face as they embraced.

Some time later there was an urgent knock on the door. "Dr. Millane."

She and Bart exchanged looks. Should they answer, or could they pretend not to be here?

"Shh." He kissed her fingers.

"I think it's the bishop."

"Dr. Millane, we need you. Something's come up."

He whispered, "Let's not answer."

"We have to," she said, and got up.

"Cavanaugh, we know you're in there." It was the colonel's voice.

"Yes sir." He was out of the tub in seconds, skinning into his clothes. "Ready in a second, Colonel." To her amazement he murmured in the same breath, "Listen, I love you."

To which she answered too quickly to stop herself, "Me too."

When they opened the door, there was a war council forming in the game room. The bishop hovered, looking diminished by two thirds. He was quite simply narrower; his face was shadowed by worry and intimations of mortality. Doc Millinger was standing next to the open trophy case, twisting his hands and muttering, and at the door Colonel Brody was a study in anxiety. Only half aware of what he was doing, he paced five steps one way and then described a tidy about-face and paced the other like a mechanical soldier that has been wound too tight. Bart gave Regan's hand a final squeeze and then drew his fingers to the tips of hers, sketching his regret at parting as he turned to go.

The bishop and Doc Millinger converged on her; she had been out for twelve hours, now it was time to take hold. She had waked up happy and rested while they were burdened by the troubles of the night she had slept through. They had spent it waiting for the attack that had not come, dealing with a possible epidemic, troubled by something Ted Beckett had started: proceeding on his own he had begun an investigation because, it was clear, somebody in the Parkhurst was collecting information and relaying it to the enemy outside. Although she did not assimilate it at the time, they were trying to tell her about something else. It would come back to her later, when it was too late to do anything. If what they implied was true, it was already too late to do anything.

It was clear the bishop was sick. Racked by cramps, weak and dehydrated, he had to swallow several times before he could moisten his mouth enough to speak. "Something is very wrong."

Studying him, she knew better than to try to get a reading on his blood pressure. "Let me give you something to make you comfortable."

He grimaced. "It's not important. Something strange is happening. My men, some of the others . . . It's getting out of hand."

"And another thing," she said. "Water's short, but you are going to have to replace fluids. You're dehydrating."

He was almost doubled over by a fresh spasm but he seemed determined to finish. "They're taking things into their own hands and we're going to pay the price. We have to deal with it."

"You're in no condition to deal with anything. When was the last time you got any sleep?"

"You know I can't afford to sleep."

"Whatever's going on, I'm sure the colonel will take care of it."

What had the bishop said, right before he ran, gasping, for the toilet? "I don't think the colonel can control it."

"Dr. Millane." Doc Millinger took her elbow gently. "I wonder if you'd mind looking over here." The trophy cabinet was ruined. The glass front had been smashed and its contents scattered.

"What's missing?"

"Barbiturates, stimulants. What you would expect." He rumpled his thin hair in distress. "But here, of all places. Our hospital."

"What we get for leaving them in plain sight, I guess. At least they were selective. Most of the antibiotics are still here."

The doctor's head was trembling on his fat neck. "I guess we should have known better than to trust people."

"I should have been on duty," she said, and flushed.

Poor old thing, he was exhausted. Still he managed the smile that must have seen him through a thousand difficult bedside moments. He patted her hand. "Don't forget, I chose to give you a sedative."

"I guess you did."

"Your ordeal in the cellar, that horrible woman . . ."

"What's happened to her?"

The old doctor's face was grey with worry. "That's another thing. But that's not the worst of it. Something strange has happened to our convalescents in the garret. They're gone."

"Gone!"

"I think Beckett's done something with them."

So she didn't know where to start: in the wine cellar, looking for Madge, or in the garret. The old doctor did not give her much choice. In the wake of the first wave of the attack and the water shortage, people all over the building were sick. They were weakened by diarrhea in what could be the first wave of anything from dysentery to cholera, so Regan spent the better part of the day going from one apartment to the next, assailed by the stench of illness and toilets that would not flush, and garbage that would not go away, helping the sick where she could and trying to find ways to protect the rest. She gave Mrs. Imelda Maddox something for her tachycardia and then spent the better part of an hour instructing her on which things to boil, which to scrub and which she had to find some way to dispose of. Then when she had answered her last call she headed for the wine cellar. It seemed important to check on Madge.

The floor was still damp. From the bottom of the stairs she could hear the sickening *thwack* of leather on flesh and she shouted "Stop!" as she ran toward the grotto where she had been trapped. The bishop's men were torturing the prisoner. Madge slouched in the corner where Regan had first seen her, bloodied and defiant, with Brewster—or was it Dexter—standing over her. "What the hell are you doing?"

"Doctor, you don't belong here." The look the two men turned on her was one of feral wariness: animals interrupted at a feast.

"This is terrible. Madge, are you all right?"

The dumpy captive saluted her with a weary wave.

"She says they're going to get us, but she won't say how."

Dexter—or was it Brewster—peeled off his driving gloves. "Maybe with a little sodium pentothal. Doctor? Your bag?"

"You're insane." She pulled away from him.

"I think she's just about to break."

Madge groaned in despair.

As she did so, Regan heard somebody coming down the stairs, somebody moving slowly along the corridor, and when she turned saw Mr. Parkhurst, who seemed to take in the scene all at once. "Whatever you're doing, stop."

"We have our orders, Mr. Parkhurst."

"I said, get out." Abel was imperious. "I have to see the prisoner."

"As you wish." The two faded to a discreet distance. One of them said, sharply, "But remember, we have our orders here."

"Mr. Parkhurst, I'm glad to see you. They've been—"

"I see. Please come in. I need you."

"Yes."

"Miss. Mrs." Madge snarled at the old man, who persisted. "I have to talk to you."

Regan said, "Have you been here ever since?"

"I've been so bombed I didn't care."

"I thought they took you out too."

"Well, they brought me back. Who's your friend?"

"My name is Abel Parkhurst. Are you all right?"

"Are you kidding?" If her expression changed at the name, she did a good job of covering. "Where were you when those two yoo-hoos started taking me apart?"

"More to the point, where was I," Regan said, using some antiseptic on Madge's face. "The doctor gave me something to knock me out."

"Miss . . ."

"Madge."

Abel went on urgently. "There's something I have to know."

"Just get me out of here."

His expression was complicated. "I'll try. But first . . ."

"I knew there would be a catch."

"It's about my daughter. What she might be doing. Whether."

"Who?" Her expression changed. "No. What?"

"I'm begging you to tell me what you know."

Regan sat back on her heels and regarded him. She did not know what was going on here or why he imagined this miserable woman would know anything about that pampered daughter of his. "You mean Sarah?"

"Oh." Madge began muttering and counting on her fingers. She looked up with a fearsome grin. "You mean that bitch."

"You know her?"

"Crap no, but I know about her."

His voice spiked. "What do you know?"

"He never loved her, he was only using her. Trouble is, she doesn't know it," Madge said cryptically. "Do us all a favor, why don't you, and break the news to her?"

Regan had just given Madge a shot of B-12 and she looked from her to Abel in confusion. "What does Sarah?"

"I don't know. There's someone staying with her, so it's all right."

"Sure it is." Madge's face split open and she began to laugh. When the old man touched her arm, begging her to explain, she only rolled away from them, still laughing, a sound as terrible as a pneumonic cough. It was, as it turned out, the wrong thing for her to do because the bishop's men had detached themselves from the grate and were coming in. One had a chain wrapped around his fist, a remarkable piece of equipment for a weedy curate, and the other was tapping a short length of pipe in the palm of his free hand.

"That's enough," one said.

The other said, "Time's up."

Mr. Parkhurst turned to face them. "I don't think so."

"We have work to do."

"We have our orders."

With unexpected swiftness, the old man produced a gun. "I'm sorry, I'm still in charge." Regan did not know whether it was the assurance with which he took aim, that was born of generations of shooting for sport, or whether it was Madge's infuriated growl or only that there were three of them, counting herself, and Mr. Parkhurst had a gun, but the two curates backed off. With a deep bow, Mr. Parkhurst stood back so they could go through the gate first. "After you, my dears."

Regan was not surprised when, at the top of the stairs, Madge turned a corner and bolted. Under the circumstances, she would have done exactly the same thing.

Bart followed Brody out of the game room with the idea that they were going to arrest the spy, and his ears buzzed because he had a good idea where they were going. No matter how much Abel counted on him, he was going to have to do this right. If the colonel had proof, they had no choice.

"You have evidence?"

"You'll see."

They went up in the elevator without any further conversation. If Brody had proof, he would find out; he kept quiet on the off-chance that this was about something else, and the colonel was fixed on his own preoccupations and did not speak until they got out of the elevator and proceeded down the long hallway to the garret stairs. Bart looked over his shoulder once. What was Sarah doing? He had left Archer in charge because the old man wouldn't hear of anything else. Could Archer prevent her from sending messages? If not, he was bright enough to turn her in. If she was the spy. But here they were going up the stairs, Brody muttering.

"I think we have a problem here."

"What do you want me to do?"

"Stand by. If we get out of this, I may need you to testify."

The garret was in good order, so quiet it was sinister. Everything was stowed according to category: crates and barrels here, ammunition here, provisions here. It was clear that, with or without the colonel's permission, somebody had been to the wine cellar and the storerooms to stock this operation, which seemed to be self-contained. Things were already headed this way when he was here with the doctor, Bart saw, and wondered what he could have done. The men had been divided into shifts; half rested while the other half manned the rifle slits and gun emplacements and one crew stood by the catapult. As Bart and the colonel came into the garret the nearest crew turned as one, not aiming at them, exactly, but with rifles at the ready.

Brody barked, "At ease."

They held the position. Yesterday they had been individuals; today they all wore approximations of Beckett's khaki shirt; they were a unit now.

"I said, at ease."

"Sorry, sir. Can't, sir. Orders."

"Whose orders?"

"General Beckett's, sir."

"Beckett, you son of a bitch!" Brody's voice dropped so only Bart would hear. "That's one thing I had to show you. When you have to lie down, you are bound to get dirt on you. Beckett!"

"How do you stop something like this?" Bart muttered.

"That's the problem. You can't even head it off."

"As you were." Approaching, Beckett tossed something in his mouth and swallowed it without water. Bart saw the riflemen's pupils were like Beckett's, reduced to points. What were they all taking? Beckett was smug. "As you see, Colonel, we're holding our own."

"On whose authority?"

"You always were a tin soldier. Now it's my turn."

"I need to use your observation post." Brody proceeded as if Beckett hadn't spoken. "Try to remember, we're all trying to do the same thing here."

Beckett spat. "Or not."

Looking over the ledge, Bart could see straight down into Abel's empty park, and to the demolition derby that ringed it, protecting the west wall of the Parkhurst: the colonel's rampart. From here the guards posted behind it looked like toys. The buildings on the far side of the avenue were more or less ruined by Beckett's bombardment, and at the moment the avenue was empty. Yet even from here, Bart and the colonel could see that the side streets were packed solid, people seething just out of range, with here and there a crudely armored vehicle, and everywhere every variety of weapon, from rifles to pikes to heavy artillery, everything massed just out of range of the roof batteries and who knew how many more of the enemy out of sight behind the buildings that were still standing.

The colonel said, in a low voice, "And that's the other thing I had to show you."

"Surrounded."

"We knew it was coming. They're waiting for it to get dark."

"What are our chances?"

"Pretty good for tonight." The colonel went on, through his teeth, "But you can see we have this other situation to take care of."

Behind them Beckett snapped, "If you're finished whispering . . ."

"Hold your water." Brody went on in a stage voice that carried halfway across the garret. "As you can see we are going to have to find some way to send a message. Blinkers are out, there's too much crap between us and the river."

Bart shouted, "I gather the radio is useless."

The colonel bugled, "They're jamming everything."

Ted Beckett's volume matched theirs. "I *said,* if you two are finished?"

"Smoke signals." Bart swallowed a fearsome giggle. They were like little kids up here, Beckett looked like a damn fool in his idea of a uniform, down to the belt with the sabre; the colonel looked ready to kill and able to do it with his bare hands if he had to, a two-hundred-pound parody with clenched teeth and bulldog muscles, and they all three sounded like actors in a high school play about World War One.

The colonel caught Bart's tone and grinned. "Or we can send Beckett here, on his tricycle. Smoke signals. I'll put someone on it." He took his sweet time getting down from the platform and Bart took his sweet time following, while Beckett fumed and waited for them to get out of his territory.

"We can get Archer to burn all of last week's newspapers." Bart dropped his voice. "Hey, I forgot to tell you about his mother."

The colonel silenced him. "We recovered the bodies."

At their heels, Ted Beckett swallowed a sudden gasp and Bart turned to see him covering his mouth with an anxious grimace. "What bodies?"

As if this was what he had been waiting for, Brody wheeled on him. "What's it to you?"

Bart had no way of knowing what Beckett was covering up, but it was obvious he was covering. He dithered and came up with a hastily constructed answer. "I hadn't heard about any deaths. If there were deaths, why didn't you notify me?"

"You'll hear plenty about them when the time comes." In spite of his best efforts to be cool, Brody grabbed Beckett by the neckerchief and twisted sharply. As he did so, they heard the clatter of a dozen rifle bolts. The colonel twisted just long enough to let Beckett know he was not afraid of anything, not him, not his riflemen, and then released him. "Plenty." Then he turned as if it had been his idea to leave and strolled out of the garret, whistling.

Once they were safely away, Bart said, "What are you going to do about that crazy guy?"

"Nothing right now. We need all hands."

"But he's dangerous."

"Can't afford to break step right now. Can't afford to do anything but get ready."

"They were ready to shoot us."

"Don't worry, I'll handle it when the time comes."

Bart felt his hairs stand up. "We could have been wasted."

"Let's just get through the night," the colonel said. "When the place is secured I'll take care of him."

He led Bart through the lobby and into the courtyard, where in the middle of battle preparations Archer Livingston was playing with an enormous bag of popcorn. He was—he was feeding the pigeons. Wait a minute, Bart thought. I told him to look after Sarah, and here he is feeding those flying rats. "Hey Arch."

Archer waved.

"Did you do what I told you?"

Archer nodded.

"If you did what I told you, where is she?"

Archer pressed his hands together and laid his head on them.

"Asleep. All I can say is, she damn well better be."

But Archer had gone back to playing with the pigeons. Bart wondered what kind of diseases they carried, and thought maybe he ought to take Archer with him, let him go out with them to inspect the rampart, where the colonel was going to issue final instructions. If he did not do this it was for several reasons, not the least of which was he might find out Archer had not really kept track of Sarah after all, which meant he, Bart, was going to have to answer to Randolph. Maybe he didn't want to keep track of her, they had been friends in the sandbox and he didn't really want to know what she had been up to. Archer looked happy enough, playing with the flying rats, and Brody was already at the gate, waiting for him with a look that let Bart know he would not be pleased by any distractions.

"Cavanaugh!"

"Coming."

Outside, at the rampart, the armed men and women looked tired but cheerful, and they refused to be relieved when Brody offered to replace them. Bart was surprised to find Randolph holed up behind a Cadillac, and as Brody went on down the line, patting shoulders, answering questions, Bart stopped to speak to him.

"Randolph, what are you doing out here?"

Randolph's look was so hopeful that he faltered. "Were you able to do what I asked you?"

Bart answered guiltily. "I have Archer seeing to it."

"He's only a child."

"If you want to know the truth, I don't know how else I could have done it. Mr. Parkhurst was ready to kill me for implying anything."

Those may have been tears in Randolph's eyes. "You were my only hope, sir."

"She's his daughter. He thinks she's perfect."

"I thought if anybody could do it, you might be able to. He thinks of you as his son." Randolph said, heavily, "So if you can't, nobody can."

"Even if I'd caught her in the act. When people don't want to see something, nobody can make them. Oh hell, Randolph, I am sorry."

Bart would be forever grateful for Randolph's painful smile. "Thank you anyway."

"Look, you shouldn't be out here on the front line. You mean too much to everybody. Let me take over. They need you inside."

"I requested this."

"Anything could happen to you."

Randolph's sigh rattled his huge frame. "I should prefer to be here for the time being. To tell the truth, sir, if there's trouble about Miss Sarah, I don't want to have to see."

"I don't think Mr. Parkhurst can do this without you."

"He's all right. The doctor gave him something to make him sleep." After a long pause, Randolph added, "Please tell him I did my best."

"I guess it's all anybody can do."

"And tell him I send—my warmest regards."

Randolph looked close to tears and if he stayed here any longer Bart would be crying too. He shook the old man's hand and in the next second began pounding him on the back in a valedictory embrace. "You can tell him yourself, as soon as this is over."

"Perhaps."

Wanting to give Randolph something more, Bart added, rashly, "Maybe it isn't Sarah after all. And if we end this soon enough, he may never have to know."

Perhaps understanding how badly Bart was torn, Randolph created one last smile for him. Then he said the one thing that would allow Bart to turn and go. "Perhaps not, sir."

Dipping his head, Bart trotted back around the rampart of ruined cars, following the colonel.

They were almost at the gate when the amplified voice started.

"YOU CAN STILL GIVE UP."

It was a man's voice, harsh and triumphant.

"SURRENDER OR DIE."

It was the first time the enemy had addressed them directly. Bart was surprised by his response: rage, as if somebody had smashed him in the belly. This thing had just become personal.

"GIVE UP," the voice said, magnified a thousand times. "YOU ARE SURROUNDED."

Brody was already bolting for the ballroom observation post. Bart followed.

"YOU CAN SEE THERE IS NO HOPE."

At the observation post, the bishop stood aside with an agonized look and handed Brody the telescope. He had shrunken terribly; he looked like a deflating balloon, but his eyes burned brightly, as if with a new vision.

"He says it's the revolution. He says we are the last holdouts." The bishop's expression was complex: relieved, in part, perhaps because it was important to him to think he knew what they were dealing with; dedicated. "At least now we know it's ideological."

"It's what?"

"There is a logic to it. It's not just another riot that got out of hand. Maybe it's for the best."

Brody was angry. "This siege is for the best?"

"The poor, rising against us. They've had enough of our affluence, and I . . ." The bishop touched his shrinking belly, "I think I understand it. Maybe we're the sacrifice—to change."

Even without the telescope Bart could see blades raised on spears in the park, and rising above the wall, grim faces under makeshift helmets. "They look like two-bit crooks to me."

"We're just as dead either way." Brody was squinting through the telescope. "It's that son of a bitch in the turban."

"GIVE UP. COME OUT. OVERTHROW YOUR LEADERS." The speaker was on a platform planted in the middle of the park and as the colonel handed over the telescope Bart got his first squint at him. Who was he anyway, and what did he want from them?

"THEY HAVE BETRAYED YOUR DEAD." A dozen amplifiers picked up the words and hurled them like boulders at the east wall.

Bart looked at the colonel. "What does he mean?"

"YOU ARE NEXT."

"That's it!" Brody's entire aspect was changing.

"SURRENDER TO THE BARON."

The echo reverberated. "*Nnnnn . . .*" The last sound spun itself out and as it did so, Bart heard the colonel groan as if he had been split wide open.

"Beckett! I was too hung up to see it."

"What?"

"What he did with the wounded."

So without wanting to, Bart understood the puzzle of the missing wounded. "The catapult. The bastard!"

"Lofted them out like so much furniture."

Archer was in the courtyard trying to make up for what he did. He was after pigeons, popping a net over the first one that slowed down long enough for him to bag it. So far he had managed to catch six of them, not bad for an afternoon's work. It was not as easy as it looked. First he had dissolved all his mother's Valiums in warm milk and soaked the popcorn in it, then he'd scattered it and settled down to wait. At first the damn things hardly noticed, they were too busy picking at the garbage that had begun to collect in the courtyard, but after a while he gathered a crowd. In a while he thought he saw a couple of them staggering around looking sleepy, and the minute one of them slowed down he made a grab. After he got finished with the ones he caught he gave them bread soaked in uppers and turned them loose. If this worked out he might end up a hero, and even if it didn't, he would have tried. Just trying made him feel better. If this worked he might make it up to Bart.

The reason he felt the way he did, which was terrible, was, he had not done what Bart told him, and when Bart came through the courtyard a while ago and asked, he had let him think everything was fine. Everything was not fine. Sure he had watched Sarah for them, he had followed her around all afternoon yesterday and stayed in her bedroom most of the night. *Most* of last night, he thought with a guilty pang. And that was why he felt rotten now. What happened was, she asked him could he give her just a minute to herself, one little minute, and even when she offered him money he screwed up his face and shook his head. Then she started begging and finally scolding, but no matter what, Archer held his ground, sitting crosslegged on the velvet puff in the corner of her bedroom and pretending to be friends.

So she had to pretend to be friends too and she started telling him stories, especially one about a prince and princess who were in love and wanted to change the world, and how the world was going to be when they had finished changing it. It might seem hard to people, but it was for their own good. What the prince and princess were going to do was get rid of the rich and take everything and give it to everybody that didn't have anything, and the people that helped were going to have a special place in the new government, she said. Archer, for instance. He could be one of the main people, then he could get back at everybody that was ever mean to him, which was what the prince and princess were going to do. Listening, Archer didn't know if she was trying to buy him off or only put him to sleep, so he yawned and kept sitting crosslegged on her velvet puff until she got mad at him and pushed him off, after which he just stood up and got back on.

"Oh Archer, for heaven's *sake!*"

After that she started taking things out of her jewel case and laying them out for him one at a time, starting with a medal she had won for archery at Farmington, a diamond necklace, a gold tank watch from Cartier. He could not help admiring the watch and before he knew what she was doing Sarah had put it on his wrist.

"*Now* will you leave me alone?"

How could he? He had promised Bart.

Then she glared with eyes that went right through the front of his reindeer sweater and his smelly shirt to his pale quivering belly and down his belly to his—my gosh!

"If I let you see me naked will you go away?"

What could Archer say? He couldn't even talk. He was fizzing like a glass of Alka Seltzer but nothing came out. If the words had come, what would they have been?

"OK, Archer, what do you want to see first?"

When he just goggled she shrugged her shoulders and to his positive horror began undressing right there in front of him, dropped her jeans and started unbuttoning her shirt. So Sarah got what she wanted after all, he was so overturned by this, so seduced and menaced that he got down off the velvet puff and fell all over himself like a damn fool getting away from her. If he knew why he was running, the reasons were buried deep. It was not because he was not dying to see a woman naked, because he was; the spit still dried in his mouth when he thought about it. He was terrified because it tore him right in two, with half slavering like a dirty old man at a porn show and the other half wanting to hide in a corner and cry like a baby for his mother, that was supposed to take care of him, cry for what she and Granger did. Undressing, Sarah touched some dark and painful area that lay waiting inside of him; it was as if she had poked a stick into the hurt spot and started twisting. He had to run.

So all right, Bart, he left her alone for fifteen minutes, curling up like a dog in front of her closed door, and when she called him back inside she had on her flannel nightie and everything looked more or less the same except for the window curtain, which had been left awry. Wait, maybe all she wanted to do was open it and throw something out. Whatever it was she was all done with it and now she was climbing into bed.

"Night, Archer."

He looked at her in dumb reproach.

She must have seen his unhappiness, the questions chasing around his face. She could probably also see how bad he felt; they had been friends since he was two, they used to drop dimes off the roof together, the story was if you hit a person you could kill them dead; she had even taught him to ride his two-wheeler in the garret, so nobody would see if he fell. Right now all she said was, "Hey Arch, it's three A.M. Why don't we get some sleep?"

He shrugged.

"Let's lie down now, OK?"

His knees were wavering.

"I'm finished for the night, OK?"

He cut his eyes at her.

"I promise not to move," she said, covering a little chain of yawns. On the table next to her was a bottle with a half-glass of water next to it. Downers, Archer thought. "Night, Arch."

What should he do? He had followed her like a dog all afternoon, they had eaten supper together, and danced to her cassette player and tried on her clothes. She had played Atari with him by the hour, and except for that short ten-minute lapse and once when he had to go to the bathroom, he had not let her out of his sight. He dragged the velvet puff in front of the bedroom door so she could not get out and then curled up on it and went to sleep. When he woke it was the middle of the day, according to his new tank watch, and Sarah was still asleep. All those downers, he thought, whatever she had to do that Bart was afraid of her sneaking away and doing, she'd already taken care of it. His gut twisted, whether with fear or remorse or hunger he could not say, he only knew that he had to get away from her, could not stand it another minute, and he ran out. In the kitchen he bolted a bunch of stale croissants and some orange juice and then went into the maid's john to pee in the dry toilet before he left.

It was on his way downstairs that he got his great idea. They were in bad trouble, they were going to be attacked again tonight, everybody looked desperate and they were running out of everything, they were never going to make it through this without help. The trouble was nobody outside knew it was going on, and it came to Archer in a flash that made him deeply proud, that when this happened in his World War One book, they sent carrier pigeons out with the news. There were about eight million pigeons living on the ledges and under the gables in the Parkhurst, Randolph was always complaining about their droppings in the courtyard so why not send messages out with some of them, why the hell not?

What he did was stop in his own apartment and pick up some stale bread and three bags of popcorn and half the contents of his mother's pill cabinet and some of the stuff from his father's desk. As an afterthought he took his butterfly net and, from Granger's room, the phony fishing net with floats that he had hanging above his bed. He did not go near the living room, where he supposed his father was still waiting under the paisley throw where he had composed him, nor did he let himself think about the smell. Once he had made his preparations he went down to the courtyard and began. While he was waiting for the pigeons to collect he wrote about two dozen HELP notes and knotted each into a rubber band so if he caught a pigeon he could just snap it on its leg. The notes, on his father's FROM THE DESK OF, were short:

STUCK IN PARKHURST
SEND HELP

Once he had caught his first few pigeons and banded them, he chased into the center of the flock and flapped and yelled at them in a desperate attempt to make them take off. He could not bear to look because he would have to find out which of his loaded birds flew, or whether any of them flew at all, or only just hobbled around the courtyard on heavy feet. He just shooed them blindly and hoped some of them would make it through the half-open bronze gates. Within a few minutes Bart and the colonel came back in and the gates clanged shut but Archer went on chasing pigeons anyway, in hopes some of them would make it to the roof and get to Jersey on the down draft. If he could just send out enough notes, then maybe somebody out there would get one of his notes. He was having a hard time with this last pigeon, he had the net over it but it kept scrambling along under the string and every time he tried to cup his hands over it, the damn thing would scurry out of his grasp. He was intent on this, chasing the dumb bird across the cobblestones, when he was knocked off his hands and knees by somebody who had come thundering out of the front door and down the steps under the porte cochere, and was heading at a dead run for the main gates. He was bowled over and kicked in the ribs by this raging tornado, who howled at him in a voice that he knew even before he realized it, screaming blue murder.

"Out of the way, you little creep!"

Then Archer, who recognized her—amazing! Archer was screaming back.

"You get out of the way," he roared like a tiger, and he was less surprised by the sound of his own voice than by the shudder of recognition that rocked him like an earthquake and in a terrible stab brought everything back. He grappled with her until the guards came and pulled her off, and as they did so, all at once Archer knew:

He knew who she was.

He knew what they had been doing that night when he got out and she grabbed him and he vomited up the Parkhurst birthday cake, and he knew more than that, saw again the one with the silver cloth wrapped around his head, the cloth that had . . .

That had slipped right before he threw his cookies, remembered seeing the . . .

The color of the hair.

So he knew who the leader was. He had known it all along.

"Hey Bart, Bart, son of a bitch!"

Knew why Sarah was dangerous.

"Son of a bitch, emergency, disaster, Bart!" He scrambled out of the tangle, hollering. "Emergency, hey listen, hot news."

Bart was in the ballroom with the bishop and the colonel, the three of them huddled over the Centrex while somebody on a loudspeaker shouted outside, he kept on yanking on Bart's arm and screaming at him to listen and finally his friend looked down and picked him up with a distracted frown, probably to silence him.

"Archer, would you *mind.*"

"Emergency. Disaster."

"Hey, he's talking."

"Big stuff, really."

"Hey Archer, you're talking."

"No time to waste." So it all came out after being stuffed up in there for days now, it was one hell of a relief. "I came to warn you about Sarah."

"Broad daylight," the colonel growled, "they're going to attack us in broad daylight . . ."

Bart was grim and preoccupied. "We know."

"The hell you do," Archer cried.

"That's how confident they are. We're going to have to show the bastards," Brody said.

Archer hit top volume. *"Sarah Parkhurst is the spy."* He expected everything to change, but nothing did. Nothing was happening.

Rather, nothing was happening except that Bart still held him around the middle so his feet dangled, while Colonel Brody gave a signal and all the guns on the roof went off all at once. As they did, the people in the park began to scream as if every one of those throats had been torn open at the same moment, after which there was an awful hush. The next time they screamed they would not stop, Archer realized; they would all let go at the same time, all of them charging the Parkhurst all at once.

"Tonight." The bishop crossed himself. "I thought they would wait until tonight." He had a strange visionary look, as if he imagined he could pray hard enough to hold them off.

The colonel took a rifle from the stack, shooting the bolt. "We're in it now. Might as well get it over with."

"The spy is Sarah," Archer screamed, trying to wriggle out of Bart's grasp. "Didn't you hear what I said?"

"We know that." Bart put him down and armed himself.

Archer did not know what to do to make them understand. He ran at Bart and scaled him like a tree, shouting, "The big man out there is Sarah's boyfriend Lawrence, he used to hang out here. It's *Lawrence,"* he said clearly, as the human tidal wave outside began to swell. Then everything stopped for a minute: Bart, Colonel Brody, even the bishop, Archer's heart, and in that arrested moment he saw it plain: what was going to happen next. That he had come up here to tell them. That he had the power to prevent. "She's on her way down there to let him in."

"She's what?"

Archer said, clearly, "She's down there opening the private gate."

"Lord," Bart said. "You're right. Brody! Quick!"

They caught Sarah in the secret archway, inside the hidden family door with her key already rattling in the lock. Old Mr. Parkhurst must have come down here and tried to stop her; he was lying on the cobblestones with a statue on the floor beside him and blood coming out of the place where she had bopped him, staining the white hair. The grownups were so caught up in the capture that they didn't even notice Archer, that he was there at all, or that he was close enough to hear what Sarah called Bart when she tackled him, close enough to see his response and hear the *thwack* her face made on the cobblestones when he threw her down. He understood she'd almost had the door open, one more minute and they would have found her old boyfriend Lawrence and his gang already piling in, and Archer did not know why this left him laughing and sobbing, but it did. Then the colonel and Bart started wrestling Sarah through the door to the service stairs. If they even saw Archer they were too preoccupied to pay him any mind, and Archer—Archer was distracted for the moment, he had bent over to pick up something off the floor. He was studying a handkerchief that looked familiar when the others went out. At the same time there came from outside a sound straight out of mortal hell, as of a million devils screaming, and the attack began.

On the cobblestones, poor old Mr. Parkhurst was stirring and Archer went to him. He still had his mother's handkerchief, he put it to his nose, knowing ahead of time that it would smell like *her.* Was he going to find anything worse? The broken chain from her charm bracelet, maybe, the heart-shaped charm with his birth date and name, or some of Granger's hair caught in the lock?

On the cobblestones, old Mr. Parkhurst kept stirring and groaning, his face whiter than his hair in the pale light from the electric sconce. Archer went over and started dabbing at the bloody spot with his mom's handkerchief. He could not be sure whether Abel saw or heard but he spoke anyway, just as the sound outside broke like a wave from the inferno, and the attack began.

"Mr. Parkhurst, are you all right?"

11

"It's my fault," the colonel said, regarding the carnage.

A light rain fell in the courtyard, where he and Bart stood in the first shadows of late afternoon. The slanting light made jagged masks of the faces of the survivors, and from here Bart could see Ted Beckett strutting on the cobblestones just beyond the porte cochere. He had come down from the garret to accept credit for his surprise maneuver, which he would claim had driven the enemy away. He might even expect them to ask him to take command. He was slapping an empty carbine against his riding boot and moving from one group to another, as arrogant and cocky as if he alone had brought them victory. It was Beckett who had dumped industrial solvent on the forces that swarmed over the colonel's rampart to the west, while Brody's men unleashed a barrage of firebombs from the eastern parapet. At the same time Luigi, the demolitions expert, organized the riflemen who were protecting their flanks. At the signal they put down their rifles and let fly a barrage of pipe bombs. The effort was coordinated, desperate; they had let the enemy have it with everything except the furniture and silverware, which were already being heaped, in case.

In short, they had used up almost everything they had.

Mysteriously, it worked. For the moment, for whatever reasons, the enemy had withdrawn. It was only for the moment, Bart thought. For all he knew they were out there putting together the elements for the next surprise. In any case it was only a matter of time before they regrouped. Looking at the colonel's face, he had the idea it would be the last attack. Even with the temporary respite, the quiet punctuated only by the amplified voices railing at them from the park, the peace was illusory at best. So was their little victory. It had cost them everything they had. In spite of the fact that Ted Beckett was jubilant, striding and preening, they had next to nothing left. He himself had next to nothing left, Bart realized, and the colonel . . .

The face the colonel turned to Bart looked flayed. "What have I done?"

"You can't blame yourself."

Brody's expression told him otherwise, but what he said was, "On top of everything, Beckett's stupid trick . . ."

"He bought us a few hours."

The colonel grimaced as if at a knife twisting in his midsection. "We still had men out there."

Bart tried to bring him back. "We have people to see to here."

In the courtyard around them lay the wounded, the ones they had gathered in from the rampart in the last moments before the enemy stormed it and swarmed over as easily as children vaulting a hedge. Lying among them were the dead: the perforated and broken bodies brought down from the ballroom, where the enemy bombardment had broached the wall; from the upper floors, where armored windows had been penetrated by weapons nobody could have guessed the enemy possessed. The Parkhurst itself was broken and perforated and bleeding in places; Bart thought he could hear its agony—the rattle of roof plates sliding off, the occasional rumble of stones spilling, the sporadic snap of parting ribs. He wondered where old Abel was now, and hoped he was still out cold in the archway to the family entrance, where Sarah had felled him with the Cellini maquette right before she tried to wrench open the family door. In the tumult of the capture and the beginning attack, Bart had forgotten. When they caught Sarah did they ask someone to see to Abel or did they just leave him lying there? Wherever he was, Bart hoped he was sleeping or unconscious, and a secret part of him hoped the old man was dead. He should not have to know what was going on. It would be too much for him to bear. It was almost too much for Bart to bear.

They had driven the enemy back all right, repelling all boarders, but Bart felt none of the excitement or satisfaction the first victory had brought. The first time they had won easily, there were a few people hurt but nobody was hurt badly. When the buildings he had wired blew, it was magnificent, and he remembered the rush: *Again.* This time his mouth was sour and his belly was sour. Everything was sour. There had been no big moments, really, just exhausting work and bad times and the uneasy relief that came with a temporary respite. All right, they would not have to do this for a little while. But now they knew there were municipal fire trucks, hook and ladders and bulldozers and tanks massing on the avenue, just out of range, and the building shook with the rumble of giant cranes moving up, and now they were running out of things to throw at their attackers. They had nothing left to keep the enemy from closing in, which meant it was only a matter of time before somebody got a ladder up or nudged the granite façade with bulldozers until the stones parted and they came swarming in.

Next to him, Brody was knuckling his temples. This military lifer who had given orders with such assurance was busy somewhere deep inside himself, considering. This left Bart to consider his own landscape: the damages, the cost. Had Brody made the right decisions? Had he? When you chose to defend yourself, which decisions did you sacrifice to somebody else? Brody never intended for Beckett to jettison the wounded, or sacrifice the people on the rampart to drive back the enemy. He did intend to protect the Parkhurst —did that mean he'd given up the right to pick and choose? Was a Beckett inevitable? They were all right for the time being, granted, but all the wrong people had died. Bart wanted nothing more than to turn his back on all this and go and find Regan and bury himself in all her soft places, but next to him the colonel was grappling with his own furies and Bart had to examine himself. Were they fighting for their ideals here or was this a matter of expedience? Was survival an expedient, or a necessity? Was what you did justified if you pulled through? The trouble was, all the wrong people had died.

Randolph had died out there on the rampart in the early stages of the attack, when it was still possible to go out and drag the dead and dying inside. He had brought Randolph's body in and could not efface the memory of their last conversation: what they knew, and had no power to forestall. Randolph was lying under that canvas over there, and he was probably better off dead. This meant he would not have to see Sarah handcuffed to the flagpole by Beckett's men, or be there when Mr. Parkhurst found out. The bishop was dead too; he had died defending the opening in the ballroom wall. Bart saw him make the sign of the cross over each victim, friend or foe, as the assailants came through the jagged hole. He was making the sign of the cross over a punk kid with a .357 Magnum and a John Travolta haircut when a virago with a machete hacked into his midsection and he fell. Bart took her out with his first shot. It was the first time he had ever done this at such close range and she was dead; he watched the light go out. She was dead and Dawson was dead and so was the gentleman publisher Zane Richmond, who moved in with Bart to replace Ransom Hickox when he fell. They were crouching behind an overturned brocade sofa, firing at whatever appeared in the opening, two of them in concert until something exploded Richmond's head. Mrs. Imelda Maddox was dead too, her basket of doughnuts hopelessly scattered on the bloody parquet. She had been running coffee to the contingent in the ballroom; in spite of his warnings she was proffering a paper cup to Bart with a cocktail napkin and a gracious, hostess smile, crazily out of place here, when a crimson flower opened in her broad belly and she fell. In the final few minutes, after the fireball from the roof removed the last few faces from the opening and it was clear there would be no more coming for a while, Bart pulled down the smoking ballroom curtains and stamped out the flames the fireball had started. He stood for a second, light-headed and drained. Then he went down into the courtyard, looking for the colonel. He caught Madge trying to wrench open the huge inner gates, heading for the double bronze doors that would open the building to the outside, and now Madge was dead, and he knew that for each of the dead there were dozens of others he had not even seen, all of them felled like so many trees. The Parkhurst contingent was sadly diminished.

"It was my fault," the colonel said so unexpectedly that Bart jumped. Brody was back from whatever interior voyage he had made but it had left its mark on his face.

"You didn't bring this down on us. Nobody knew it was coming."

He tilted his head. "I had an idea it might. When you've spent half your life going to wars, you end up looking for wars to go to."

"But you didn't cause this. From what you say, it was going to happen anyway." Regan: what had Regan said? About Mardella.

Brody was brooding. "I should have gotten these people out before it did."

"They wouldn't have gone with you." She'd said: *There was nothing you could have done to prevent this. You can't eat yourself out over something you could not have known.*

"But no, not me. I had to make a stand." Brody was shaking his head. His face was scored with pain. "It doesn't matter that I didn't know."

"I think it does," Bart said, out of his new knowledge. "We never know half of it, but we have to keep going anyway. What you end up doing is just the best you can. It's all you can do."

Brody said, "I should have called up the house guard and marched these people out of here Friday afternoon."

"You think Mr. Parkhurst would have let you?"

"Let's say I could have forced the issue."

"No you couldn't," Bart said.

"Whether or not I could, I didn't, I wouldn't. After that damn thing tore into the ballroom I wouldn't have given it up for anything. You know what I was thinking when it started?" He flashed an uneven grin. "I thought, *This one is mine!*"

"You didn't have much choice."

"What do you know?" Brody's face changed for the last time. He said, with a clear, steady look, "I know it was my fault. Hubris. Call it what you want. It was my fault. *I wanted this.*"

Beckett's voice fell between them. "Damn right it's your fault."

Bart wheeled. "You two-bit murderer."

"Our friend is going to have a lot to answer for when we get out. I'm going to take the matter to Washington."

Bart looked into Beckett's smug face. It was clear he didn't imagine for a moment that they might all die here.

Brody said, "*If* we get out."

"You're going to answer for your incompetence."

Bart was ready to lunge but Brody held him back. The colonel turned to face his old acquaintance directly. "I remember what you did to your platoon, my friend. And I know what you did up there on the roof."

"Do you think anybody cares? I'm getting it done."

Brody flared. "That's all you care about, isn't it? Getting it done."

"I'm not the only one, and you know it."

Brody raised his gun. "Shut up and get out of here."

"Touch me and my men will blow your head off." At Beckett's signal two of the complement from the garret stepped forward.

The muzzle of Brody's pistol did not move. "Cheap at the price."

"Put that thing down."

Brody did not falter; his expression was drawn in stone. Bart knew he would just as soon shoot Beckett as not. Now Beckett knew it too. With a murderous look he turned slowly, as if it had been his idea to leave them. He gestured to his men and the three of them moved out. They went to the opposite side of the courtyard to the flagpole where Sarah Parkhurst was handcuffed, with her head bent against the soft rain.

"He's going to be a problem for you," Brody said.

Bart's head jerked back as if he had been hit. "What did you say?"

"I'd like to take him out before I go, but he's got too many men on him."

To his surprise, Bart understood what the colonel meant without having to be told. "You're going for help."

"Can't do this without reinforcements."

"We're still surrounded."

"It's almost dark."

"It's not nearly dark. What if you do make it? What can you do?"

"Maybe I can get a message off from Riverside Drive."

"I just wish you wouldn't."

"Somebody has to."

"You might not make it."

"If anybody can do it, I can. I'm a Marine."

Bart was astonished by the emotions that moved him to say, "You're needed here. I'd better do it."

"You don't have the training." Brody was striding toward the lobby door.

"I'm better than you think."

"That's why you're staying here." Brody tossed this over his shoulder without looking back.

Bart followed, double-time. "What do you want me to do?"

"Help me get ready."

When they returned to the vaulted archway just inside the secret door Bart noted with relief that old Abel was gone. Had the trusted Randolph found him and carried him to his room? No. By the time they caught Sarah, Randolph was already posted on the rampart, and now he was dead. Brody was pulling a black ski mask over his face. He put on his flak helmet and quickly took it off. Everything else was black: his clothes, his boots, his expression, and in the pale flicker from the electric sconce he looked like a double negative. Could he really slip through their lines? If he did make it to the banks of the Hudson, could he really get off a message? Could he make it to the other side? Would he make it back with help? Looking at the hawk profile, the resolute line of the shoulders, Bart realized this man would come back from the grave if he had to. Right or wrong, he kept his word. *I am a Marine.* He cleared his throat and found he had too much to say. He did not know where to begin.

"OK, Cavanaugh, I guess this is it."

"Yes sir."

"This leaves you in charge."

"Wait." In another second Brody was going to douse the light and slip out. "What about Beckett?"

"Do what you have to."

"Mr. Parkhurst!"

"See you, kid."

"Wait."

Brody set his flak helmet on Bart's head. "You're in charge now. Break it to him any way you want."

"But this is his building."

"Sometimes people don't know what's best for them." That was the old Brody, grinning confidently.

"What if I do it wrong?"

"You won't. You're the best I've got." The colonel doused the light and slipped out. He just went through the crack in the door like so much smoke.

12

So the Parkhurst was his to defend; the responsibility descended with the weight of the building: granite walls, towers, all those living souls, everything. *Oh well,* Bart thought with a wavy little grin, *maybe this is one way to make up for everything.* This hope flickered like a flame in a wind tunnel before it was swept away by a hundred new concerns: how bad it was, what they had left to fight with, how to defend. This time the masses had attacked in broad daylight; there was no guarantee they would wait for dark to attack again. The Parkhurst contingent had to get ready quickly, which meant rallying all those exhausted people and sending them back to the barricades; they thought they had been pushed to the limit, they were grieving and diminished, and he was going to have to ask them to begin again. With any luck this would be the last time; if they could hold the fortress this once, maybe Al would get back with reinforcements, and if he didn't . . . Bart could not think about it now. He had too much to do.

He began in the ballroom, where only two people were posted, keeping their Thompson guns trained on the crowd on the other side of the avenue. The rest, gunners and riflemen alike, were slumped under the gun slits, sleeping sitting up. Daylight shone on bare floor in several places where the apertures were undefended, and Bart realized they'd lost more people than he'd thought. The survivors were surrounded by spent cartridges and empty cartons, and it was clear they had very little ammunition left. Setsu, the Parkhurst houseboy, gave him a listless wave. Because he didn't have the heart to disturb the sleepers, Bart crouched next to the houseboy and kept his voice low. "How are things?"

"Terrible," he said with a sigh. "Outside they are telling us to give up while we still can. What do you think? They say if we put down our weapons they will give us safe conduct. They want us to open the gates."

"So they can roast our asses."

Setsu grimaced. "They are going to roast our asses in any case."

"Not if I can help it. Not without a fight. Right?"

"We don't have much left to fight with. What if we just . . ."

"Never," Bart said, trying to lift his spirits with his bare hands. "They can't do this to us. Right, Setsu?"

Did he look a little better? Bart thought so. "Right."

"Going to throw the kitchen sink at them. What I want you to do is organize these people. When it comes down, they should fire in turn so they don't blow all our ammunition all at once. And somebody should collect all the knives and skewers and cleavers from the kitchens—anything that's sharp."

"Kamikaze." Setsu managed an evil grin.

"That's my boy. But we're going to get them before they can get us. What's the matter?"

"I don't know if they will do what I say."

"Wear this." Bart took off Brody's flak helmet and set it on the houseboy's head. The minute he did this he felt fifty pounds lighter, but the lift was temporary. "And get somebody to move the library tables in front of the weak spots; we want to make it as hard for the bastards as we can. That's a good man. Damn the torpedoes, right?"

"Whatever you say, sir." Setsu doffed the helmet in a salute. "Banzai."

Like it or not, he was still in charge. He mounted the last flight of stairs to Beckett's garret bastion with misgivings, because the tin soldier's people were not going to welcome him.

At least the defense was proceeding, he thought as he came into the open space. Here again they were low on ammunition but they had piled heavy furniture by the catapult: sofas, benches, wrought-iron furniture, and there were stacks of chairs, small tables and other pieces of lighter stuff at intervals under the long skylight. There were a few more drums of Beckett's industrial cleanser heaped and waiting, and in a corner three women were busily making Molotov cocktails from whiskey bottles, decanters, anything else that came to hand. Unlike the ballroom, the place was neatly organized. It was also almost empty, except for the two guards who leveled rifles at him as he approached. He noticed uneasily that they were wearing khaki shirts like Beckett's and they had pieces of red stuff knotted around their arms.

"Where is everybody?"

"Downstairs."

"Downstairs? Why?"

"Orders."

"Well get them back. They're going to hit us again and we need every hand we have."

"They won't come back until they're ordered." Beckett's man looked at him indifferently.

"Well I'm ordering. Colonel Brody's authority. I'm his second-in-command."

"General Beckett has ordered them to the courtyard. *General* Beckett."

"That sleazy little . . ." There it was again; the sound of rifle bolts. "I want you to give General Beckett a message from me. Tell him we can't fight these people from the ground. We need his forces here."

"I'll tell him," the guard said in an it's-your-funeral tone.

He spoke stiffly. "Very well."

"*If* I see him," the guard said.

He wanted to go to the opening and look out at the west side, but he could not afford to turn his back on these two. He was fairly certain they were surrounded; what he did not know was whether there were already people directly below them, planting charges against the west wall. Did the enemy want to keep this building in one piece for political reasons, or would they just as soon blow them all to hell? He didn't know. He did know it was one thing to be told you were in charge and another to prove it to the people you were supposed to defend.

"But you guys are on duty here," he said finally.

"Yes."

"Then you'd better get your asses over to that skylight and keep an eye on things. If we stand here jawing long enough, somebody's going to sneak up and make a great big hole in your west wall."

He stayed just long enough to see that they were going to do what they were told.

It should be easier on the parapet, he thought, going back along the top floor to the northeast tower. The colonel had supervised the cannoneers, the lookouts, the people with the firebombs. They had orders to use the lulls to replenish their supply of Molotov cocktails, to rearm, regroup, do everything they could to prepare. The door to the parapet opened easily and he was surprised to find nobody there. The woman who guarded the tower door was gone, the cannoneers were gone, the heaps of empty bottles were still empty and the tins of gasoline still closed. Somebody had abandoned the pile of sheets intended for wicks; the entire operation was out to lunch. There was one kid left, sitting on the gravel with his back turned to the avenue. He did not bother to look up.

Bart yanked him to his feet. "Who the hell are you?"

"None of your business. Now let go."

"Where is everybody?"

"Gone downstairs. They left me in charge, my name is Chester, now let go!"

"You're in charge?" Bart tightened his grip. "You're in charge and they're all downstairs and those bastards across the street are just about to rush us. They are going to rush us as soon as they get it together and all these people are downstairs."

"The general wanted them."

"The general!"

"General Beckett. He said he needed all hands for the rally in the courtyard, would you please let *go?*"

Bart dropped him and did what he had been putting off until now. He went to the railing and looked over and down at the scene on the far side of the avenue. The enemy spread like a living carpet, studded here and there by pieces of heavy artillery and spotted with bulldozers, cranes, fork lifts, other pieces of heavy equipment he could not identify. Even at this distance he could see they were moving carelessly, in the leisurely arrogance of conquest; he thought he saw people passing bottles and sacks of food, walking in the open without a glance for the gunners in the ballroom. Why weren't they firing? Had Beckett co-opted them too? Were they out in the courtyard picking their noses and waiting for Beckett to pull the strings so they could dance? It was clear that Lawrence or Baron or whatever he wanted to call himself thought he had nothing more to fear from the people he had besieged.

In an open space directly across the street they were erecting a platform and draping it with more of that silver stuff Lawrence had wrapped around his head. An ice cream cart had popped up from nowhere and the operator was handing out ice cream sticks; the siege was turning into a party, and, watching, Bart began to understand the nature of the power this man had exercised over Sarah—the irresistable combination of sex and drama and righteousness, a Robin Hood act that blinded her to the reality of terror and blood. If she did the unforgivable she was only playing at the story he had created for them. If she was the princess in the tower waiting to be rescued she could do this precisely because she could not see outside. Right now Lawrence, no, Baron and his disciples were passing food and drinking from bottles, scratching their bellies and taking turns with the bullhorn, rattling off lists of accusations, naming war crimes and appropriate punishments, spinning out insults, warnings, anything they wanted because they were on top of the situation now and they could take their sweet time moving in for the kill. They would parade and harangue for as long as they got off on it, there were people down there taping the whole act for posterity, and then, if Bart's people did not crack and surrender, they would split the building open and empty it like an oyster shell.

They're getting careless, he thought.

Maybe we have time.

The abandoned battlements, the apathetic lookout and the threat Beckett posed made Bart's teeth rattle. He pushed the kid aside and went down the tower stairs with a wild urgency that propelled him at top speed until he reached the lobby and found himself stopped cold by the fact that so far he was alone in this, unarmed and empty-handed. He knew he had to do this, but at the moment did not know what to do next, or how. He felt like a Mickey Mouse balloon, almost weightless, with great floating useless hands. *How am I going to get them to listen to me? I'm only a young guy.* As soon as he formed the question he knew the answer. He was going to have to use Abel, whether or not the old man was up to it. Abel had to do it. Didn't they both want the same thing?

The old man was lying on a mattress under the lobby stairs, where Archer had dragged him after Sarah bopped him with the Cellini bronze. The kid was still standing guard, bright-eyed and charged with excitement. "I've been taking care of him."

"That's great." The old man was protected by a heap of quilts. Bart studied him, wondering, was he up to it? It didn't matter. He had to be. "Mr. Parkhurst. Abel. It's me."

"I don't think he wants you to wake him up."

"It's all right, Bart." The old man struggled back to consciousness. "I was hoping you'd come."

"Archer, would you get us some coffee?" He bent to help the old man to a sitting position. Abel did not look at him directly. Instead he reached past him to take the coffee from Archer, who had returned almost before he left. "Are you OK?"

"Thanks to Archer, here. As a matter of fact, he and I . . ."

"He keeps trying to give me presents," Archer said. "I can't take them because I was dumb."

"I don't get it."

The kid put his knuckles in his mouth like a squirrel trying to eat an outsized nut. "It's my fault Sarah got away."

Bart thought, *Not you too!* He had been blinded by guilt for two years and now this ten-year-old kid had a case. "Cut it out. Forget it. It's not what you did that matters, it's how you make up for it."

"Is that true?"

The very idea made him feel better. "I think so. It might be the main thing. Look, Arch, I have to talk to Mr. Parkhurst. I want you to go get us some brandy and him an electric razor and a clean shirt." Archer was glowing like a little jack-o'-lantern. Bart touched his forehead in a salute and sent him off. He said, to Abel, "We have to talk."

"I know." On the bed Archer had made for him, Abel was looking at his fingers, as if trying to number the losses he had suffered in the past few days. "I think we are very close to the end."

"Not if I can help it," Bart said through clenched teeth.

"I'm glad you're here."

"I need you. We have work to do."

But the old man wasn't following. Instead he said, thoughtfully, "It's funny, you go along thinking you are doing one thing, and it turns out you've done something completely different."

"That's what the colonel said." He was about to tell the old man about the colonel, to lead him step by step to the conclusion that they had to confront Beckett in the courtyard, but Abel cut him off.

"When my great-great-grandfather built this place, he was creating an ideal; he thought he and his descendants would live here forever, preserving everything beautiful: the culture of the ages, the arts of his century. Perhaps it was folly, but we all lived by this; we memorized what he wrote. He wrote: *No matter what happens outside, we will keep this as a reminder of the way things ought to be.* Pretentious? I don't know."

"I don't know either," Bart said.

"We were the custodians, and now it's all slipping away. Did I guess how it was going to end? Perhaps I did." Abel's face had been refined by suffering; he seemed to be midway in the transition from flesh to pure spirit, and Bart was going to have to arrest the process for the time being because he needed the old man. "When my grandfather died, I was five years old. I was playing on the tiger skin in front of the fireplace. I used to think his bedroom was like a king's room, with the skins and the tapestry: Shadrach, Meshach and Abdenago walking through the fire. I thought he must be the happiest person in the world, and then he called me to his side. I wish I could tell you exactly what he said before he died but all I can remember was the way he looked—tickled to death to be escaping, for one thing, and the other . . . sorry for me."

The old man was so frail that Bart did not know how he was going to get him to his feet and out into the courtyard; some time in the past few days Abel had become that which he was defending, which meant that all the ruptures in the building were duplicated in his body; if the roof was torn it was marked by the gash Sarah had put in his head. "Let me help you."

"In time." Abel waved aside his hand. "My father would never talk about any of this, but when he died I was on location with a film company in Nepal. He died and God help me, I knew. I also knew we were all the same person: Grandfather, Father and I." His breath quavered. "And here I am. I tried to make the perfect home and my wife ran away from me. I tried to be the perfect father and could not keep my daughter. I tried to give the perfect party, to bring her back, and now . . . It's no accident that she hit me with the Cellini. It's the most precious thing I own."

"That's one of the things we have to talk about. Sarah. She's . . ."

"Which is why I'm counting so heavily on you. Why I kept track of you even after you and Sarah ceased to be friends. It's clear I'm not going to live much longer."

"Of course you are."

"Don't condescend. And when I go I want to leave the Parkhurst in good hands."

"I can't talk about this right now. There's trouble in the courtyard. The colonel left me to deal with it, and I need you."

"I was hoping you cared as much as I did."

"I don't know what I care about." Bart's tone was altered by the complexity of the questions troubling him. "Right now we have to get through this. The thing is, the colonel's gone."

"Gone!"

"He's trying to get a message out." Bart dropped his head for a minute. "He wanted me to take charge."

"That seems appropriate." The old man was distressed. "The colonel went out."

"He said if anybody could make it he could." Bart could see reflected in the old man's eyes visions of Brody staked out in the rubble, or Brody disappearing under a swarm of attackers, or lashed to a lamppost and being doused with kerosene. He knew better than to ask what Abel thought. Instead he said, "For our purposes, we're going to have to act as if he can."

"You're right. I think you'd better help me up."

Once Bart had him standing, he stood back, assessing. Could he make it? Bart didn't know. Could Bart make it? He was going to do his best. "There are a couple of problems in the courtyard."

"What do you want me to do?"

"I think it would be a good idea if you showed yourself."

"I am still the Parkhurst," Abel said, resigned.

"I'm afraid so. The colonel sort of left me in charge but nobody is going to believe that unless you back me up. Look, here's Arch with the stuff."

The old man refused the shirt; he began with the brandy and then ate the sandwich Archer had made with the deliberate air of somebody who had been given a necessary medicine. Then he let Bart comb his hair and, leaning on him and tottering only slightly, he launched himself across the lobby and down the steps to consider the scene outside.

Bart imagined what it must look like to him. The fountain was dry and the plantings were ruined. His bandstand was still in place but the canopy was gone, along with the lanterns and bunting strung for the anniversary. Tiles had slipped from the roof into the courtyard and people were sweeping up the shards and heaping them where only yesterday there had been unexpended piles of ammunition. There were groups of people standing everywhere in the beginning twilight, looking sullen and sinister. Helping the old man across the courtyard, Bart realized that he had kept the worst part from him for a reason, and in the failing light Abel did not immediately see the figure chained to the flagpole. Instead, he was drawn to the heap of body bags, canvas from the Parkhurst laundry shrouding large and small alike.

"I would not have imagined there would be so many dead. Who?"

"Abel, you don't want to know."

"Tell me the worst," he said, but was drowned out by the amplified voice, which had resumed.

"THUS END THE PLEASURES OF THE RICH."

"Don't mind them. They've been at it off and on since they pulled out."

Abel said, "You know, I never wanted to be rich."

"GREEDY KILLED PIG."

"I tried to be responsible."

"You could have given it all away and things still wouldn't be any better," Bart said. "Or any different. You wanted me to tell you who was killed."

"FIRST YOUR MONEY." The amplified voice seemed to rattle the gates.

Abel cried, in answer, *"I tried to share."*

"We lost a lot of cops and some of the guard and most of the people from the rampart . . ."

"THEN YOUR LIFE."

"Listen, out there," Abel shouted, *"I don't have it any more!"*

"We lost Randolph and Mrs. Maddox, among others."

"Randolph!" Abel was weeping. He finished. "I don't have anything."

But the voice in the park was not going to leave him alone in his distress. It hammered at them. "SO GIVE UP NOW!"

"Never!" Abel cried so loud it stopped Bart in his tracks. Shaken as he was, distressed and ill, the old man was not going to surrender; he was not even going to give in to his own frailty, Bart realized. He was glad because it solidified his own position; if they had to go down they were going to do it with all flags flying. "You might as well tell me who else we've lost."

"The bishop, among others." To his surprise Bart's voice shook. "He wouldn't keep his head down."

"Poor Bertram."

"At the end he ran around *blessing* people." Bart was outraged. "The air is filled with flying crap and he's blessing people, as if that would make a difference. It was so weird."

"He was more of a man of God than he wanted to admit."

"If he hadn't been so damn busy praying, he'd still be here."

"We make our own choices. We do what we have to."

As the old man went from one body bag to the next, touching each in a valedictory gesture, Bart considered this. The colonel had expected him to take over, which he supposed meant stopping the Beckett thing and getting these people organized. Looking around the courtyard at the miserable, the angry and the disaffected survivors, he did not know how easy this was going to be. Which of them was likely to be loyal to the Parkhurst family? Did they even know, or care? The high spirits and excitement of the early hours had been dispelled by the losses of the past few days: the injuries, the illness, the shortages, the deaths. Could he rally these people to oppose Ted Beckett, or should he get Beckett to help prepare for the next wave? If the enemy held off now, it was because Lawrence wanted abject surrender; he was out there with the bullhorn, haranguing them, alternating threats and promises. As he looked at the clumps of survivors in the courtyard Bart saw them weighing this; did any of them really believe they would be better off if they gave up? Should he jump on the bandstand and tell them about Granger and Mrs. Livingston? He had to do something, and soon. With no more to go on than the colonel's orders and the authority of this indomitable old man, he was going to have to proceed.

"One of us is going to have to make a speech."

Abel ignored this. If he had not seen Sarah at the flagpole he knew she was there anyway. Now he was tugging Bart along. "I must see my daughter first."

"After what she did to you?"

"She's still my daughter," Abel said.

"I don't know if she wants to see you." Bart could guess what she would have to say, if she said anything; at the moment she stood as if completely alone. She was listening to the amplified voice with an intent look; she had already cut herself off from everything that happened here. She dropped her head, sullen and remote.

"I know." Abel sighed. "I should have listened when you tried to warn me, but I still hoped."

"I should have turned her in anyway." Bart shrugged. "It isn't anybody's fault."

Abel rushed forward. "Sarah, my dear."

Even in fatigues spattered with Abel's blood, she was beautiful. She stood with her shorn head bent. Someone had run the cuffs through a loop on the pole so she could not slip them up or down. The face she raised was caught between expressions—relief that they were people she knew and had at one time loved, and anger because she had been caught. "Are you going to get me down or what?"

Abel lifted his hands to her. "I love you, but I can't."

"If you care at all, you'll get me down."

Lord, Bart thought, don't let him ask me to unshackle her. He was aware of movement at his back: a small group approaching, but he would not look behind him. Instead he looked at Sarah, who had been his friend since the sandbox, who had been caught in an ugly adult act that she thought of as a game, and he said, "Hello, Say."

"Hi, Barty. How about you let me down?"

"I can't."

When she spoke again it was in a voice so low that at first he could not be certain she had said anything. "Then when he comes, you'll be the first to pay."

Abel's voice quavered. "Oh, Sarah, are you all right?"

"What do you care? You," she said with contempt. "The Baron is going to nail you to the wall for what you did."

"But I love you. I love you and I've always tried to do what was right. Always," he said brokenly. "I haven't done anything."

"Did, didn't do. It's all the same. When you get yours I'm going to be glad."

"Please, why do you hate me when I only want the best for you?" He was supplicating with his eyes, his voice; if she had gotten free and made a run for it he would have tried to protect her with his own body, standing between her and the fire of the guards. If she'd tried to kill him at that very moment he would have died holding out his hands to her. "What have I done wrong?"

Behind Bart, Beckett grabbed his arm, hitting a high-pitched bark. "Cavanaugh."

Bart shook him off. "Sarah. Say, what did you think you were doing?"

She answered both of them. "You know damn well."

Abel said, "My poor dear!"

But Sarah was looking over their shoulders at Beckett, and Bart thought he saw a crack in her expression: the scared kid peeking through. In the next second her face closed. She had, after all, a position to defend. "So you might as well let me go," she was saying, as if she had explained everything. "I am in a position to do you all a few favors. Let me go now and I'll put in a good word for you when Baron gets in. Otherwise, there's going to be hell to pay."

"Never," Beckett snapped. His little corps of followers stirred.

Abel said, "My dear, I have to keep you here, where you'll be safe."

Bart added, "Where we'll be safe."

"Then I don't care what happens to you."

Abel leaned heavily on Bart. Behind them Beckett was clacking with impatience and Bart stabbed him with an elbow. He heard Beckett hiss as if he'd been punctured and knew from the ominous stir behind him that he had not bought much time. Abel was still holding out his hands to his daughter, saying, "I'll always love you. You'll always be my daughter, no matter what you do."

"That's funny," she said with a vulpine grin, "You were never my father, you know?"

Abel cried out as if he had been hit.

"Never."

"Sarah, I love you."

"If you cared about me at all you would open those gates and let my lover in."

"I'm your father, but I'm this too." Abel grew taller as he spoke. "I am this, that I must defend."

"This is all you are," she said bitterly, dismissing him. "It's all you ever were."

"All right," Beckett said. "It's time for us to begin."

Bart wheeled. "What?"

"Rallying point." Beckett pushed past him to confront Sarah. "Sarah Parkhurst you are a traitor and a spy."

Abel said, "But she's sorry!"

"Like hell I am." Her face had turned to marble and her eyes glittered. "I'm glad."

"Oh, my dear!" With a sigh, the old man kissed his fingertips and touched them lightly to his daughter's forehead so that even as she jerked away violently and her head clanked against the metal pole, she had to suffer her father's loving touch. "I tried so hard."

Poor bastard, Bart thought. *All that effort, over all these years.*

"I loved you so much. I wanted so much to do it right."

All he was trying to do was the right thing.

"I wanted to give you everything." Abel turned from her with his face wet and Bart could not be sure whether those were tears or drops of her spit or only light spring rain that the old man wiped from his face. "I tried so hard to do it right."

"Well you were wrong."

The right thing. Here was Abel, brought to despair, Abel, who had spent his life trying to do the right thing. Looking at the old man, Bart knew that even if he had been warned, even if he had foreseen this, he would have done precisely the same thing, and something exploded inside his head and time stopped while he considered it.

"All right," Beckett was saying to Sarah, "we don't have much time . . . Do you want a lawyer or will you defend yourself?"

Beckett droned on but by this time Bart was deafened by a humming in his ears, as of suspended movement—the pause before a rush of flapping wings. So he was struck in his tracks by the complete vision of himself in flight, the gorgeous spectacle of Bart scot-free in the clear blue, beyond guilt and obligation—the seduction of the moment before he plummeted into oblivion. No wonder he had tried to kill himself.

Climbing back from that moment hand over hand, in the hospital and in Cambridge and especially here, he had imagined life as a matter of doing things right, in the right order, in some reasonable expectation of reward. If you could manage this and this and then that, everything would be OK. When he remembered how he lost Mardella the black holes would stop opening; when he acknowledged his guilt he would be able to read; if he could do something big to make up for it, he could go back to his life. It had all seemed neat, completely logical, yet here was Abel, who had spent all his life trying to do the right things in the right order, and look at him. He had tried to protect and preserve this place and it was a shambles; he had tried to give Sarah the best and she spat in his face. Bart had been busy putting one foot in front of the other in confidence that if he did, everything was going to come out all right. Now he understood that there were no guarantees. It was clear that there might not be any rewards for any of this, unless he was willing to count process, which meant that he was reduced to two choices: giving up or going ahead anyway. No wonder he'd wanted to fly.

He and Abel had been bumped to the fringes of the circle around the flagpole, where Beckett finished saying whatever he had been saying to Sarah and turned, raising his voice to the clumps of people in every part of the courtyard.

"We're going to make a public example of her."

Stricken, Abel cried out, but his voice was lost in the rising clamor.

"OK," Bart said, because, for the first time since the colonel turned the place over to him, his course was clear. His voice lifted. "OK!"

Abel turned to him in confusion. "What?"

He put his mouth close to the old man's ear. "Come with me. I think I've just figured out how to do this. We have to go inside and get a couple of things and get ready."

"But they're going to . . ."

"I think I know how to stop them."

He did. He also knew that the choice between giving up and going on was illusory. No matter what happened, no matter how it ended—well or badly, he was going to go ahead with it. If the guards caught him at the top of the science building and snatched him off the ledge before he could fly out of his life, it was because he had guessed all this and still wanted to live. He was Bart Cavanaugh, who could not give up. He would always go ahead.

"That's it. Let's go. There's somebody we have to find."

Regan and Doc Millinger were finishing with their last patient when the bishop's man came for them. The evil-looking fool with the cadaverous face hung over them as she finished setting clamps to close poor Dawson's cut. Something about this made her take her sweet time. They were low on supplies, she had nothing left to give Dawson for pain and she had no idea when or how this was going to end but she was a doctor, and for as long as she was needed, she would take care of the wounded here.

"General Beckett wants you in the courtyard," he said for the third time.

"You mean Ted."

"I mean General Beckett."

"I thought you worked for the bishop."

His tone chilled her. "The bishop is dead."

She had felt in vain for poor Bertram's pulse and then composed his face. "I know."

Doc Millinger's voice was edged with fatigue. "I think we should stay here, in case we're needed."

"I'm sorry," the bishop's man said, pushing the doctor roughly. "You have no choice."

"Let go of him or we're not going anywhere." Regan glared. Her hands were shaking and her mouth was dry from the long afternoon of attending patients. Exhausted though they were, she and Doc still had rounds to make.

Regan stood her ground with a sense of outrage. What right did this weedy curate have to order them around? She let her soiled lab coat drop without bothering to see where it fell. She undid the kerchief that held back her hair and looked at the bishop's man. Was this Dexter who was regarding her coldly, or was it Brewster? Some time in the last few days they had begun to look sinisterly alike. This was Beckett's man now, with his long blue jaw scored by fingernail marks—Madge's?—and his lips tight. As she confronted him he raised the barrel of the rifle he was holding, using it as a prod. The disheveled clericals were filthy, the collar sprung and the whole more or less covered by a khaki shirt that was unbuttoned down the front. He had tied a piece of red cloth around his arm just above the elbow—Regan thought it was a piece of the library draperies—and she understood that although he had no sense of costume, he had been instructed to come in uniform. He stood for something more than he really was.

"Are you coming quietly?"

"Who the hell are you to ask?"

"Get moving." He used the rifle to nudge her in the ribs.

"You know some of these people could use a little religious consolation, or have you forgotten who you are?"

"That's all gone by the board," Brewster said. "Everything has changed."

"What's the rag for?"

"It's not a rag." He scowled. "It's a badge."

"The shirt!"

"Uniform. Are you with us or not?"

"I told you, we have patients to see."

"Not now, you're wanted in the courtyard. He wants everybody in the courtyard, regardless."

"What for?"

"Never mind. Orders."

Regan dug in her heels. "What does he want us for?"

"None of your business." Brewster prodded her with the rifle barrel, nudged Doc Millinger. "Just keep moving."

Coming outside, Regan was surprised by the number of people wearing khaki shirts with scarves tied at the elbows. "What's going on?"

"Shut up. The commander is speaking."

"That isn't the commander."

Brewster turned with a sly grin. "He is now."

"What happened to the colonel?"

"Who gives a damn what happened to the colonel?"

"Stop that!" He had insinuated the steel tip of the rifle into the soft spot between two of her ribs and now he twisted it with an expression that was nakedly sexual. She grasped the metal and removed it. "Leave me alone."

"Not yet. We need your vote." He lowered the rifle and gripped her arm with his free hand, kneeing her until she stepped up on the low stone rail that bordered the steps under the porte cochere. "Stand up. Stand up there so you can be counted."

"You have all suffered enough," Ted Beckett said from the bandstand. He had taken the microphone and was addressing the crowd in the courtyard. Regan could not figure out why everybody seemed to be muttering in agreement. What had happened here, and where were Mr. Parkhurst and Al Brody? Her heart skidded. Where was Bart? Beckett was pacing like a petty demagogue, filling the air with his self-important rambling.

"What's going on?"

"Shut up."

"Enough of old leadership. Enough of losing. Now we're going to win this," Beckett ranted, unchallenged.

"This is crazy."

Brewster gave her arm a savage twist. "Now listen."

"I'm going to take care of you all . . ." Beckett raised his arms, calling for approval. "But I need a vote of confidence."

When he dropped his arms the shout rattled the building.

Beckett's goons, or whoever they were—the others with khaki shirts and red scraps tied at the elbows—stood in a loose circle at the edges of the crowd Beckett had gathered. As Regan watched others came out of doorways in the west wing, and from the underground garage; they were all armed and as she studied them she began to be clear about who had stolen the drugs from the trophy case and what had been done with them. Pulled together by this self-important bastard and identified by the uniform, they might have done his bidding anyway; fueled by uppers and whatever else they were popping, they looked ready to do anything. Even some of the wounded had been turned out on crutches or on litters, and every time Beckett made a point they shouted in agreement. The effect was chilling.

There were people in the courtyard Regan had never seen before—a couple of cornets from the orchestra, along with the entire string section, carrying instruments; the crews who must have been working on the generator, gunners—who was defending the ballroom? There were vestiges of the Parkhurst staff, refugees, others she could not identify. Whoever they were, they were all sadly altered by the events of the past few days. Their clothes were filthy and bloodied in places; their hair was matted and their eyes were dulled by illness and exhaustion. In their misery, they looked ready to do anything. Even the Parkhurst matrons had been changed by hardship and circumstance; their tatty costumes had given way to raincoats or robes, anything that covered them, and they brandished canes or held handbags like blunt instruments. On the platform above them, Ted Beckett seemed to know they had been pushed so far that he could get them to do anything he wanted. He was pacing back and forth with a hand mike, working them like a Vegas emcee; when he reached the end of the platform and made a turn, he flipped the microphone cord like a practiced entertainer.

"Today we fight. Tonight we celebrate."

Everybody cheered.

"The best of everything for everybody."

Somebody started the chant: "Beckett, Beckett, Beckett!"

"I knew I could count on you. Now, I want you to show me your colors."

Several people waved their red scarves.

"And now. The vote. All in favor . . ."

Regan shouted, *"No!"*

She was drowned out by the others. Brewster's breath came out in a little "Pah!" of satisfaction and he left her. As he did, Beckett silenced the crowd with the assurance of a star. Without thinking Regan jumped down from the rail, crunching through the ornamental flowerbed. She reached the base of a garden statue and mounted it. From here she could see two of Beckett's people marching a woman up the steps to the platform, kneeing and kicking her as she struggled.

Beckett shouted. "No mercy."

A dozen voices picked it up. "No mercy!"

"We will show no mercy!" Beckett sounded like a revivalist. "Do you hear me?"

"We hear you." The response came in a series of jagged echoes, as people jumped and waved in a passion to be seen shouting.

The woman looked like . . . Was. It was Sarah Parkhurst. What were they doing with her? Sarah was in a frenzy of defiance, tossing her head and struggling as they tied her to one of the supports. She faced her accuser in a fury.

"Court-martialed, convicted," Beckett shouted.

Wait.

"Convicted of treason!"

In front of the platform, loyal Dawson, who used to take Sarah in her stroller to the park, was shouting, "Treason." A dozen others picked it up. Soon there would be hundreds.

"Fairly convicted," Beckett shouted. "Now for the sentence."

"The sentence!"

The mob in the courtyard seemed to be pulled in several directions by calls for hanging, shooting, whipping. The ugly tone was clear, as was the intent. Sarah was going to be punished for everything that had happened to them. Regan had been hanging on to the tail of a stone lion; she hoisted herself up on its back, thinking if she could only see better she could begin to make some sense of this. If she could locate Mr. Parkhurst, or catch sight of Bart. Better yet, if she could speak to Bart . . . But all she saw was Billie Beckett coming out from under the platform with one of the waiters from the anniversary ball; he lifted the bunting so she could duck out from under it. They were brushing sand from faces that looked blurry and sated, and she realized that these two events—Beckett crying murder from the platform and Billie down here with another lover—were directly related. Screwing as though the siege had catapulted her into full season, Billie had been here, there, everywhere with a string of men. Regan had been dimly aware of this as she went about her own urgent business, but saw it demonstrated now as Billie's husband saw it demonstrated, publicly. It was as if the projectile in the ballroom had shattered the protective outlines of their everyday lives, catapulting them into a no-man's-land of extraordinary situations and unpredictable responses. This was not like anything any of them had ever known. The world had flopped over, overturning all of them as it did so, wrenching all their assumptions out of place so that nothing pertained, and nothing could be predicted.

The rules had changed, along with their expectations. Sitting astride the stone lion, Regan was surprised by a kind of guilty excitement because in the chaos she had somehow escaped her life, like a schoolkid playing hooky.

The divorced woman who went her rounds in the gray old hospital in the real world seemed remote; if she had drunk too much because she had to just to make it through the day, it was for reasons she couldn't even remember now. Everything had changed, she thought. She had changed. No matter what happened after this she was a different person. Wild as this was she realized now that she'd rather be here, under siege and in real danger, then back in her old life. It crossed her mind that they might be in siege here forever, and she welcomed the idea. So long as they were, then certain things would remain suspended. She was so lulled by this that she watched almost dreamily as Ted Beckett raised both hands and called for a voice vote, and she was not surprised when a dozen voices seconded his motion for execution and the courtyard rocked with the shouted "Aye."

"Very well," he shouted, "am I authorized?"

The shout was hysterical, *"Aye!"*

"No!" Regan was crowded suddenly, dazzled and almost blinded by light; it was as if somebody had dropped a hornets' nest directly on her head, every insect a whirring point of fire. She dragged her hands down her face, trying to clear the air so she could see and hear. OK, she realized. If this was panic she had to fight it. Whatever she had imagined this was, that was happening, had begun to change. The tin general up there on the platform had just been authorized to put that girl up there to death. She remembered herself in childhood, too tired to quit playing: *Regan, it's time to come in to supper,* or on Halloween: *Now it's time to take off the masks.* The exhaustion and urgency and false camaraderie of this time of siege had left her confused and strangely vulnerable; the others must be feeling some of the same things. If they did not stop now they were all going to do something they would be forever ashamed of, and she could not for the life of her figure out how they were going to stop.

Beckett shoved the microphone in Sarah's face. "Any last words?"

"Hell no." Her expression was changing; the look of defiance slid away, revealing the frightened girl. She grabbed the mike. "I didn't do this. You can't kill me."

At a signal from the bishop's men the crowd began: "Beckett, Beckett, Beckett . . ."

"It was my father," she cried, and her amplified voice drowned out theirs, pinging back and forth against the courtyard walls. "It was all his fault."

Did the people outside hear? Regan thought she heard an answering cry, the stir of the last wave of attackers gathering, preparing to break over them.

Beckett snatched the microphone and hurled it down. He backed the length of the platform with his pistol raised while Dexter and Brewster turned the desperate girl so she would be completely exposed, so that it was clear to everybody that they really were going to execute her and she began to cry helplessly. Beckett took careful aim and Regan began screaming, not words, just pure sound with no beginning and no end.

As she did so several things happened at once: the platform, the people on it and everybody in the courtyard and even the walls began to vibrate with what Regan only later identified as the aftershock of several simultaneous explosions outside. A trio swarmed up the steps of the platform in the confusion and before Beckett could recover his balance Bart had pounced on him from behind, hooking an elbow around his throat and thrusting the muzzle of a pistol in his ear. Swathed in a boat cloak, Abel Parkhurst crossed the platform, drawing on what must be his last bit of strength. He picked up the microphone and the air shuddered with his sigh. Behind him was the blunt-faced Luigi, the demolitions expert, who beamed and clasped his hands in the air above him like a prizefighter taking a bow.

Beckett's people raised their weapons uneasily, while all around her people stirred and murmured, completely confused. Dexter and Brewster were in disarray, waving their guns without knowing where to point them because Bart was using their struggling leader as a shield.

Abel began to speak. "If you want to shoot anybody, shoot me. One way or another, this is all my fault."

Bart crossed the platform in seconds, dropping the gun to sieze the microphone before the old man could continue. The sound system relayed his aside to Abel. "Cut it out, that's enough of that."

Riveted, Regan was peripherally aware of another sound that must have been going on for some time at a great distance; within seconds the source had begun its approach. But she was watching Bart now. His face was flushed and his voice vibrated with energy as he commanded the microphone. He was brand-new.

"OK, people, let's get our act together. Luigi just lofted three frag bombs out of here. Now we've got to cut all this crap and get back to our posts."

Did Regan hear something approaching, and did the others? Were they all aware of it as they decided what to do? They were all watching Bart now, ignoring the angry Beckett, whose knees were buckling as he struggled to breathe. Some of Beckett's people had trained rifles on Bart and others were crowding them aside, bumping the guns so that even if they did fire, the shots would go wild. Beckett was trying to loosen Bart's arm so he could draw enough breath to speak and in the next second Bart had brought the mike up and smashed it against the side of his head with a sound that amplified itself like the bang at the end of the world. Then in a broad gesture he whirled, lifting the deflated figure and throwing it off the platform like a broken toy.

Without even looking to see where Beckett landed, he faced the crowd with a grin of pure triumph.

"OK, gang, are you with me?"

People began shouting, "Yes!"

If he had been a confused kid when this began he was sure of himself now, grinning and brilliant and strong, and, watching him, Regan let herself believe in happy endings in this context—that these extraordinary events had indeed lifted her out of her life. But running under the cries of assent she heard a beginning murmur that gathered momentum as the distant sounds came near enough to be identified. By this time the metallic racket made it necessary for Bart to shout.

His bright, loud voice rallied the crowd. "OK, people, we've bought some time. Now we've got to hit them again, and soon. Setsu, you take the ballroom. Dawson, the parapet. Brewster and Dexter, the west side. It's do or die, people, all right?"

Regan heard somebody, perhaps Dawson, raise the first shout: "All right!"

On the platform, Abel Parkhurst stood with his head lifted and his face streaming with tears of gratitude and relief while the bishop's duo exchanged looks and then moved so they were standing more or less behind Bart, in hopes they'd be taken for allies.

"All right?"

At the back of the platform, Sarah had raised her shackled wrists to her face and was rubbing hard, as if the face she wiped away could be replaced by one everybody would like. The racket overhead grew louder but the crowd was fixed on Bart now, in a thunderous assent.

It was as if they could not fall in fast enough, the hasty outcry raised to efface that earlier, shameful moment when they had voted for Sarah's murder.

They were all shouting now, "*All right.*"

But as they did, Bart looked up at the sky and began to laugh. He dropped the microphone, shaking his head in an amusement that Regan did not immediately understand because she was still caught up in the drama of the execution, dizzied and confused by how quickly things were moving and too distracted to see what was coming, what had been coming from a long way off even before Beckett's rally began.

Around her, people were changing before her eyes, muttering and shifting, dropping weapons and changing alliances with manic speed, as if they had to dissociate themselves from their recent shame before . . . before what? Now she saw khaki shirts and red scarves being removed and hidden and she saw Bart looking over the edge of the platform where he had shoved Beckett and then facing the crowd with a driven, vindicated look of savage joy; by that time the metal swarm was directly overhead, dozens of heavy helicopters and a couple of light ones, filling the twilight air. The huge machines passed over while the light ones began a descent into the courtyard. Regan understood for the first time that she and the others were being delivered. Outside the heavy helicopters would be fanning out to settle on the streets and avenues; she supposed troops would jump down to disperse the swarm in the park. She suspected it would not be hard even for a handful of troops because of the force they stood for, the implied forces. The hand of the government would scatter this enemy as carelessly as it might a flock of geese—the followers frightened and the leaders taking cover quickly, before they could be identified and apprehended. In a few hours the terror that had held the city would simply cease to exist.

Is that all it was, Regan wondered. *Something they could settle with a few hundred troops? If that was all it was, what were we doing?* What would happen to their positions, she wondered, all the gallent and craven gestures, these life-and-death decisions?

In the courtyard, the crowd Beckett had gathered was dwindling as people backed away from the two perching machines. They began to disappear into doorways and through arches as if they could somehow erase the past few minutes and be rendered innocent. If pressed they would all deny what they had almost done here. The helicopters had landed neatly and Regan found herself laughing and sobbing at the same time as uniformed officers jumped down from one and a team of spanking-fresh medics hopped out of the other, handing down cases of drugs and cartons of dressings carelessly, as if they knew they had enough to last forever. She saw Doc Millinger going down the steps to greet the medical crew and understood with a groan of relief that her days as field surgeon were over.

What else is ending, she wondered. She turned her back on this question and headed for the platform. There were only a few people left in the courtyard, which made her passage easy. She did not know what she expected to do when she reached it; slip her hand into Bart's and try to pull him along with her, into her future? Take some part in the liberation? She did not know. What she did know was that it seemed important to be with him.

She made it up the steps just behind the captain of the rescue squadron, who looked so bright and shiny that he might have been freshly minted. The captain saw Abel totter, and moved to keep him from falling. "Who belongs to this old man?"

"My name is Abel Parkhurst." Abel pulled back from the captain with a look that forestalled pity. "I am the owner."

"I'm sorry. You looked so . . . what happened here?"

"We've been under a strain," Abel said coldly. "We did what we could."

The captain looked around the ruined courtyard. "I'm sorry we couldn't get here sooner."

Abel turned to Sarah, who was loose now and standing quietly as if drained of everything: blood, anger, will. He said, "I'm sorry too. So many things might have been prevented."

"Terrible bureaucratic foul-up."

"I see."

The captain shrugged. "You can imagine."

Abel was distant: the householder who has been slighted. "I'm afraid I can't. Mr."

"Gavin. Captain Rex Gavin, U.S. Army. Those are Army units out there doing the mopup," he said with an air of pride.

Abel was rattling with exhaustion but he seemed to regain his sense of himself as he spoke. His tone was imperious. "Why weren't you here before?"

"It was a jurisdictional thing."

Bart said, "During which, we had to hold the line."

The captain shrugged. "It looks to me as if you didn't, really."

"Wait a minute," Bart said.

But Gavin had turned to Abel, who drew his arm across his breast so that the sweep of boat cloak covered his soiled shirt. "To tell the truth, sir, it was a matter of which branch of the service was responsible, whether it was even a job for the armed forces. As a matter of fact, there was a heavy sentiment for leaving the whole thing to the city police."

"So you leave us . . . ."

He cut Bart off. "Then another faction thought the state highway patrol ought to move in and then there was the matter of whether this was a national thing or strictly a domestic thing, whether the state National Guard units ought to handle it or whether the federal government was responsible. Nobody signs an emergency order without committee advice and it takes time to convene the appropriate groups, so you can see why we couldn't cut through the red tape until today. But I want you to know those are U.S. Army troops out there taking care of your problems, which is the best the country has to offer, as you know."

Bart groaned and held his head.

"As a matter of fact, we're all on hazardous duty pay, it's the only way we could manage to move in right away. Without the proper authorization it would have been morning before we got this operation launched."

"We could have been dead by morning," Bart said.

"Oh no. The situation has been carefully monitored."

"Monitored!"

"We had to wait until all our systems were go."

Next to Regan, Bart stirred. "But then you got our message."

"What message?"

"I mean, Brody made it through."

"Who?"

"Al Brody, colonel, USMC. The one who brought the message."

"Nobody brought us any message."

Bart said, urgently, "He was ready to die for us. The Marine."

Gavin said, "I'm sorry."

"Then how did you find out?"

"I must have done it," Archer said. He had scrambled up the steps in the middle of the confusion and now he stood next to Abel, who put one arm around him so he was partially wrapped in the cloak.

"Who are you?"

"It was one of my pigeons," Archer said, stepping in front of the old man without letting go of his hand. "I sent the messages, first I grabbed them and then I tied things to their legs . . ."

"Captain, this is Archer Livingston," Abel said. "He's begun to be very important to me."

"Carrier pigeons, like in World War One," the little boy said.

Abel spoke over his head. "Archer is an orphan."

"I saved everybody."

"I'm going to take care of him from now on."

Gavin shook Archer's hand without even looking down. "As a matter of fact we've known about your situation from the beginning. Our helicopters reported your enclave the first day . . ."

"The beginning!" Bart went on under his breath. "Son of a bitch."

"What's that?"

"Nothing." Regan could feel Bart shaking, was afraid for him and then understood; he was—he was *laughing,* rocking silently. "Not a damn thing, Captain, sir."

She was outraged. "You mean you people knew?"

But Gavin ignored her. He was speaking to Bart and Abel, because they were the men here. He said, apologetically, "You know how these things are."

Regan repeated, "You knew and you didn't do anything?"

Abel was distracted, tousling Archer's hair as if it was the most important thing he had to do. "I'm sure you had your reasons."

"Perhaps if we'd had any idea how badly your people would bungle it . . ."

"Wait a minute, wait a *minute.*" But Bart was shh-shhing in her hair. She persisted. "You don't know what it was like."

Bart said, "We did the best with what we had."

Abel overrode him. "Naturally I and all my people are grateful to you."

"Yeah, right," Bart said distractedly. Regan did not know what he was thinking about but it was clear he had gone beyond her. "You don't know what it was like." He went on, laying it out carefully, "Nobody knows what it was like."

"Oh, Bart," she murmured. *He's right.*

Everything was changing now. Rather, she thought, everything seemed to be changing *back.* She put up her hands as if she could somehow stop it, at least long enough for Bart to have his triumph and for her . . . she did not know. In any case, it was already too late.

If Abel had depended on Bart for everything in the past few days he had not forgotten, exactly, but rather displaced the recollection, moving it to one side so he could resume being that which he had been for most of his life until now. "I know what you did for us, and I will always remember."

Bart shook his hand. "It's OK."

"You know you will always have a place here."

"I can't stay," Bart said, with immediate certainty. "And I don't think you want me to."

"But I thought of you as . . ." Abel dangled the prospect in front of him like the keys to a new car. "As a possible heir."

"Thanks but no thanks. I have to get back to my life."

Regan tightened her fingers around his hand. Did that mean she had to go back to her life? *Not yet,* she thought, *not yet.*

"Very well." The old man took Bart's right hand in both of his. "Whatever happens, you will always have a place in my guest room. Now I think Archer and I had better go inside and see to things—perhaps a cold supper for our rescuers."

"Wait a minute, Daddy." It was Sarah.

"Dr. Millane, I haven't thanked you properly."

The angry, defiant woman who had betrayed them dropped ten years in ten seconds. She sounded like a little girl. "Daddy, what about me?"

Abel turned to the captain. "I hope you and your men will join us at dinner, as a partial expression of our very great thanks."

The captain said, "Who's supposed to be in charge?"

"Bart is," Regan said.

"As the owner, I . . ."

Bart grinned at the captain. "Looks like you are, Captain Gavin, sir."

Sarah was grabbing at Abel with shackled hands. "Aren't you going to take me with you?"

Abel gave her a long, thoughtful look and in the next second turned and started down the steps. As he did so Sarah dropped her hands and began rubbing her wrists with a strange, green glare of concentration, the silent watchfulness of someone whose inner furniture is rearranging itself. At the bottom of the steps Abel halted and drew the cape around him like a stricken

Nelson or the dying Roosevelt at Yalta, saying, "Captain, tell your men we dine at eight."

"Poor old bastard," Gavin said as Abel stumbled and Archer caught him. "He should take better care of himself."

"He's been through a lot," Bart said.

Regan finished the thought. "Everybody has."

"What were they all doing when we came in?" Gavin regarded Sarah, who flushed and dropped her eyes. "What was going on?"

"They were trying to . . ."

Bart cut her off. "Nothing much. We had a problem that almost got out of hand. I turned it around, that's all."

"But this woman's wrists. The damage. The place is a wreck."

"It could have been leveled," Bart said. "We kept it in one piece. We settled the problem and we held the place."

Wait a minute. Aren't you going to tell him about Sarah? "It was more than a problem," Regan said.

Bart silenced her with a look.

"These people," Gavin said. "They're in worse shape than the ones outside. What was the problem?"

"No problem."

"But it looks like Nagasaki—or worse." He turned on Bart and Regan as if they were somehow responsible, reproaching them as if they had failed in a stewardship. "These people are half-dead."

Regan said, coldly, "We did what we had to."

"Well, somebody made a mess of it."

"I guess you had to be here," Bart said.

"So much destruction," the captain said sadly. He made a slow lighthouse turn, taking in the scope of the wreckage, the boarded-up windows, the ruined shrubs, the garbage, the stacked body bags and the few survivors who had not fled the courtyard to prepare their faces for the liberation. He completed his survey, fixing on Sarah Parkhurst's bloodied wrists, the shackles. "All you had to do was hang on until we got here."

Regan said, bitterly, "We didn't even know you were coming."

"We didn't know anything," Bart said thoughtfully. "We didn't know and we did it anyway."

"Terrible mess." He was studying Sarah. "This poor girl."

"Wait a minute," Regan began. "You don't know what she did. That's Sarah Parkhurst, and she . . ."

But Bart was pulling her along the platform. *"We did it anyway."*

Together they went down the steps. "Wait a minute," she cried, pulling against it one more time.

"Don't," Bart said in an undertone. "Come on, it's over."

So she yielded all at once. He was right. It was.

Behind them, Regan could hear Gavin asking Sarah: "Who's that crazy kid?"

"Old friend of the family." Sarah's tone was weary and voluptuous. It curled around them and lingered. "He's nobody special, just a kid I used to know."

"But those handcuffs. What happened to you?"

"It's a long story," Sarah said. "If you could get somebody to take these things off . . ."

Regan said, to Bart, "You're not going to let her . . ."

"Shh."

The captain was saying, "You didn't tell me who you were."

"Sarah Parkhurst. I'm the new owner."

"But the old man said he was the owner."

"Poor Daddy," she said silkily. "I'm not at all sure he's competent. If you don't mind, please—these things are hurting my wrists."

"Corporal, the bolt cutters."

"Yes sir."

"Just like that," Regan said.

Bart pulled her close to his side. "Right," he said. "Just like that. Her lover is a wipeout. The whole operation is a wipeout, but she has this to fall back on. She always did. That's the whole thing about the rich."

"Bart, she betrayed us, you saved her life."

"And now it's over," Bart said. They stood together at the base of the platform for a moment, Bart with his arm around her and Regan pressing close. "If you think she wants to remember what she did, or any of them want to remember what they did . . ."

"I remember what you did."

His voice soared. "Me too."

There was a stir at the gates, which opened to admit motorcycles escorting a guard surrounding a prisoner. The captive struggled and spat and lashed out, snaking his red head this way and then that. Somebody had bound his wrists with a length of soiled and shredded silver cloth. As the group crossed the courtyard, Bart said, "Watch this."

"Who is it?"

"Lawrence. The Baron. The big guy."

"He looks just like anybody else."

"Right. For a while there he was the new leader. Now he's trying to figure out how to get out of this. Watch Sarah. Watch what she does."

As he spoke the captive saw the group on the platform and called Sarah in a desperate, guttural shout. When she did not turn but only went on talking to the captain, he broke free of his captors and lunged for the platform steps, calling her name again and again even as the guard tackled him and brought him down. As he fell she murmured something to the captain, who barked:

"Take this man away."

Ted and Billie Beckett emerged from the lobby and crossed the courtyard just as the captain turned to ask Sarah where they ought to lock the prisoner up. The Becketts were both scrubbed and carefully costumed, so earnest and capable that it seemed logical for the captain to ask them for help. So Ted and Billie mounted the platform and began an earnest discussion of the relative merits of the wine cellar and the underground garage where, they said, there were certain security risks.

Bart took Regan's hand and led her away. They retreated to a stone bench in a far corner of the courtyard, where Bart sat down with his arm around her and tried to get her to stop trembling. "It's as if none of it happened."

"It's OK," he said, "it's OK."

"But after everything, after what they *did* . . ."

"It doesn't matter," Bart said. "If they want to go back to being what they were, we can't stop them."

"Lord, is this all it's going to amount to?"

He was grinning. "Depends on what you want from it."

"But you were so . . ." She swallowed the last word because she could not decide on any one that would sum it up.

"I guess I was. Had to be. We were in the middle of it." After a pause he went on thoughtfully. "I guess you do a thing and then you look around and you say, Look, everybody, did you notice? I did this, so where's my thank-you present? Where's my large cash prize? The thing is, there isn't necessarily going to be a present."

"I know." She sighed. She did. She had stopped trembling.

"What you get is that you did whatever it was that you did. But you know you are going to keep on with it, whatever it was." He weighed it before he went on. "So I guess the test is, whether you can go back to real life and be just as good. Which I have to find out sooner or later, you know?"

She could hear the clatter of fresh helicopters setting down outside the wall, yet another detachment on the way. From outside came the sound of heavy fire, the spatter of rifle bullets as the federal troops dispersed the few people remaining. *By tomorrow,* Regan thought, *we're going to wonder what we were making such a fuss about.* Around them, the captain's men had organized crews to clean up the courtyard. Weapons were being stacked over here, next to the stone lion; bodies were being loaded, to be flown out. Over there, somebody was filling a pickup truck with the heaps of roof tiles the Parkhurst contingent had gathered for its last stand. In the game rooms the medics would be seeing to the wounded, and Regan knew they would be tsking over makeshift splints and hasty sutures, complaining about her emergency procedures. Somebody would be bound to make note of the unsanitary conditions. They might even ask her and old Doc Millinger for an explanation. Nobody who came in from outside could possibly understand what they had been through. Through the open gates she could see twilight settling on the deserted rubble where Bart had blown the buildings; soldiers were walking here and there with their helmets off, as careless as sightseers. The siege was over.

Bart kept his arm around her waist. "Do you think we can be alone?"

"Not now." She saw a corpsman coming down the steps from the main entrance; she already knew he would be looking for her, saw Billie Beckett pointing in her direction. "By tomorrow I'll be on my way back to Boston."

"You know I'm going to be in Cambridge. There's a lot of stuff I have to start doing."

She caught her breath. "Me too." *All of it.* If she'd had a vacation from her life, it was over. If he could see it, at his age, she could certainly see it at hers. The corpsman was approaching, already opening his mouth to speak.

Bart said, "Do you think we'll see each other?"

"Not right away." Drawing back in the moment before she kissed him and turned to face her responsibilities, she saw how very young he really was. He was high as a kite, delighted by his existential conclusions, that she recognized as existential only. He looked fine, he looked wonderful with his unlined, hopeful face, and she realized that she had already spent too much time being that which he was only now becoming: a sober adult, and now that the time of siege was ending she would go back to her life not so much restored as reinforced by what she had survived; by his love. She was, she thought, much too old for him, but he was pulling her close and because he thought he loved her and right now she loved him, she let him hold her, saying, "I don't know. We'll see. When it's all done, let's see how we are."

About the Author

Kit Reed is the author of ten novels, including *Magic Time, Captain Grownup* and *Armed Camps.* She is a regular contributor to *The Magazine of Fantasy and Science Fiction,* and her short fiction has also appeared in *Transatlantic Review, Cosmopolitan, Ladies' Home Journal* and *Redbook;* her stories have been collected in *Other Stories and: The Attack of the Giant Baby, Mr. Da V. and Other Stories* and the forthcoming *Revenge of the Senior Citizens.* She lives in Middletown, Connecticut, and teaches a fiction workshop at Wesleyan University.